The Syrian Dandelion

Thaier Alhusain

Copyright © 2025 T Hashem Alhusain

All rights reserved.

ISBN: 9798305629675

DEDICATION

To my parents, who raised us to be kind-hearted and just, shielding us from the storms of political and religious divisions. Who bore burdens that would make mountains crumble. To my beloved, forgotten city of Ar-Raqqah, a place I endlessly long to return to. To our selfless heroes, whose bravery I can only admire but never hope to match.

ACKNOWLEDGMENTS

Since the summer of 2013, when I left my city of Ar-Raqqah, starting over from scratch has become a way of life. Over the years, I have called more than twenty houses home, spread across twelve cities and five countries, carrying with me little more than a passport, a mobile phone, a laptop, and a suitcase of clothes to last the year. Writing this book has been a journey of finding closure to those years spent wandering, seeking to re-root my life and grow anew.

Thank you to everyone whose paths have crossed mine and who played a part in helping me complete this book—a chapter of my life. Your support has allowed me to move forward, finding a new home and a new land to call my own.

Prologue

January 3rd, 2013

Killing should come with hesitation—a flutter in the chest, a paralysing doubt even. Instead, Shamil found something else entirely: a quiet, unnerving calm, as if the act belonged to someone else, and he was merely a spectator in his own body.

The choice felt foreign to him, yet it was his own: Auburn Beard must die first; Black Beard must then swiftly follow.

Blood trickled down his forehead, warm and sticky, filling his eyes and turning the world into a smear of crimson blur. He didn't want to harm anyone. Not again. He had seen enough death for a hundred lifetimes, but none of that mattered now. The logic was simple: hurting the two men blocking his path to safety was the only way to stop them from hurting him.

He traced their carotids with his gaze, pulsating with the certainty of life that neither of them knew was about to end.

"If you're not a spy, the Emir will spare you," Auburn Beard rasped, his voice a thin veil over a threat.

Shamil didn't answer. Words were useless now. Long ago, he learned that words could be twisted; silence could not. He'd seen the lies of men like these, wrapped in soft voices and outstretched hands until the knife appeared or the gun fired. He wouldn't make the mistake of trusting them. Not again.

Running wasn't an option. Shamil had already measured the hopelessness of his odds. Barren fields stretched as far as his screams could reach, a desolate expanse where no cry would be heard. Where no one but God would see him end their lives. It was just the three of them on a desolate path south of the Syrian-Turkish border. Even with his broken glasses, he could almost see his family waiting by the border gate. He hoped they had made it.

"To the car, now," Black Beard barked, striding ahead with his comrade as if they were overlords in a land that already had enough overlords.

They didn't check Shamil. They didn't pat him down, tie his hands, or point their Kalashnikov rifles at him. They saw what they wanted to see: a wreck of a man, too weak to pose any threat. And maybe they were right. His white shirt was soaked red, his bruised ribs strained with every breath, and whatever blood was left in him had barely kept him on his feet.

"It's self-defence," Shamil whispered, as much to justify as to believe. Thirst clasped his parched throat, and he could taste it on his crusted lips—sweat and blood, both dry and fresh. The pain melted away, replaced by a heightened sense of purpose, and the concealed pistol now felt almost weightless in his hand.

"Forgive me, God," he prayed, tightening his grip on the frigid handle. Each heartbeat sent searing pain up his neck as the moment arrived—kill or be killed.

Auburn Beard must die first; Black Beard must then swiftly follow.

The Syrian Dandelion

Bang.

Chapter 1: London

December 20th, 2012

In a secluded office, tucked away from the frantic Emergency Department, Shamil sank into his weathered swivel chair as he typed the notes of the last patient he had seen. Each keystroke was careful, leaving no space for mistakes. As usual, his documentation had to be immaculate; only the notes weren't routine this time—they carried a warmth that lingered in the corners of his heart. A newly pregnant patient had asked for a letter. She needed it for her boss, a small written plea for some time to tend to this fragile, miraculous thing growing within her. Shamil couldn't say no. His patient's happiness when he shared the good news lifted some of the weight off his shoulders, the kind borne from long hours and the relentless beeping of machines. Life had strange ways of asserting itself in the sharp fluorescent edges of the hospital, where despair often outnumbered hope. There were moments like this when life declared itself precious and undeniable.

Leaning back, he let the worn chair creak beneath him and stretched his arms behind his head. He couldn't wait to peel off the blue scrubs clinging to his skin, escape the sterile confines that had held him captive, and discard the suffocating mask, the weight of which throbbed in his ears.

Removing his round glasses, Shamil rubbed his weary eyes, tracing the contours of exhaustion dug beneath them. He massaged his scalp in a futile attempt to alleviate the burdens that weighed upon him. It had been five years since he last saw his family. Five years, two months, and three days—he had been counting. As his fingers weaved through his straight black hair, a few strands surrendered, cascading gently onto his desk. Why were the black strands the first to yield while the stubborn grey ones fought tooth and nail, defying the natural order of things?

He ruffled his hair into a semblance of presentability with a quick adjustment, his reflection in the monitor serving as his final judge. Hastily rising from the chair, he switched off the lights and made his way to the hospital's main reception. Freedom beckoned, and he hurried through the glass doors, the chilly air embracing his face and cooling the perspiration on his neck.

Shit. He stomped his foot on the ground, bolting back toward the Emergency Department. Somehow, he had forgotten about one of the patients he had started to examine before he was called away. Unforgivable. It had never happened before. Perhaps it was the news reports of clashes in Syria that had caught his attention and corrupted his memory.

He knocked on the door of cubicle three gently before entering. His gaze fell upon Mrs Turner, her face worried, her hands slightly shaking as she clutched a worn handbag.

"Mrs. Turner, I'm so sorry for the delay," Shamil smiled warmly. "Just one more blood test, and we'll have everything sorted."

Mrs. Turner's eyes met his, her anxiety seemingly giving way to trust. "Do what you must, Doctor," she said, smiling as she extended her arm for the blood draw.

"Any plans for the holidays?"

"Oh, nothing too exciting, Doctor," a soft chuckle escaped Mrs. Turner's lips. "Just a simple Christmas dinner with my family. How about you?"

Shamil's gaze briefly wandered, his mind whisked away to his homeland—Syria. Being apart from his wife, Laila, and his son, Zain, was a constant ache. He missed the warmth of their presence, the comfort of their voices, and the peace of knowing he could keep them safe.

Swiftly regaining his focus, he replied, "I'll be working, I'm afraid."

"Oh, bless you," Mrs. Turner murmured, her voice hinting pity as Shamil carefully gathered the blood samples. This was exactly why he always avoided talking about his home or family. Whenever the conversation drifted in that direction, it always brought those same familiar, pitying looks. Shamil never knew how to deal with pity—it wasn't a role he recognised for himself. He was the one who helped others, the one who made sure everyone else was okay. The idea of being the one who needed help? It wasn't worth entertaining.

Wishing Mrs Turner a Merry Christmas, he left the cubicle and walked through the bustling corridor connecting the Emergency Department to the laboratory, briefly glancing at the security cameras above—a habit he could not rid himself of.

As he dropped the blood samples into the lab collection window, his colleague John burst through the lab doors, a wide grin spreading across his face. "Sham, my man! Of course, you're still here. Thanks for picking up those shifts—you're the boss."

Shamil turned to face John. "It's nothing," he nodded, wishing his family was celebrating Christmas with him in London. Instead, he was on his own, covering the holiday shifts to give his colleagues a chance to celebrate with their families.

John clapped Shamil on the shoulder. "What're we gonna do without you, honestly."

Shamil smiled. "Well, since you're feeling grateful, can I entrust you with a patient?"

"Of course," John replied, retrieving a pen and a crumpled paper filled with notes. Though there was barely any space left on the page, John managed to squeeze in some additional information—Mrs Turner's identifiers and which blood tests to chase.

Thanking John, Shamil's task was complete. Finally, he could leave the hospital in peace and make his way to his modest room, where he would collapse onto his bed and surrender to sleep until it was time to work again.

"Doctor, thank God you're still here." A breathless nurse, Beth, ran after Shamil. "Aidan is holding a knife or something. He's threatening to kill himself."

Shamil's eyes darted to the commotion unfolding across the Emergency Department. A jolt of adrenaline rushed through his arteries, and suddenly, all that day's weariness had vanished.

"Call security," Shamil instructed, his voice steady, as he analysed Aidan's location: cubicle 8—the psychiatric patients' assessment unit.

Aidan stood there in his usual grey tracksuit, pressing a shard of broken glass against his neck. His piercing blue eyes, now rimmed with red, flickered between fear and anger.

How had he even gotten hold of the glass? Shamil's mind raced as his eyes darted around the scene, instinctively taking in every detail with the precision of his training. Aidan had concealed blades in his trousers before—sharpened pencils, compasses, wires, and cables—anything that he could use as a weapon to harm himself or create a scene. On the pale tiled floor, shards of a broken mug scattered around a large splash of spilt tea. That explained it.

"I swear I'll cut my neck if you come any closer!" Aidan's voice reverberated through the air, veins swelling on his neck as a trickle of blood coursed down the sharp shard.

Three hospital security guards positioned themselves at a cautious distance from Aidan. In a previous encounter, Shamil had wanted to intervene; however, the attending consultant had forbidden him, insisting that the hospital security disarm Aidan before the medical staff approached. The outcome had been disastrous. Aidan had accidentally slashed his neck, almost hitting his carotid artery, and it took a miracle for the surgical team to save his life.

History wasn't going to repeat itself, even if it meant defying orders.

Aidan's eyes locked with Shamil's. "They're not giving me the meds, Doctor."

Shamil took a step forward, but John's grip on his arm tightened—a silent plea to reconsider.

"I'm good." Shamil gently freed his arm from John's grasp. Time was of the essence.

"Aidan, I need you to put that down," Shamil said, his voice calm and firm. "We've been through this before."

Aidan's eyes wavered momentarily, but his grip on the shard only tightened. Shamil held his gaze, his tone unwavering as he took another cautious step forward. "Aidan, you know I always listen to you."

"Yeah, but they don't," Aidan responded, briefly waving the shard at the guards before pressing it back against his skin, smudging the blood already staining it. It was becoming harder for Shamil to assess how much damage Aidan had already caused.

"Step outside, please." Shamil looked firmly at the guards.

"Doctor?" The guard closest to Shamil questioned, almost objecting.

"You can leave the door open," Shamil insisted. He knew that Aidan was impulsive but had never been suicidal; and that once the outburst of anger was managed, he would return to his usual self. He might even feel silly about all the drama he had caused — he had done it before.

The guards hesitantly stepped back but wouldn't leave the room, their body cameras recording Shamil's gamble.

"I got this; he won't hurt himself," Shamil persisted.

"I just want my shots, man," Aidan's voice quivered, his hand too close to his neck for Shamil to make a move.

"Morphine or something else this time?" Shamil asked, stepping closer and minding the spilt tea on the floor. He couldn't afford to slip.

"You know what I want. Why are you asking?" Aidan retorted, momentarily retracting the shard from his neck to wave it in frustration.

That was Shamil's cue.

With swift precision, he seized Aidan's wrist, his thumb digging into Aidan's skin near the carpals, forcing him to release the shard. The hospital guards instantly joined in, subduing Aidan and restraining him face-down on the cubicle's bed.

"Get me Lorazepam, four milligrams," Shamil instructed Nurse Beth as Aidan's anguished cries echoed throughout the room.

"Four milligrams?" Beth questioned.

"Yes, NOW!" Shamil asserted firmly before turning his attention back to Aidan. "Aidan," he said, laying a hand on his shoulder as he thrashed about. "We're getting you your medicine, okay?"

Aidan continued to cry out, attempting to bite the guards as they held him down. Who could blame him? Countless attempts at dialogue had failed in the past, resulting in self-inflicted harm. At least this time, Aidan had not succeeded in slashing his own neck, and now he would receive the care he needed.

Passing through a silent crowd of onlookers, Shamil leaned against a nearby wall. His breathing gradually returned to normal as his heart burned away the remnants of adrenaline.

What would he say to his supervising consultants? Surely, they would question his methods and perhaps reprimand him. It didn't matter—a slight blemish on his otherwise impeccable professional record seemed insignificant compared to the importance of preserving a life. Aidan was safe, and his immediate crisis had been averted.

Glancing at his mobile phone, Shamil realised it was already well past his duty hours. He sighed, feeling the hunger creep up his stomach. If he left now, he would still have enough time to put together a semblance of a wholesome dinner, which he would devour before collapsing onto his single bed with the comforting drone of a television in the background. The white noise helped ward off the profound solitude that accompanied his nights and the ghosts of 'what ifs' that plagued his dreams after every shift.

Just as he was about to stow away his phone, a message from his father illuminated the screen. His stomach sank—late-night messages from his father were seldom bearers of good news.

With a quick swipe, he unlocked his phone and read the message.

Salam. Zain was arrested. Call me.

Chapter 2: The Passenger

Shamil arrived at Heathrow Airport three hours ahead of his flight. Somehow, he had managed to make a last-minute reservation. The news of his son Zain's detention by the police felt too surreal to be true—how could his father, Mudhar, have allowed it to happen? And how could his uncle Jassim, the head of Syrian Air Force Intelligence, SAFI, have let this slip through his grasp? Surely, his informants would have made him aware of it hours, if not days, before it happened.

Shamil needed answers.

"I'm at the airport now," he said into his headphones, speaking to his wife, Laila, on the other end of the line.

"You don't have to come. Zain is home now," Laila said. "It was a misunderstanding, and we sorted it out."

"Why was he arrested? Where was Jassim?" Shamil asked, struggling to hear her answer over the cacophony of the crowd around him. "Laila, give me a minute." He put her on hold as he noticed John's call coming through.

"Are you all right, mate? You didn't show up to work today," John said.

"It's a family emergency. I informed HR this morning. I need to take a few weeks off," Shamil explained quickly. In the background, the airport intercom announced a flight delay.

"Wait, are you at the airport?" John's voice rose.

Shamil frowned, unsure of how to respond. He had kept his personal life private, avoiding conversations about the conflict in

Syria. Everyone expected him to choose a side—either the rebels or the regime. But he stood with those caught in the middle, the ordinary people who only wanted to survive. For this, both sides scorned him, labelling him a grey person—someone too weak, in their eyes, to stand up for what he believed in. "John, I have to go," he said, reaching for his headphones to remove them.

"No, wait! Talk to me, man. You're not really going to Syria, are you?"

"It's just a short trip. I've booked a return ticket," Shamil replied.

"What if things go wrong? Have you sorted out your citizenship interview?"

Shamil hesitated; the interview was crucial for his citizenship application, but rescheduling it wasn't a major issue. "I'll handle it when I get back. I'll be fine."

"I don't know, man. Think about it. You're heading into a war zone—do you think the UK will just let you back in?" John's question planted a seed of doubt in Shamil's heart. "Have you thought this through?"

Of course, Shamil had thought this through, but what choice did he have? Exhaling heavily, Shamil stepped back, motioning to the passenger behind him to take his place in the security line. He had hoped to keep Zain's arrest a secret, but John was different. He was Shamil's closest colleague in the UK, perhaps the only person he had ever confided in about his family matters.

"My son is in prison for protesting against the regime or something. I have to get him out," Shamil lowered his voice.

"Can't your uncle help? The military big shot?" John asked.

Shamil had already asked himself that very question. "He'd only make things worse. I'm sorry about the Christmas shifts—I'll make it up to the department."

"Forget the Christmas shifts," John shot back. "I'm more worried about you."

"I'll be fine, John. I'm sorry, but my wife is waiting on the other line. I'll call you when I arrive."

Shamil ended the call with John and returned to Laila's. All he wanted was to hear Zain's voice, to know his son was safe at home. That small reassurance would buy him enough time to delay his departure and make it to the citizenship interview.

"Put Zain on the phone. I need to talk to him," Shamil said as Laila's voice filled his ear again.

"He won't speak. He's just being stubborn," Laila responded.

"Laila, is he there or not?" Shamil's patience wore thin. Was she hiding the truth again?

"He's here, I swear on my mother's soul. He's just upset with everything."

Shamil paused, torn between his desire to trust Laila and his lingering doubts. This wasn't the first time his family had concealed truths under the guise of kindness, sparing each other from painful revelations. A few years back, when Shamil's cousin Adil was martyred, Jassim and the rest of the family had fabricated a tale of a three-month mission before finally revealing the heart-wrenching news to Adil's mother.

They feared the shock might exacerbate her recovery from a stroke, perhaps even claim her life. While done in kindness, such deceit was still just that: deceit. Shamil wouldn't want his family to treat him the same. He wanted the truth, always.

"I'm coming back," he conceded, ending the call and proceeding through security checks.

Chapter 3: Aleppo

At a discreet corner near the boarding gate, Shamil angled his body carefully, ensuring no one could glimpse the content of his laptop screen. His fingers moved with urgency, opening tab after tab in his browser. Each search brought up more questions than answers.

Who are the fighting factions in Syria? Who fought where, and who gained what land? The names blurred together like a mosaic of chaos: groups splintered, alliances formed and broken, each claiming a cause and carving out pieces of the land like scavengers circling a carcass.

What are the possible ways out of Syria? Now, this was the real question, the one that mattered. The simplest option was to go through Lebanon. He could take Zain and Laila there, find them a modest flat to stay in while their visas were being processed, and have them fly directly to London. It seemed straightforward.

The more complicated and much more dangerous alternatives were smuggling routes through deserts filled with mobsters or perilous treks over mountains, where the cold could be as deadly as a bullet. Those routes were a gamble he couldn't afford to take.

He researched the matter as if decrypting a complex medical case. He had to read all the signs and symptoms of the "illness" spreading across his country and find the safest and fastest way to exit the chaos.

Hours later, his flight was ready for boarding. He erased his browsing history with a few clicks and opened a few random medical articles before switching off his laptop. He slipped his headphones on and blasted "Magic Fly" on a loop. The outside noise was subdued, while the one inside his head rumbled to the loud electronic beat. Two weeks only. He revised his plans repeatedly: Plan A, Plan B, Plan C, D, E. Nothing could be left to chance—he had to be back in time, or else risk losing his job in the UK. Before he could finish revising Plan E, he was disembarking in Aleppo.

The unforgettable odour of the city assailed his senses. An icy breeze, tinged with the stench of sewage and a hint of linden trees, blew right through him, messing up his black hair and landing dust on his glasses.

Not much had changed in Aleppo's depressing airport. It was still a stark, rectangular structure enclosing an ever-shrinking waiting area. Posters and banners plastered every surface, each depicting the face of the country's so-called saviour—not Jesus, Mohammed, or even Moses, but a figure whose reign had been marked by disappointment—now glorified with slogans and quotes.

Shamil quickened his pace through the dark, brown-walled corridors, which were unusually clean, save for the corners of the faux-wooden ceiling where flies lay trapped in ancient webs. The air was thick with stagnation, the weight of years of disillusionment pressing down on every surface.

"Where are you heading?" asked the disinterested customs officer, flipping through Shamil's passport before glancing at his monitor. His thinning, light-brown hair was gelled and combed back, and his clean-shaven face bore the typical look of a government employee.

"Ar-Raqqah city," Shamil replied. There was no point in lying to the officer.

"Alone?"

"Yes."

The officer glared at Shamil, then shifted his scrutiny to the passport, the luggage, and finally returned to fix his gaze on Shamil again.

"Take off your glasses," the officer instructed.

Shamil complied quietly, choosing to bow his head and avoid unnecessary conflict rather than invoke Jassim's name and end up indebted to him.

"Are you coming here to join the demonstrations?" The officer frowned as though Shamil had already answered yes.

"What demonstrations?" Shamil replied instinctively. It was the most challenging question he'd practised answering. He had to feign ignorance.

"You being a smartass?"

"I thought it was all fake news."

"It is fake news," the officer jeered, shoving Shamil's stamped passport back at him. "I'd watch what I say if I were you, Doc."

Shamil said nothing and slipped his passport down his pocket. 'Hakim' would have been a more respectful way to address a doctor, but the officer opted for 'Doc' instead—an insult in disguise.

"And shave before we do it for you," the officer added, pointing at Shamil's stubble. "A little thicker, and we'd mistake you for a terrorist."

Shamil kept calm. He had no time to waste addressing the officer's rudeness and wasn't above showing some obedience to get his way. "Of course, sir. You have a good day," Shamil said with a forced smile before picking up his passport.

Wherever he went, at whichever airport he found himself, customs officers always seemed the same. Whether reacting to his name, birthplace, accent, or stubble, they all felt compelled to remind him that granting him passage was an act of grace, not a right. It no longer mattered; the senseless interrogations were over. He hurried through two sizeable automatic glass doors into a deserted arrivals hall. The cafés were shut, their tables stacked and chairs upside-down in the gloom. The currency exchange office was locked, a faded sign flapping listlessly against the door. In the waiting area, the monitors flickered with those same old propaganda reels, glorifying the Al-Baath party as if anyone still believed them. The chants droned on, monotonous and heavy, the kind of sound that doesn't just fill a room but seeps into one's mind, reminding him that the state didn't just own the streets—it owned the air he breathed, too.

When Shamil stepped outside, silence met him. The usual mobs of taxi drivers were nowhere to be seen, replaced by a small group huddled a safe distance away.

"Taxi, sir?" shouted one man.

Shamil declined, pulling out his mobile to check for his ride. And even if his ride was delayed by hours, he knew better than to take a taxi from the airport and risk being robbed when he left the premises.

As he waited for the call to go through, stomach growling and feet aching, a dark green camouflage jeep screeched to a halt in front of him. He stood his ground, knowing his papers were in order and influential contacts were ready if needed. A soldier stepped out of the jeep.

Tall and well-built, with tattoos covering half his neck, the soldier glared at Shamil as if the two were acquainted. Shamil tightened his grip on the bag in his right hand and sized up the muscled man striding toward him. If it came to a fight, Shamil would give him a run for his money, but the soldier would win. Shamil knew his limits and respected them. He tried to keep a straight face, but his composure faltered as the soldier drew closer.

"Dr Shamil, you're coming with us."

Chapter 4: Laila

In the tranquil embrace of her bedroom, Laila sat on the ottoman, her eyes scrutinising her colourful reflection in the mirror. Makeup had never been her ally—she detested how it felt against her skin and couldn't fathom how other Middle Eastern women endured it clogging their pores, especially in scorching weather. But today was exceptional—Shamil, after a gruelling absence of five years, was finally returning home.

He wasn't particularly a fan of makeup, or so he used to say, but what if all those pretty British women, with their extravagant makeup, whom he had been working with, talking to, or, dare she think it, sleeping with... Laila quickly tapped her temples. She didn't want to entertain such thoughts.

She deftly tied her wavy black hair into a high bun and adorned her ears with penguin-shaped gold earrings. Retrieving the copper bottle holding her cherished kohl eyeliner, a gift from her late mother, she delicately drew lines accentuating her fiery hazel eyes. "That's enough," she chided herself, mindful not to overdo it and risk looking like a clown.

Dusting off residual powder from her blue dress—the one Shamil had sent her from London—she surveyed the bedroom one last time. Clean, creamy-white sheets adorned the tidy bed, with dry towels and fresh clothes thoughtfully arranged nearby. She had hidden away the floor mattress he used to sleep on during those months leading up to his departure to London, now wishing to share the bed with him again.

Her expectations were modest—years of separation had tempered any grand hopes. Yet, in the depths of her heart, a longing for his presence remained, a longing she didn't fully understand.

Stepping out of her bedroom, Laila caught a glimpse of the TV screen in the living room. Another news report celebrated the army's triumph over the rebels in Aleppo. A victory that came at the cost of hundreds of families going homeless. She let out a dismissive sigh. The truth about Aleppo remained a twisted puzzle, and she knew better than to trust the narratives fed through the media, surely nothing but a web of lies.

The ever-changing labels—rebels, Islamists, terrorists—only added to the confusion. She had lived in Ar-Raqqah long enough to know that reality was far from the neatly packaged stories presented on the screen. Though whispers of discontent and sporadic protests echoed through the city, she had yet to witness the horrors that were broadcast on television. Ar-Raqqah was safe, unlike other cities, and the majority were too busy making a living to protest the regime.

Grabbing the remote control from the coffee table, she swiftly changed the channel to a lively music station. With the melodic tunes filling the air, she made her way towards Zain's bedroom, matching her steps to the beats. It had been so long since she'd danced that she had almost forgotten how to do it.

"You're still in your pyjamas?" she asked Zain, curled up in his bed, tired brown eyes consumed by his laptop screen. His room was suffocating with the smell of his sweat, the thick curtains drawn tight, enveloping the space in darkness. What would

Shamil say when he saw that? "Your father is arriving any minute now; go shower and get ready."

"I'll shower when he arrives," Zain replied, scratching his head before giving his unruly black hair a vigorous ruffle as if coaxing it awake.

Laila made her way through the clothes scattered on the floor and opened the curtains and the windows, allowing a gust of fresh air to breathe life into the stuffy room.

"It's cold!" Zain complained, pulling the duvet tighter around himself.

Laila shook her head as she collected the laundry and deposited it into a basket under Zain's desk. She couldn't have placed that basket any closer to where he spent most of his time, yet somehow, he had barely used it. "I'm raising a raccoon; I swear to God."

"Ugh," Zain grumbled, shutting his laptop and springing off the bed. He reached for the basket from Laila's hands and planted a quick peck on her cheek. She smiled, momentarily overlooking his untidiness. As long as he remained safe, the state of the flat didn't matter.

Last week, when the police came knocking, she was in shock. She couldn't believe they dared to arrest Zain, the grand-nephew of Jassim. But they did. They took him away while Ameena, Laila's mother-in-law, locked arms with her, trying to stop her from rushing to the police station. Only shameless women went to police stations—one of many societal rules Laila despised.

For nine agonising hours, she waited; the police had kept Zain locked up before Jassim intervened and brought him back home into Laila's waiting arms. When she asked Zain what had transpired during those hours, he remained silent, assuring her that Jassim and Mudhar would explain everything later. They never did. The next thing she knew, Mudhar had spoken to Shamil and told him that Zain was still under arrest, urging him to return immediately. Perhaps it was all a ploy to get Shamil back.

"Do we have any yoghurt left, or have you used it all on your face?" Zain teased, interrupting Laila's train of thought.

A blush rose, and she took a deep breath to steady herself. The last thing she needed was for her efforts to be undone by a sudden hot flush.

"Is it that bad?" she inquired, glancing at her reflection in the mirror on Zain's desk. She may have overdone it a little.

"You look beautiful, Mama," Zain reassured her, carrying the laundry basket towards the bathroom. "He doesn't deserve you."

"He's your father!"

"Who's in London hooking up with God knows who," Zain said, emptying the basket into the washing machine.

Laila's heart sank, and an overwhelming desire to wipe her face swept over her. Reality crashed upon her like an unforgiving wave—Shamil had likely moved on with his life, and his return was merely for their son's safety.

"Zain!" Laila's voice rang out firmly. No matter her feelings towards Shamil, he was still his father, and she insisted on a level of respect.

"Relax, I'm only saying this to you," Zain retorted, playfully tossing his shirt into the laundry. He sniffed his underarms, making a face like someone who had just caught a whiff of an old pickle. "Yep, definitely a raccoon."

"God help me," Laila chuckled, shaking her head at Zain as he wet his black hair and combed it into a makeshift mohawk.

"Are you gonna tell him the truth?" he asked, his face turning serious as he checked himself in the mirror.

Laila's stomach churned, unsure of the truth he was alluding to. Was it another one of his digs or ill-timed jokes? She couldn't make sense of it.

"Truth?" she hesitated before blurting out, almost defensively, "I don't hide anything from your father."

He squinted, locking eyes with her, and said nothing as if waiting for her to admit to something she couldn't quite grasp. But what truth was he referring to? She couldn't place it, so she kept her silence.

"Never mind, I was joking," he brushed down the mohawk, then held his bottoms with both hands, sporting a cheeky smile. "Pants coming off in three, two…"

"You…" Laila quickly closed the bathroom door behind her, her mind still preoccupied with Zain's cryptic words. "Leave some hot water for your father, OK?"

"Mhm," Zain said, then blasted loud music on his phone—a habit he'd picked up from her.

Laila remained near the bathroom door with a lingering sense of confusion. She closed her eyes and shook her head, attempting to rid her mind of the thoughts Zain's words had stirred up.

As far as she knew, she had been honest with him ever since she and Shamil had separated. After all, that was their agreement—always to tell each other the truth, regardless of the circumstances. Was Zain referring to the fact that his arrest wasn't as significant as they had made it out to be? But she had already shared that with Shamil, and he chose not to listen.

Anyway, she had no time to dwell on it now. Ameena would need her assistance in the kitchen. There was still much to prepare for Shamil's arrival.

Five long years.

If someone had told her that she would miss him this much, she wouldn't have believed it. After all, she was the one who encouraged him to leave and go abroad, unaware that the ache of his absence would settle deep inside her, growing heavier with each passing year.

Shamil had been in her life from the first day she stepped foot in Ar-Raqqah. His wide brown eyes had settled on her, holding her gaze just a moment too long—it left her feeling a mix of unease and curiosity. She'd always thought men were worthless, her father being the prime example.

Shamil was an exception, she realised in the months that followed. She found comfort in knowing that he would protect her from the hungry boys who followed her home and the older men who sought to bargain for her hand in marriage. Thankfully, none of those offers were ever close to what her father had in mind for her. She was, after all, the most beautiful among her sisters. Skin naturally tanned and smooth, plum lips, and wide hips—words her father used to describe her when discussing her worth with interested men. She had yearned to confront those men herself, but societal norms dictated that women should be obedient lest they bring shame upon their families. She loathed the constraints of such a culture, but the web of tradition was inescapable.

Marrying Shamil was the solution. He was her guardian, and the more time they spent together, the more she warmed up to him and accepted him as part of her life.

If only she hadn't pushed him away.

Wiping away the tears that had threatened to fall, she headed into the kitchen to wash her face. What was the point of wearing makeup when the pain and turmoil underneath it all remained the same?

Leaning over the sink, she heard the doorbell ringing, interrupting her thoughts.

"One second," Laila called out, hastily dabbing the corners of her eyes with her sleeves.

"Laila, daughter, it's me," came a familiar voice behind the door. It was Shamil's father, Mudhar.

Laila swiftly opened it, offering a warm smile. "Welcome, Uncle; I was about to come help Auntie."

"Mashallah, wow," Mudhar exclaimed, his brown eyes studying Laila as if he were seeing her for the first time. You look..." He appeared to be at a loss for words.

Blushing slightly, Laila glanced away, tucking a few strands of her hair behind her ear. "Ridiculous, I know."

"No, no. You look majestic, like Cleopatra," Mudhar gave her a rare compliment.

"You flatter me, Uncle," Laila replied, making way for him to come inside.

Once in the corridor, Mudhar's expression turned serious. "Did Shamil call you?"

"Not since this morning. He should be arriving now, no?"

"The plane has landed, I checked. I thought he called you."

"No, he didn't," Laila replied, her mind racing with anxiety. Where could Shamil be?

Mudhar pulled out his mobile phone, scrolling down to Shamil's number. The line was busy.

"Well, he's speaking to someone," Laila said.

"It's been like this for over two hours now. I don't think it's just busy," Mudhar said. Not exactly the reassurance Laila was hoping for.

"Jassim would know where he is. Why not call him?"

"He's in an important meeting until six." Mudhar sighed, exchanging worried glances with Laila.

"So, what now?" Laila asked, her voice shaky.

"Don't worry, daughter," Mudhar said, slipping his phone back into his pocket. "He must have found a way back. We'll just have to wait."

Chapter 5: Jassim

Jassim clenched the golden letter opener in his hand, its dull end pressing against his temple. The incessant ringing in his ear infuriated him. He loathed the distraction, the weakness it represented, and it seemed to amplify on days when his patience wore thin. The urge to drive a rod through his skull, silencing the maddening noise, grew stronger with every pulse of pain. He'd rather be deaf than distracted.

Once these incompetent recruits finally completed the simple task of hanging the painting of his late son, Adil, he would drown out that noise with pills. Only then would he check the progress with his informants. Protests had become a daily occurrence in the city, and he couldn't help but wonder if he had been too lenient with the protesters. Calling for bloody freedom, as if they weren't free enough.

"The artist really puffed up his arms. He looks like Rambo now," one of the young recruits had the audacity to comment as they observed the portrait.

Jassim's eyes flared with anger at the recruit's insolence. Adil was perfect; he didn't need an artist to enhance his image.

"Pull up your sleeve," Jassim scowled, his authoritative tone cutting through the air, and the recruit complied.

Seizing the recruit's arm, Jassim dug his thick fingers deep into his flesh as if searching for the nerves to incarcerate them against the bone. The recruit winced in pain, nearly falling to his knees.

"Sir," the recruit pleaded, trying to free his arm from Jassim's unyielding grasp as the others watched in silence.

Easing off a little but maintaining a firm grip, Jassim's face contorted with anger. "If either of you had one-tenth of Captain Adil's strength, those terrorists wouldn't have stood a chance in this country."

"Sir, please, I beg you," the recruit cried out.

What a weakling. Jassim released him with a dismissive wave of his hand. "Grab something to eat on your way out. Any skinnier, and your arm would have snapped."

The recruits bolted away with a salute, leaving Jassim to straighten the painting, the last piece of décor his new office needed. His assignment to head the Aljazeera branch of the Syrian Air Force Intelligence, SAFI, felt like a slap in the face. All those years of unfaltering loyalty to the regime, even losing his son in service, and the regime rewarded him with a post in a combat-free zone to babysit protesters. How insulting.

He would show them what he was capable of. The intelligence his late son Adil had managed to collect before ascending to heaven would undoubtedly aid in defeating the rebels in the north. His son's name would be immortalised, and his family's honour restored.

Sitting on his ivory-adorned armchair, Jassim narrowed his eyes with dissatisfaction as he grasped the file resting on his desk—Zain's file. His fingers deftly flipped through its pages, devouring the contents of the attached reports. What a shameful situation Zain, his grand-nephew, had put their family in. Conspiring with the rebels, spying, inciting violence—actions that would have ensured Zain never saw daylight again had it not been for Jassim's intervention. But that would all end soon; he was sure of it. His family's honour would not be tarnished by the actions of a fatherless teenager.

He reached for the satellite phone securely strapped to his waist and dialled one of his trusted informants. The voice on the other end confirmed what he already knew—Shamil had arrived.

"Good," Jassim's voice held a steely edge. "Bring him to me."

Chapter 6: The Way Back

"Hold on, Brother. I need to make a phone call," Shamil scrolled to Jassim's number and dialled it. The line cut instantaneously, so he dialled again.

"Colonel Jassim sent us," the soldier said, stepping closer and extending his right hand. "We're your escorts."

Shamil stared at the soldier, unwilling to shake his hand before confirming that they were indeed Jassim's men. His father Mudhar had assured him that his escorts would be dressed up as civilians, not soldiers. Something wasn't right.

"What's your name and rank?" Shamil asked firmly, his thumb hovering above Jassim's number.

"Nizar Feratly, private security," Nizar replied, easily lifting Shamil's bags onto the jeep.

Shamil glanced at his phone—there was barely any signal. "What's Jassim's surname and last post?" he asked, the bare minimum Jassim's private security should know.

"Look, if we were going to arrest you, we wouldn't be having this conversation now," Nizar said, holding the jeep's door open.

"Surname and last post," Shamil insisted.

"Al-Sayed. Jermana. Good enough?"

Shamil's eyes scanned the jeep - an easily escapable all-terrain vehicle - before he got in the back seat.

"Welcome, Hakim," the driver said, barely smiling as if forced to fake politeness. "Forgive me for the bumpy ride ahead, but I must drive fast. Our clearance expires soon."

"What clearance?" Shamil asked.

Nizar adjusted his seat next to Shamil and pulled out a pack of cigarettes. "We need it to pass through checkpoints." He lit a cigarette and offered it to Shamil. "Do you smoke?"

"I don't, thank you." Shamil reached for the window knob, but it would not budge. "Could you open your window, please?" he said to the driver.

"Sure." The driver partially lowered the window. "Pass me one," he asked Nizar for a cigarette.

Shamil sighed. He may as well have joined their smoking fest, given how smoggy the back of the jeep had quickly turned. Their story holds, though. They spoke to him respectfully and were on the right path to Ar-Raqqah city. Still, Shamil had to confirm their intent before he could rest. He rechecked his phone, but there was no signal.

"So, Colonel Jassim says you're his nephew; how come you look nothing like him?" Nizar asked, turning to face Shamil.

"What do you mean?" Shamil said, coughing. The smoke was getting thicker.

"Well," Nizar hesitated. "He's very dark-skinned, and you're quite pale."

The driver chimed in, "And Jassim is bald."

"Very bald," Nizar cackled. "You two have the same sharp eyebrows, though. The same angry look."

Well, of course, Shamil was angry. He had had a long trip, and the only expression his face could display in that suffocating jeep was 'repulsed'.

"If I spent as many hours under the sun as Jassim did when he was young, trust me, I would be as dark," Shamil replied.

"Your dialect is different as well; it doesn't sound Raqqawi enough," the driver smirked as if his own accent was 'Raqqawi' enough.

Shamil cleared his throat, glaring at Nizar's cigarette, his face saying what his lips were not. He could have reached for the cigarette, grabbed it out of Nizar's hand and tossed it out of the jeep, and Nizar would have said nothing. He possessed Such privilege for being Jassim's nephew, but Shamil had never abused that power, and he wasn't about to start then. It wasn't worth it. "I've been abroad for a while; that must be it."

Nizar frowned, putting out the cigarette on the bottom of his boot. "Are you back on another mission then?"

"I'm sure Jassim has briefed you on why I'm back," Shamil said, turning away. He knew better than to answer Nizar's 'innocent' questions; intelligence operatives were never 'just curious'; every question they asked had a purpose.

"Well..." Nizar began before his phone pinged. He quickly eyed what looked like a concise text message and put it back in his pocket.

Shamil checked his phone again, but still no signal. What network was Nizar using?

"Is that a satellite phone?" Shamil asked.

"I wish," Nizar said, lighting another cigarette. "It's a new model, though."

Shamil's phone was also new, so why was it disconnected? Perhaps Syrian networks didn't accept foreign SIM cards? He would look into it once he was home.

Resting his head lightly against the window to his left, gentle vibrations spreading across his forehead, Shamil spaced out as he observed the desolate countryside. The sun was setting in the west, casting a golden glow over the war-torn lands of Aleppo. His chest ached with every shallow breath he took in the smoky interior of the vehicle, and he watched the rolling hills covered in lush green carpet, yet the valleys were strewn with filth and litter. Plastic waste lined the roads; even the few farmers tending to their fields carelessly left their refuse by the wayside. Even without the war, the land would have decayed with such neglect.

"We're almost there," Nizar said, his ash-coated hand patting Shamil's shoulder.

I know. Shamil nodded.

He could never forget the entrance to his city, where towering eucalyptus trees stretched towards the sky, their branches entwining in a ceaseless dance with the wind. He could almost taste the sweet flesh of the artichokes that dotted the banks of the nearby canals and smell the calm, crisp waters of the Euphrates.

Silent as a shadow, Shamil gazed at the road with an almost tender melancholy as though he had stumbled upon a long-forgotten lover, one he had once left behind but was now inexplicably drawn to once more.

"Breaking News Alert," the radio speaker announced, snapping Shamil out of his trance. "Our sources in Ar-Raqqah city inform us the rebels have taken over the northern countryside and are mounting an assault on the city in the next forty-eight hours. We can neither...." The driver turned off the radio.

"Turn it back on," Shamil sat up straight, quickly glancing at the road ahead.

Where are the rebels? Where is the fighting they had just spoken about?

"It's propaganda," Nizar scoffed, pointing at the road ahead. "Do you see anything around you? It's all fake news."

Shamil took another look around, his eyes carefully scanning the landscape. There were no signs of the conflict he had braced himself for—no fire or smoke, no tanks rolling ominously over the horizon, no militants lurking in the shadows of the valleys. Instead, the scene was disarmingly ordinary. The familiar sights of mud houses lined the riverbanks, their thatched roofs blending into the earthy tones of the land. Cattle herds meandered lazily across the green islets, utterly untroubled by the world beyond. It all looked peaceful until the jeep slowed down to a stop a few metres away from the southern entrance to Ar-Raqqah, where soldiers had set up a checkpoint, scanning through a long queue of vehicles seeking to enter the city.

"Clearance?" one of the soldiers asked, a Kalashnikov strapped to his chest, and Nizar quickly flashed a piece of paper in front of him.

"Who's the civilian?" the soldier asked, looking at Shamil.

"He's with Colonel Jassim," Nizar answered.

"Jassim from SAFI?"

"That's the one."

The policeman stepped back. "Get moving."

It was that simple; no one dared upset Jassim.

As the jeep drove away, Shamil couldn't help but glance back at the checkpoint. The soldiers had then pinned two men to the ground, their Kalashnikovs trained on them.

"You weren't kidding about the.." Shamil began before the air was shattered by the sound of gunfire as the soldiers fired two warning shots into the sky, causing the other travellers to cower in fear.

"They wouldn't shoot people, right?" Shamil asked Nizar, his mind drifting to the images he had seen online of soldiers shooting at civilians in other Syrian cities.

"Jassim wouldn't allow it," Nizar replied, unfazed by the incident, puffing on his cigarette.

"They'd tell you it's fake news, Hakim, but I'm afraid we're weeks away from having to abandon Ar-Raqqah," the driver said.

"And you would just hand the city over to them without a fight?" Shamil asked.

"Ignore him," Nizar sneered. "We'll kill every single one of these bastards before they step foot in the city."

"You stay and fight," the driver interjected. "I'll take my family and leave."

Nizar spat in disgust. "I won't leave this city until I run out of bullets."

"Ok, enough now," Shamil interjected. "You can fight over this when I'm not with you."

Nizar grunted, looking at his phone again. He must have received another text, one that made him scoff. He looked at the driver. "Change of plans; we're dropping him off at his parents' house."

The hair on Shamil's neck bristled with unease. Where else would they have dropped him? Jassim had planned something for him; he could feel it in his bones.

"We'll be there in two minutes," the driver said, speeding by the city's Clock-Tower square.

Shamil bit his lip, deciding it was better to feign knowledge of Jassim's plans and maintain some dignity than to appear panicked. They were only a few blocks from his parent's house, and he didn't want to complicate matters further.

His phone vibrated twice. Could his SIM have registered on the network at last? He hastily checked it; there was still no reception. Then it vibrated again, and a received text message icon briefly appeared before vanishing. He undoubtedly needed a new phone.

Looking around the square, Shamil's confusion grew even deeper. Pavements were cluttered with vendors hawking their wares of colourful fabric, trinkets, and cheap electronics.

The throngs of passersby were so thick that they overflowed onto the street, forcing the jeep and other vehicles to slow down. The square's frenetic energy, which pulsed with life unlike anything Shamil had seen before, struck him.

Everyone seemed oblivious to the news reports and dismissive of the gunshots that had just echoed not far from them. Men, women, and many children gathered around barbeque kiosks, waiting their turns to be served. The smoky aroma of sizzling meats filled the air, and the piles of deeply fried falafels neither stirred his hunger nor eased the churn he had felt watching the police officers fire their Kalashnikovs.

"Watch where you're walking, Sheep," Nizar shouted at passersby.

"Fuck off," one of them responded.

"Your mum's the sheep," added another.

"Kiss my ass."

The profanities exchanged only escalated the tension. A young man even punched the window beside Shamil, making him flinch.

"I'll fucking kill you," Nizar shouted, jumping out of the jeep, but the young man vanished into the crowd.

"Are they for real?" Shamil asked, bewildered by the unusual sight of ordinary people challenging the military.

"They're all displaced from many other cities, Hakim," the driver said.

"Those bastard rebels, they go to civilian areas and force them out of their houses and into Ar-Raqqah, and now we have to deal with this mess," Nizar said, climbing back onto the jeep.

"It will only get worse," the driver remarked, steering them further into the city.

Shamil wiped his clammy forehead, mulling over the driver's grim prediction. He stared out the window, taking in the scene: people hustling along eroded, muddy streets, beggars more conspicuous at every corner. Police officers slouched in their roadside cabins, their eyes pinned to their mobile phones, indifferent to the chaos around them. This was Shamil's birthplace—busier now, perhaps, but its soul remained unchanged. The city he had tried his best to get over, but to which he inevitably returned.

Chapter 7: Home

Laila paced the length of her in-laws' balcony, the rough tiles cold beneath her bare feet. Her patience frayed with each restless step, her mind looping through the same question: Who could Shamil possibly be talking to for over two hours? She glanced at her phone again, the screen blank, staring back at her.

She told herself there was no need to worry. Syria wasn't some lawless wasteland, no matter what the news reports might suggest. It's just that Shamil wouldn't disappear like that; he had always kept her in the loop.

Carefully plucking the dry leaves from the spearmint plants, hoping the task would provide a momentary distraction, she tucked the leaves into her pocket. Later, she would use them to brew a comforting cup of tea—something she desperately needed.

"He's here, come down," Mudhar's voice called out, a summons that sent Laila's heart into a frenzied dance. She hastily tucked the gathered leaves into her dress pocket as she gazed at a military jeep easing to a stop.

"Auntie, he's here," she called out to Ameenah, then hurried downstairs without hesitation, dusting off her dark blue dress on her way.

And there he stood—a familiar yet transformed figure, surrounded by his loved ones. His black hair, now streaked with a bit of white at the temples, lent him an air of distinguished grace. The new round glasses highlighted the kindness in his brown eyes, enhancing his charm. And he still favoured his white shirts, a detail that sent her heart racing in an instant.

Crossing her arms as if stopping her body from propelling itself towards Shamil, she watched Ameena envelop him in a tight embrace, almost trying to make him a part of her once again. Who could blame her? He was her only son.

"You're the light of my life," Ameena said, tears welling up in her honey-brown eyes, before Mudhar playfully intervened.

"Give us some space, woman," he said, peeking from behind Ameena.

For Laila, it was an extraordinary sight. Mudhar, usually reserved with his emotions, now revealed a rare display of affection as he drew Shamil closer. She'd never seen him hug anyone before, other than Zain, but on that day, embracing Shamil with both arms, he was as if an expert in awkward hugs, bringing a smile to Laila's lips.

Now, it was her turn. As Shamil's eyes met hers, Laila felt her heart thud against her ribs, pushing her ever closer to him. Should she reach out and hold his hands, or would prying eyes condemn their intimacy? Could she dare to kiss his cheeks, feel the soft brush of his beard against her skin, or would propriety deem it improper?

Could she kiss his lips? She trembled at that last thought, biting her own. Though fifteen years had passed since they last tasted each other, the memory lingered—a phantom sweetness she yearned to savour again.

When they would be alone, she would do it all, but for now, a gentle peck on the cheek wouldn't offend anyone.

She felt him take a deep breath, relishing the familiar fragrance of the perfume she wore—the one he always liked. Her soft lips imprinted on his skin as she greeted him with a gentle peck on the cheek. His fingers brushed her arm, a touch so light it sent a ripple of warmth through her. When his hand rested on her hip, it felt steady, grounding. She couldn't stop the smile that spread across her face, her chest tightening with emotion as her eyes met his soft, brown ones—so familiar, so kind.

"You really came," she whispered, her voice filled with the joy that threatened to spill over.

"Of course I did," he said, his gaze locked on hers. "Where is he?"

Laila's heart faltered. Amidst the excitement of Shamil's return, she had forgotten about Zain. "He's inside. I'll go and get him," she said, smoothing her hijab before she hurried upstairs to their apartment.

"There will be a feast in Shamil's honour this Friday. Everyone is invited, OK?" Mudhar's voice echoed, announcing to the gathered neighbours.

Obviously, it would be Laila and Ameena preparing that grand feast, yet Mudhar would gladly take credit for it. She didn't mind that time— her heart was whole, knowing that Shamil was there, safe and sound—home at last.

"Zain," Laila called out as she entered her apartment, her voice echoing in the quiet hallway. The only response was the soft rustle of the wind beneath Zain's closed door. She urgently opened the door to an empty bed and an abandoned laptop on the desk. The room was immaculate; Zain must have tidied it up with meticulous care. But where was he?

She checked the kitchen and the bathroom, peering into every corner of the apartment, but he was nowhere to be found. Panic started to set in as she searched the balcony and her bedroom — still, no sign of him.

Perhaps he had already gone to his grandparents' house, but she was sure she hadn't seen him pass by. Reaching for her phone, she dialled Zain's number, hoping for an answer, but he didn't pick up. She tried again, only for him to hang up abruptly.

Laila's anger rose, momentarily overshadowing her concern. She hadn't raised him to be disrespectful. Whatever was going on, she needed to find him, and she wasn't going to let him evade her.

"Where are you?" Laila complained into her phone the moment Zain picked up. Silence greeted her, accompanied by muffled voices in the background. Although she couldn't hear everything clearly, snippets of the conversation reached her ears.

"Two, three weeks at most..."

"We need to keep the pressure high until..."

"Obviously... Casualties..."

Was he at Amr's? Laila tugged her hijab away from her ear and pressed the phone hard against it, desperate to hear more clearly. Zain had sworn he would stop communicating with the rebels, yet here he was, breaking his promise. Jassim warned them that if Zain continued aiding the rebels, he wouldn't be able to protect him anymore.

Laila's pulse quickened as she strained to identify the voices on the other end. Amr's voice was unmistakable, and she was almost certain she heard Muhammad's as well—two of Zain's closest friends. This offered her heart little reassurance. In fact, it deepened her worry, for when those three were together, trouble invariably followed.

Disappointed in him, Laila continued to listen until a gentle tap on her shoulder from the back sent her panicking as if a ghost had touched her. Gasping, she turned to find Mudhar standing there, looking perplexed and perhaps even guilty for startling her.

"My God, daughter, it's just me," Mudhar said.

She hung up the phone in panic, not wanting Mudhar to know about Zain's whereabouts. The last time she had confided in him, Zain ended up in prison—a mere coincidence, she knew, but the association lingered in her subconscious.

"I'm sorry, uncle, I didn't know you followed me," Laila said, attempting to regain her composure.

"I came to get the cable for the generator. Zain took it this morning but didn't return it. We'll need it later," Mudhar explained.

"Of course, I'll get it for you. You don't have to wait," Laila replied, making her way to Zain's room. She knew her son's habits well— whenever he did a quick clean, he would stash everything he found lying around in the bottom drawer.

True to her expectations, Zain had nestled the cable among a jumble of unfolded clothes, chocolate wrappers, and even an empty bag of crisps. She sighed, half exasperated by his clutter and half relieved the cable was there.

As Mudhar took the cable from her hands, he inquired, "Where's Zain?"

Laila mustered her best fake smile. "He went to drop off a bag of clothes at Amr's place. He should be back any minute— I sent him a text." The lie came effortlessly.

"Well, call him. See if he needs me to pick him up," Mudhar said, his fingers deftly wrapping the cable into a wreath.

She had already called, of course. She had already heard what she dreaded and hoped not to hear again. Mudhar had to leave, but she couldn't just tell him that. It would be unusual, rude even.

"Uncle, pardon me, but I really need to use the toilet before coming back down," her voice wavered as she spoke, her fingers fidgeting with the hem of her hijab. Two lies in a row were a bit more than she could endure.

"Oh God, yes, sure, daughter," Mudhar stammered, turning his face away awkwardly as if Laila was suddenly naked before him.

"I won't be long." She closed the door.

Chapter 8: A Piece of Heaven

The ground floor's hallway carried the lingering aroma of freshly brewed cardamom coffee. Shamil smiled, taking in that precious scent as he followed his mother, Ameena, into the cherished courtyard, where treasured family gatherings unfolded.

For a second, his steps faltered as he looked back at the metallic front door. The years had slipped by, yet the holes he had made as a resourceful teenager, a desperate measure whenever he forgot his keys, remained untouched. A rush of nostalgia swept over him, momentarily easing the anxiety that had built during his journey back home.

Why did Laila leave so suddenly? He couldn't suppress that nagging thought. Surely Zain knew he was arriving any minute, so why wasn't he there with the rest of them?

He needed to let go; there was no point in worrying when everyone around him seemed so relaxed. Settling into a chair next to Ameena, he let the soothing ambience of the rock fountain and the heavenly scent of his father's beloved grapefruit tree envelop him. His gaze turned towards the tree, its branches stretching like supportive arms across the second floor, as if it held their entire home together. When his father, Mudhar, first acquired the plot of land on which he envisioned their family house, it was nothing more than a humble expanse housing two mud-walled rooms and a grapefruit tree.

The previous landlords had advised Mudhar to dismantle the aged structure and level the ground for an apartment complex. A tempting proposition, no doubt, but Mudhar found himself drawn to the tree's allure.

"How can I cut down a piece of heaven?" he had mused to his architect friend as they discussed the blueprints. And so, the architect had designed a two-story house that would coexist harmoniously with the majestic tree. A gap in the ceiling, covered with a transparent plastic sheet in winter and thick cardboard in summer, was meant to maintain the tree's prominence while offering protection from the elements.

An architectural disaster indeed it was.

When it rained, they drowned in an indoor pool, and when it snowed, their bones ached. As for the notorious August, no one dared to test the architect's vision during the peak of scorching Middle Eastern summers.

"Coffee? Tea? Water?" Ameena offered, about to get up.

Shamil's hand quickly landed on her shoulder. "Sit, Mama, let me see you first."

She smiled, holding Shamil's hand. Her hazel-brown eyes glistened with tears. She couldn't have adorned herself with more golden jewellery than she did that evening, a gesture reserved for the most special occasions. As a child, Shamil could never have imagined a day when he wouldn't be in the same city as his beloved mother.

He had always adored her, cherishing the moments when she had walked him to school, shown him how to cook, and read his poems and short stories, being his harshest critic and biggest fan both at once. She was his guiding angel, and he had promised God that he would be forever grateful for the eternal gift of her presence.

"Mama?" Shamil said, pulling her closer and kissing her head. "Those better be happy tears."

"It's hard to tell; they both always felt the same," she chuckled, wiping her face. "I thought I was never going to see you again."

"It wasn't forever."

"It sure felt like it."

"Well, now I'm back," Shamil said, grabbing a glass of water. "Is he coming?" he added, his worry growing as Zain remained absent.

"He will, don't worry," Ameena said, removing her headscarf and allowing her golden hair to breathe freely around her shoulders. "I told your father that you are as stubborn as Zain is. I knew you would come regardless of what we say."

"You didn't leave me much choice now, did you?" Shamil said, glancing at Mudhar coming through the front door. Alone.

"Zain is safe now, and you are too," Mudhar interjected as he grabbed a seat next to Ameena. He must have overheard them talking.

"Does he know I'm here?" Shamil asked.

"Yes, he went to drop off some old clothes. Bless him, he cares a lot for his friends," Mudhar explained.

Shamil nodded in silence, disappointed that he wasn't his son's priority.

Perhaps he deserved it after his prolonged absence, but if not for his son's future, he wouldn't have been absent in the first place, something they seem to have forgotten. His eyes flitted back to the open front door; it was Laila this time. She had that look on her face, which she usually had when she was nervous, embarrassed, or trying to hide something. She was terrible at lying, his sweet angel; it wasn't something she could do for long.

Her eyes locked with his for a fleeting moment before darting away, a telltale sign that something was off.

"I'll make us coffee," she scurried into the downstairs kitchen, lifting the edges of her long blue dress to keep them clear of the floor. Her toenails adorned like cute little ladybug backs—a sight he hadn't witnessed in years. He couldn't afford to be distracted, though. A gnawing feeling tugged at him, telling him they were all hiding something.

"My dear, you've lost so much weight," Ameena said, her eyes scanning Shamil with concern. "Zain is coming, stop worrying."

"He can't stop worrying; it's in his nature," Mudhar scoffed, unwrapping the cable he had in hand.

Ameena nudged Mudhar gently with her elbow. "And you're the king of cool nerves, eh? You should have seen your face last week when...."

"It's all in the past now," Mudhar interrupted, laying his hand on Ameena's thigh and locking eyes with her. She took the hint; she'd had forty years of practice.

"Yeah, it won't happen again," she said, looking back at Shamil. "It was nothing really."

"Well, it didn't sound like nothing in Father's messages," Shamil said. "Actually, after what I saw today on the road, I think you all should consider going abroad."

"We can't just leave everything," Mudhar waved his hand dismissively. "And for what? For fear of a couple of teenagers shouting around?"

"The police used live ammo today, Baba," Shamil spoke, his tone rising with emotion. Even if today's incident was an outlier, it was still serious. A sign of what was yet to come. "And on the radio, there was talk of rebels advancing towards the city. I think we should be ready to leave, just in case."

"Only traitors leave their country at war," Zain's voice echoed through the corridor leading to the front door.

Shamil's eyes widened in shock as he strained to recognise his son's voice. Leaping from his chair, he closed the distance, pulling Zain into a tight embrace, his nose buried in the soft, grey sweater, searching for echoes of the past. The once-familiar scent of milkshakes and biscuits had given way to a more mature aroma of sweat and shaving cream. His boy had changed, standing tall and thin, no longer the little one he once knew.

Zain's brown eyes mirrored the intensity of his mother, Laila, while his hair, once a light brown, had transformed into dark, wavy locks, strikingly resembling her. Zain slowly, almost shyly, wrapped his arms around Shamil, and in that moment, something inside Shamil broke.

The weight of every moment they'd lost hit him all at once, a wave of grief and regret crashing over him, leaving his heart aching with sorrow too heavy to bear.

"Look at you," Shamil said, holding Zain's face and studying his every feature.

Zain looked away. "I didn't think you'd come."

"Son, nothing would have stopped me," Shamil replied.

Zain took a step back. "Let me cut it short. I'm not leaving with you."

"Son, I..." Shamil paused, holding back his words.

He looked at Zain, standing there with his arms crossed, prepared for confrontation. His sweet boy was so cold and distant despite how close they finally were to each other. Struggling to find the right words, he looked back at Ameena, Laila, and anyone else who could back him up.

"All right, food will be ready soon. I don't want any of you to talk about politics," Ameena intervened, giving Zain a stern look. She then turned her attention back to Shamil. "We're going to have dinner like a normal family, okay?"

"Sure," Shamil replied, his gaze now drawn to a camera fastened to Zain's waist. The camera appeared more costly than Zain's budget, and Shamil couldn't recall buying it for him.

Grabbing Zain by the arm and sitting him next to her, Ameena then turned her attention to Shamil. "So, tell me, how's the UK? How's your work?"

"It's good," Shamil replied, trying to regain his composure. "Work is rewarding. And I got into speciality training at last."

"You're still in training?" Mudhar's thick black eyebrow arched in surprise.

"Yes, I just started it."

"So, how many years before you became a specialist?"

"Depends. Sometimes up to eight years."

"Eight years?" Mudhar's voice rose, disappointment etching lines on his face—a look Shamil dreaded with a passion. No matter how grown-up Shamil had become, a single dissatisfied glance from either of his parents was enough to transport him back to primary school, clutching his report card, on the verge of tears over that one subject where he hadn't entirely made the grade.

"If you were here, you would have been a consultant by now, working at your clinic. You probably wouldn't have left either," Mudhar continued. "You would have had many children, with tons of money flowing into your pockets."

"One special kid is enough," Shamil said, looking at Zain. His frown was unchanged.

"More is better. In case one of them decides to abandon you and leaves for London," Ameena said, her smile forced as she rose to head to the kitchen, her words stinging as much as Mudhar's, if not more.

Shamil needed his coffee.

He loved his family. Still, the time they spent apart had drawn deep lines onto their faces, but it had not dulled the sharpness of their disagreements.

"The city centre was so busy," Shamil said, changing the subject.

"Lots of refugees, but it'll get better," Mudhar said in his usual authoritative, dismissive tone.

"No, it won't," Zain said, trying not to raise his voice to what might be deemed impolite. "Not until we overthrow the regime, if God wills it."

"And how do you expect that to happen?" Shamil said.

"The free army will keep hammering the regime forces until they surrender and give up the city," Zain said.

"I thought I said no politics when food is around," Ameena interrupted, carrying a fruit platter. "We're now celebrating my son's return. There will be no talk of political nonsense," she added, putting the large tray on the table Zain had quickly pulled near the fountain.

"You two can talk about this upstairs," Laila mirrored Ameena's sentiment, carrying the coffee tray. "For now, let's enjoy a little peace."

"Mama, we're just talking," Zain told Laila, taking the tray from her. Following tradition, he offered the first cup to Mudhar, followed by Shamil.

Grabbing his cup, Shamil studied his son's features, now as mature as the big words he was using. Overthrowing the regime, hammering the police, surrendering the city—these were words that must have been fed to him by the rebels and their sympathisers. Words that had consequences Shamil wasn't sure Zain was aware of.

They had been talking on Skype, Yahoo Messenger and other applications that connected them, but seeing his face that close felt different. He could see every freckle and every zit. Every little scar, the ones he remembered and those he didn't, and something inside him grew even sadder. He couldn't bring back time, but he wouldn't waste another second away from his precious boy.

"That looks like a costly camera," Shamil told a silent Zain.

Zain set the tray aside. "It takes amazing photos, even from afar," he said, picking up the camera. "I'll show you some great photos I took from a rooftop."

"I see," Shamil said, looking at Zain start his camera.

"He was gonna send me a better one, but Mum wouldn't let him."

"He?" Shamil raised his eyebrows. Who could be sending such lavish gifts to his teenage son?

"Your friend Alaa bought it for him," Mudhar chimed in.

Alaa—a name Shamil hadn't heard from since he'd left for London, yet the memory remained as fresh and strong as the scent of cinnamon wafting from his teacup.

"I've had it for a year now-" Zain started, then everything plunged into darkness.

Chapter 9: Black

Laila had never been bothered by power cuts. Lights out—no problem. A candle lit in the dark was the perfect medium for her to paint for hours, the dancing shadows on the walls of her cold bedroom guiding her every brushstroke.

That, until Zain was arrested.

Now, whenever the lights went out, her stomach turned in knots. Was there going to be another protest? Was Zain going to sneak out and join them somehow? Were the news reports of the rebels advancing towards the city truthful?

Fears that clogged her mind so heavily that she stopped painting altogether—her creations had all transformed into featureless shapes of black.

Casualties, armed rebels, time's up—if only she had continued listening to Zain's conversation earlier that afternoon, perhaps she could have made sense of the fragments she had overheard. Small protests occasionally erupted near their house, lasting mere minutes before the police dispersed them, and life resumed its normal course. That was their reality. But to speak of casualties? She wasn't prepared for that.

Regardless, now that Zain was beside her, she wouldn't let him out of her sight again.

The moment the lights went out, she instinctively grabbed his arm. "Help me in the kitchen."

"But the generator," Zain turned his mobile's flash on, resisting her grip.

She locked eyes with Mudhar, his face barely lit.

She couldn't ask him aloud to start the generator himself and leave her to talk to Zain, but her face must have said it all.

"I'll do it; go help your mother, Son," Mudhar told Zain.

"I can do it," Shamil offered.

"I'll be quick, you stay here," Mudhar replied, getting off his chair and nudging Ameena's shoulder.

"You sit here and tell me about London," Ameena told Shamil before turning to face Laila. "See if the rice is done?"

Laila nodded with relief. Mudhar and Ameena were quick to her aid. She could always count on them passing instructions to each other without having to whisper a word, something she admired and envied.

With a firm grip, she pulled Zain into the kitchen on the ground floor, a good distance from where Shamil was sitting.

"Ok, what have I done this time?" Zain said, freeing his arm once they were inside.

Laila closed the door. "You're staying here with me until the lights come back."

"I wasn't going anywhere," Zain scoffed, briefly glancing at his vibrating mobile before he switched one of the kitchen's battery-powered bulbs. "I told you I stopped."

"Zain, I heard everything," she blurted, not wanting him to embarrass himself by lying to her. "The protest plans, the times, everything."

His face, illuminated by the feeble glow of the kitchen's weak bulb, appeared even paler as he gazed at her. With a nervous smile, he asked, "What protest?"

"The stupid one you've plotted with your 'friends'."

Zain's smile quickly morphed into a straight line. "I…"

"You know what, it doesn't matter. Your father is here now, and he will have to deal with you," Laila interrupted, waving her hand at Zain.

She stole a glance at Shamil through the kitchen window, and in a moment of synchrony, Shamil responded with a knowing look as if he sensed her watching. Swiftly diverting her gaze, in fear he might perceive her concerns and join them in the kitchen, she looked back at Zain. "Of all the days to go and meet them, you chose today."

Zain flicked through his phone. "So now you are spying on me?" he said, holding his phone before her. "Show me how you did it."

"You lied to me," Laila said, softening her tone. "And what's this you're wearing? Is this how one greets his father?" she pointed at his black joggers, which he had usually worn whenever he'd been to one of the protests.

"Show me how," Zain insisted, a look of betrayal on his face.

That sorrowful gaze nearly suffocated her, one that she didn't deserve. Still, even though she inadvertently 'spied' on him, she would have intentionally done so if given the opportunity. "You answered me when I called," she clarified.

"I see," Zain checked his call record. "You should have hung up," he turned to face the kitchen door, but Laila wouldn't let him leave.

"You're not going out." she blocked his way.

"I'm going to sit beside him. Isn't this what you want?" Zain uttered, his voice faltering as he focused on the door handle. His trembling hand met Laila's grip.

The pain in her chest grew stronger, and she let go. "Let's just have a normal dinner, and we'll talk about it all when we're in the flat, ok?"

"Normal," Zain scoffed, exiting the kitchen and leaving her behind.

She leaned against the kitchen door and watched him dust off his joggers before he pulled a chair next to his father.

Nothing was 'normal' in her life, but she had faith that it would all change soon. Shamil was back, and she was going to tell him everything. She only had to...

The gas! Panic surged through her as the smell of burning rice filled the air. Hastily, she turned around, rushing to rescue the pot from the stove and placing it onto the cool marble rack.

"You burned it again?" Ameena complained, joining Laila in the kitchen and closing the door behind her.

It was as if Laila needed a reminder of how inattentive she had become recently. She quickly covered the pot with a damp cloth, hoping Ameena hadn't noticed how bad it was, although Ameena's keen senses were nearly superhuman.

"Just a bit, I'm sorry, Aunty," Laila said before noticing a smudge of oil on her left sleeve. She sighed, assessing the extent of the stain. "I knew I shouldn't have worn this."

"Here, let me," Ameena offered, grabbing a lemon from the shelf, cutting it in half, and squeezing a few drops onto the stain. "Was he going to sneak out?"

"He says he wasn't, but...." Laila began before her voice faltered.

She couldn't fool Ameena about Zain's intentions more than she could fool her about how badly the rice had burnt. "I just want to protect him; why doesn't he understand that?"

"It's impossible," Ameena said dismissively as she dabbed a dry paper towel on Laila's sleeve. "If I recount the times Shamil was hurt or poisoned or.... ugh, may Allah forgive my tongue for saying this, but he used to attract as much misfortune as defrosting meat attracts stray cats."

Laila smiled bitterly; misfortune had indeed clung to her much like that stubborn stain. "Should we tell him?" she asked, her voice low, her eyes searching Ameena's face for agreement. But Ameena's expression gave nothing away. "About Jassim and..."

"Let him eat first!" Ameena cut in, her tone sharp. She reached over, brushing at the bits of dry paper towel stuck to Laila's sleeve. A few pieces clung stubbornly, but she didn't seem to notice—or perhaps didn't care enough to try again. "Now, roll it up and lend me a hand with the table."

"Of course," Laila quickly pulled up her sleeves and unwrapped the wet towel she had sealed the rice pot with. She knew she shouldn't have asked— she anticipated the inevitable refusal. Still, the anxiousness that had taken hold of her refused to let go.

She reached for the serving plates Ameena had set aside and began filling them with rice, avoiding scraping the bottom to prevent mixing the burnt bits with the good ones. She'd already embarrassed herself enough and wouldn't lose focus again— Ameena had spent hours in the kitchen preparing the food, and Laila wouldn't upset her.

"Did you season the salad?" Ameena asked, sprinkling a mixture of butter-roasted nuts over the rice. The sizzling aroma of pine nuts and almonds replaced the smoke.

"Yes, I did," Laila replied, swiftly tasting the salad and exhaling with relief as the lemon juices and salt dissolved on her tongue. "It's definitely seasoned."

"Zain, come help us set the table," Ameena called Zain, who dashed into the kitchen with empty teacups in hand.

"Grandpa wants more tea," he held the teacups before him.

"He'll have to wait," Ameena said loudly, her daring gaze directed at Mudhar. "We're having dinner first."

Laila took the cups from Zain and put them in the sink before she poured the okra stew into serving bowls. She opened the oven to heat some bread, only to find a tray of oven-baked Kibbeh steaming inside.

"You made Kibbeh?" she asked, retrieving the tray from the oven.

"There's also rice and pistachio pudding in the fridge for dessert," Ameena replied, adding more cumin to the salad before drizzling it with olive oil. "It needed an extra kick," she explained with a smile directed at Laila as if to soften the critique.

Laila couldn't have cared less.

While she had indeed seasoned the salad, her mind couldn't recall the act. Shamil's return and that damn phone call had consumed all her attention, and she was lucky she didn't double the amount of salt or, heaven forbid, add chilli pepper to the seasoning— such a blunder would have been unforgivable.

Disaster averted, and all she had to do was help set the table, have their dinner, and then head back together with Shamil to their apartment, where she could hold him close and rest her head against his chest. She yearned for a moment alone with him, inhaling the scent of his shirt and feeling his skin against hers. If only she had harboured such feelings in the years leading up to his departure for London. Perhaps then, she wouldn't have urged him to leave in the first place.

Everything would be fine— Shamil was sitting beside her, consuming the rice she had accidentally burnt and sipping the tea she had brewed. And for a moment, it felt almost normal until his phone vibrated.

A message from 'K' flashed on the screen, just long enough for Laila and Ameena to catch a glimpse before he swiftly snatched the phone from the table, nearly spilling his tea. He brought the phone close to his face, obscuring the screen from Laila's view, and within moments, he powered it off and slipped it into his pocket.

Chapter 10: Sweet and Sour

Shamil grabbed a glass of water; K's message had left his throat parched.

One thousand dollars per person? What a scam. Just yesterday, they agreed to the job for five hundred dollars each. Something must have changed, but it wasn't going to deter Shamil. It was a minor hiccup, and things were still going according to plan.

"K is for Klinton?" Ameena asked, reaching for Shamil's plate to refill it.

Shamil's pulse quickened, and he sensed the blood flushing his cheeks. Lying to Ameena was not something he had ever been successful in doing.

"Clinton with a K? Grandma?" Zain interjected with a chuckle, saving Shamil's face.

"Yes, Klinton, K, right?" Ameena asked, looking at Shamil for confirmation.

"Some are with a K, yes," Shamil said, stopping Ameena from taking his plate. "I've had my fill, Mama. I think we'll call it a night, yeah?" He glanced at Laila, who nodded.

"I'll take the bags upstairs." Zain pushed his half-finished plate down the table and got up in a rush as if he had been waiting for that dinner to end.

"You go ahead; I'll help Auntie clean up," Laila said.

"I'll do it myself, Daughter. You tend to your husband," Ameena replied, rising to kiss Shamil on the cheek. "Coffee in the morning?" she added softly.

"Of course," Shamil mustered a strained smile, casting a gentle glance over his shoulder. He then left for his apartment on the first floor of the building opposite his parents' house, Laila trailing silently behind him.

Entering the apartment, the power had already been restored, and the smog from the neighbourhood generators had begun to dissipate.

"Hurry up and shower before the lights go off again," Laila said, turning the bathroom light on before shouting, "Zain, the floor is wet again; I told you a thousand times to check after you've showered."

"I'm sorry," Zain said, dashing past Shamil into the living room, the rest of Shamil's luggage in his hands. He dropped everything near the door, then rushed back into his room, leaving Laila to mop the bathroom floor.

"Slow down. Can I get another hug?" Shamil said, standing at Zain's door with his arms open wide.

Zain swivelled in his chair to face him, then sighed. "I stink."

"You don't, Baba. You smell like heaven," Shamil insisted, approaching him and giving him a brief hug while he remained seated. "If anyone here stinks, it's me after all that travelling."

"You smell like food and expensive cologne," Laila chimed in, poking her head through the bathroom door. "The floor is dry — I'll get you some fresh towels."

"Oh yes, thank you," Shamil glanced at her. "I'll just talk to Zain for a bit."

Standing in Zain's room, he let his eyes wander. It was smaller than he'd remembered; now, a large desk filled almost one-third of it, but it still carried a warmth that felt unmistakably Zain.

The thick grey and black wool carpet was new. It stretched across the floor, soft and quiet underfoot, almost swallowing any sound. Zain's bed was where it had always been, pressed against the right corner, with dark green sheets neatly tucked in and plumped-up pillows. It looked inviting and cosy as if Zain had slept in it only a handful of times, but Shamil chose to lie down on the thick carpet instead— his spine was weary of the long, bumpy roads he had travelled, and he needed a bit of 'tough love' before he could sit up again.

"I love this carpet," Shamil said, his eyes feeling heavy. "If only I had more space in my room in London, I would have definitely got one just like this."

"You still live in that matchbox?" Zain mocked. Compared to his room, Shamil's was a prison cell.

"Yeah, flats are expensive in London, and I thought I'd save that extra money for when you and your mum move there."

"I told you I'm not moving," Zain's reply was intense.

"It's happening."

"Make me."

Shamil pulled himself up and rested his back against the bed. He hadn't returned to strong-arm his son into submission—he wasn't Mudhar. He had hoped to talk to him, to understand why he had chosen this path, and to show him that he was there for him. "Son, it's not a game," he said gently. "What you're doing is dangerous."

Zain kept silent for a few seconds; his attention focused on his desk where the laptop was.

"I'll show you," he snatched his phone out of his pocket, hastily scrolling through it as if he'd lost something on it. "You'll agree with me because it's the right thing."

"I've seen the videos; they were horrible," Shamil said, not wanting to see them again.

"There's more," Zain said, his hand shaking. "I know you're upset about the arrest, but they released me the same day, and they couldn't prove anything against me."

"Zain, it's ok," Shamil said, placing his hand on Zain's knee. "You're home safe now and won't be protesting again."

Zain pulled his knee away. "What's wrong with protesting?"

"Getting arrested again? Getting tortured? Perhaps, even shot?" Shamil couldn't hold back.

"It wasn't even a real arrest. Jassim probably arranged it to scare me," Zain said with a smirk, oblivious to the gravity of being arrested, whether real or staged.

Shamil raised his voice, "Even so, do you realise what arresting you, the grandson of Mudhar, means?"

"You're not listening to me."

"You aren't either," Shamil said, tucking a pillow behind his lower back. "Son, I don't need this headache right now. We're getting you a passport and leaving; this is the end of it."

With a flick of his thumb, Zain brought up a series of harrowing images on his phone's screen: bombed-out buildings, bloodied bodies, and wounded civilians.

Images just like the ones Shamil had seen online, but no matter how many he'd seen, he still couldn't help but flinch at the sight. "How can you condone this?"

"I don't; it's horrific," Shamil said, taking the phone from Zain's hands. "This clip is from Iraq, by the way." Shamil kept on scrolling. "And this one is from Chechnya, it has been dubbed."

"Oh my God, you're just like the regime muppets," Zain snapped. "It's all fake news, yeah?"

"Not all of it." Shamil switched off the phone. "I'm just showing you how easy it is to spread rumours and play with people's emotions."

"Even if one per cent of those clips were real, it would be enough."

"Son, what good will it do for you to get involved? What could protesting teenagers achieve with their cardboard signs? Deflect bullets and tank shells?"

"I'm not weak, like you; I'm doing what's right."

"Weak?" Shamil didn't believe his ears. Had Zain no respect for him whatsoever? "I've worked day and night for you and your mum, and this is how you thank me?"

"I didn't want you to leave."

"You were eleven. It didn't matter what you wanted," Shamil blurted, regretting those words the moment they parted his lips.

Zain's anger dissipated, replaced by a wounded expression. "Yes, I didn't matter."

"Zain, I just want you to be safe."

"With this regime, none of us is safe," a tearful Zain said softly. "There needs to be justice."

"But is this really the way to get justice?" Shamil said, his tone gentle but firm. "You're not just putting yourself in danger, but your family too."

"I didn't ask you to come. I was fine without you."

"And you getting hurt wouldn't affect me? Are you crazy?" Shamil asked, and Zain ignored him, unlocking his laptop and opening his Facebook.

"Can I get my phone back?" Zain threw his hand in front of Shamil.

"Son, this isn't how I imagined our first meeting to be."

"My phone, please?" he gestured impatiently as Shamil relented, handing it over.

Taking a deep breath, Shamil found himself dealing with a standoff he had anticipated but not so soon, and certainly not with Zain holding the moral high ground. Was it wrong to prioritise his family's safety while others suffered on the streets? Were the protests the right way forward? What could they realistically change anyway? The conflict was larger than any of them could ever hope to change. It was past peaceful protesting; the regime had murdered thousands of civilians. The only direction the conflict was heading was one of bloodshed; for once, Shamil decided to be selfish and ensure his family's safety, hoping to find ways to aid those left behind later. It was the right thing to do.

Changing the topic, Shamil asked, "You always wanted to come and live with me abroad, remember? A house with an ice cream tap? Why the change now?"

"An ice cream tap," Zain scoffed. "I'm not a child."

Indeed, he wasn't anymore. Only Shamil hadn't realised it yet. He stood there, stunned into silence. Should he resort to the same oppressive tactics as Mudhar had with him, or should he strive for understanding and seek a middle ground?

No. There was no time for dragging it any longer; it was too risky. Had they not been related to Jassim, Zain would have been another name on a long list of prisoners of unknown fates. Shamil wouldn't allow that to happen. Protesting had to stop, but for now, he needed to calm things down.

"I'll go take a bath," Shamil said, leaning forward to plant a gentle kiss on Zain's head.

Planning his return, Shamil had naively assumed his son would simply listen and comply—after all, that's how Shamil himself had been at Zain's age. Even now, at thirty-seven, if Mudhar were to ask something of him, Shamil would still do it out of respect. His initial intention was to better understand Zain before delving into his involvement with the opposition.

However, their conversation quickly spiralled into an argument that threatened any hope of future dialogue. Exhaustion had gotten the best of him— he could barely keep his eyes open, let alone engage in a reasoned discussion with his son without letting his emotions cloud his judgment.

Dragging his feet from Zain's room to the bathroom, he checked his phone. A few messages from John had appeared on the screen. Aidan had complained to the hospital and was threatening legal action unless Shamil apologised to him in person.

Shamil shook his head; he knew that his good deed would come back to haunt him. He decided to deal with it later; for now, he needed a break. Laila had already heated the water, unpacked his bags, and hung his pyjamas on the bathroom door.

"I know I said don't come, but I'm happy you did," she said, her voice trembling with emotion as she stood by the bathroom door.

Oh, how he missed her raspy voice.

"I couldn't stay away," he replied with a smile.

And it was true. Despite all their past arguments, there was nothing he wouldn't have done for her— his heart would always win that debate.

Slipping into the soothing warmth of the bathtub, Shamil surrendered to the embrace of tranquillity, allowing his mind to wander to a time when his heart was complete.

His love for her was instantaneous. She had just moved into their neighbourhood, and from the moment he set eyes on her, he felt it—the unparalleled warmth that filled his chest, as if it yearned for her presence to be intertwined with it. Her scent was unique, softer and lighter than any other girl's—like a field of lemon trees after a gentle rain. Her accent was as sweet as honey. She could have told him, "You're an absolute embarrassment," and he would have relished hearing her say it.

At sixteen, he confessed his love to her, the memory of that day still vivid in his heart.

"I want you to be my wife," he blurted as soon as they crossed the finish line at a school race.

She had laughed, but it was a sweet, musical sound that left him breathless. "You can't even outrun me in a silly race. How can you be my man?" she had said, her voice teasing.

There must have been a dozen other pupils around them witnessing his humiliation, but all he could see was her beautiful face.

"So, you'll say yes if I win?" he asked, thrilled that she hadn't said no.

"You'll never win, Sham," she replied with a grin before jogging away with her friends.

I made her laugh, he daydreamed, unable to take his eyes off her.

"Happy now? You looked like a total fool," Alaa said, Shamil's high school best friend, landing his hand on Shamil's shoulder. His eyes were as green as olives basking in a Syrian scorching sun. He had probably never run a comb through his straight light-brown hair— a couple of ruffles were all he needed to make it look presentable.

"She didn't say no," Shamil looked back at him.

"She didn't say yes, either. She actually mocked you."

"I don't care," Shamil dusted his shorts, then wiped the sweat off his face. "She thought I was funny."

"She laughed at you, you idiot. You need to ignore her and make her beg for your attention; that's what girls want," Alaa scoffed, claiming to be the expert.

"Not Laila," Shamil said, his young heart naively believing it to be true.

Unplugging the bath, Shamil sat at its edge, waiting for it to empty— had he remained in it any longer, and he might have drifted off to sleep amidst the warm embrace of the water. He dried himself off, then ensured the bathroom floor was spotless before he made his way to the bedroom. There, he found Laila seated on the ottoman, gently running a comb through her wavy black hair before gathering it up and removing her makeup. She rarely wore cosmetics, perhaps only the occasional touch of mascara or the handmade kohl her mother had gifted her. Soft and untainted by lipstick or creams, her lips had always held the pure essence of her being, like the sweet nectar of sun-ripened strawberries. Why did she bother with makeup at all? Was it to accentuate what Shamil had been missing for years? Did she even care if he missed her at all?

"You're staring," she said, looking at his reflection in her mirror: a shadow of a man burdened with guilt.

"I'm just tired," Shamil said.

He was indeed tired of not being with her, of not being there for Zain when he needed him, of worrying about everything and everyone.

"Is he going to get his passport done?" Laila asked, dotting two drops of scented oil onto her wrists, rubbing them together, and running them down her neck on each side—a once inviting ritual that he could no longer act upon. She was the reason he believed in God; her beauty was the design of a deity, not the result of numbers and probability.

"It's not that simple," Shamil said, taking in all that sweet scent.

"I told you so."

"I know," Shamil said, resting his back against the door and looking back at her perfect reflection in the mirror. "He's very passionate about this whole 'revolution' I don't know how he got there."

"He believes it's his duty."

"And he's so damn stubborn, like his mum," he teased.

"Ten times more, I'd say," she chuckled.

"We're asking him to turn a blind eye to all these injustices—it's hard to justify such a request."

"Being righteous is one thing, and being reckless is another," she said. "Anyway, let's rest now, you must be exhausted."

Shamil checked the time on his mobile phone; it was past midnight.

"We'll figure it out together tomorrow," he said, looking around for the floor mattress he used to sleep on in the years that preceded his departure to London. "Where is the mattress?"

"It's on the roof. Zain sometimes uses it there," she said, untying her hair and then lying down on her side of the bed. "You can sleep on the bed. I don't mind."

But Shamil minded sharing the bed with her; only he was too tired to object. How could he lie beside her, yearning to touch her, yet unable to do so?

"We'll find you a new mattress tomorrow," Laila insisted. "It's just tonight."

"Ok, only tonight then," Shamil surrendered, shuffling to the bed and sitting on its edge for a minute before lying down.

Why couldn't they have stayed married? He tried to drift away, the weight of the world pressing down upon him.

With Laila's back turned to him, he lay there in silence, tracing familiar patterns in the shadows cast by the chandelier. He closed his eyes, feeling the warmth of her body so close to his, almost embracing him. The soft sound of her breathing synchronised with the gentle sway of the blanket, pulling them closer together with each exhale.

Suddenly, her voice broke through the stillness.

"Is 'K' one of your lovers?" she asked softly.

Shamil froze, her words hitting him harder than he'd expected. He wanted to turn to her, meet her gaze, and challenge her to find even a flicker of another lover in his eyes. But he couldn't do it. She had asked him to let her go, and he had given her his word.

"I don't have any lovers."

Chapter 11: The Longing

Noura's snores filled the room with a comforting rattle, a familiar rhythm that eased Jassim's restless mind as he lay beside her. Each sudden and forced exhalation seemed to carry her soul to the brink of departure before she would draw it back in, an act that no longer troubled him, not since the doctors assured him it was benign.

With a bitter taste lingering on his tongue, Jassim swallowed the pill that aided his sleep. Resting his back against his bed, he reached for the situation report that had consumed his thoughts all week. He needed an explanation, one that justified his restraint from employing lethal force against the protesters without branding him as sympathetic to the rebels' cause. He would have shot the insurgents himself; that was never in question. He merely had no desire to inflict harm upon civilians in the process. He had arrested plenty. In fact, he had even authorised the torture of those who had organised the protests and aided the terrorists. But to kill civilians? That wasn't something he could order himself.

He glanced at Noura after one of her deep breaths; a rare smile adorned her lips. What could she be dreaming about? People, Jassim mused, were most genuine in their sleep— deceit didn't spill from their lips when they were unconscious. If only he could delve into Noura's mind to scout the landscapes of her thoughts. Was she visited by visions of their martyred son, Adil?

Was she happy?

Was he?

He carefully folded the report before placing it on the bedside table atop a black leather notebook.

His son Adil had such potential and a vibrant zest for life. He could have married four women at once, if not more, and Jassim would have allowed it. He could have had tens, even hundreds of children, and Jassim would have blessed every single one of them. All of it ended with one piece of shrapnel. One small, insignificant fragment of metal sliced through both their hearts.

Jassim refused to move past it— Adil's name must always be remembered, and the glory he brought to his family should last for generations.

He reached for the black-leather notebook, flipping through its pages where Adil had left notes of future plans and past encounters. Some pages bore the marks of spilt coffee, while others were stained with blood. Codenames, coordinates, and phone numbers were scattered across the paper alongside sketches of what seemed to be an enhanced firearm and hand-drawn maps outlining the terrain of the Ar-Raqqah governorate. Not all of the writings were Adil's, Jassim noted, as he closely examined the elongated K's and fat-bellied L's. They must have been Shamil's; Adil wouldn't have trusted anyone else with his plans.

Jassim's gaze halted at a page torn in half, the remnants of an ancient poem smudged upon its surface.

"May God cast blame upon the days of our separation, for no day spent apart is worthy of praise. Each passing day, filled with agonising yearning, only begets greater longing for the next. My essence is consumed by this relentless ache for their presence, leaving nothing but regret echoing within the depths of my soul. Even as my limbs tremble with anticipation, I find no respite in moments of joy."

"Curse you, Shamil," Jassim's heart wailed silently as a wall of tears blurred his vision.

If only Shamil had dissuaded Adil from leading that disastrous mission, or at the very least, went with him and shielded him from harm, Adil would still draw breath.

Shamil bore the weight of responsibility— if any shred of honour was left within him, he would continue Adil's work. Their family's legacy could not be allowed to fade so easily.

A lump formed in Jassim's throat, thick with phlegm, as he struggled to swallow. With a series of forceful coughs, sharp pains shot through his chest, and he found himself unable to continue reading any further, yet unwilling to stop. He yearned to hear his son's voice once more, even if only in a dream.

The calls to prayer reverberated through the hallways of Jassim's mansion, reminding him that it was time. He closed the notebook, pressing a tender kiss upon its cover before placing it delicately on the bedside drawer. As he extinguished the reading light, he lay down, gazing upward, awaiting the sedative's embrace. He needed to rest— tomorrow was going to be a big day.

Chapter 12: Coffee on a Balcony

Sleeping had always been a struggle for Shamil— an endless duel with the demons of his past that kept him from finding peace. But the night he returned home, exhaustion, a comfortable bed propped with silky soft sheets, and the sound of a loved one breathing beside him were like a soothing lullaby.

For a while, he drifted in and out of sleep, his mind wandering to distant places and times. But then, as if summoned by his fears, nightmares of air raids and rebels wrapping an explosive vest around Zain's waist jolted him awake. He gasped for breath at the edge of the bed, cold sweat dripping off of his face as he tried to shake off the darkness that clung to him.

Slowly getting up, he tiptoed towards the window where he heard a distant thunder— the blasts in his nightmare were real, after all.

Cold air crept through the partially opened window, bringing with it the burning diesel scent of neighbourhood generators that still lingered.

The sky lit up briefly as another thunderclap echoed through the night. He peered out from the balcony, scanning the streets for signs of the impending invasion. Clouds had abandoned the pitch-black sky, and distant calls for prayer echoed from afar. Grey doves lined the electric cables undisturbed by the man-made thunder— It seemed as though he was the only one unsettled by it.

A shadow roaming his parents' kitchen caught his eye. "Mum?" he whispered across their balconies.

"In the name of the merciful, you startled me," Ameena gasped, pressing her hand against her chest. Her face dripped with water, a cleanse before her morning prayer. "Why are you awake?" she whispered back, trying not to come out to her balcony as she wasn't wearing her hijab.

"Coffee?" Shamil said, and Ameena nodded.

Casting an eye on Zain, fast asleep in his bed, he snuck outside as quietly as the creaking front door allowed him to be and didn't put on his shoes until he was a safe distance away. He slipped inside his parents' house unnoticed. Ameena had left the front door open for him, and he waited for her on the balcony. Moments later, she joined him, carrying a coffee tray. She had just finished her morning prayer, a duty Shamil had abandoned the day he moved abroad, except for the odd days when he desperately needed divine guidance.

"Do you still pray?" Ameena said, setting the tray on the balcony's round table.

"Not as often as I should," he said, pulling the hoodie over his head. The streets went quiet, and the sky was beginning to lighten up. "What was that noise all night? It sounded like thunder."

Ameena took a deep breath in. "They weren't always this loud," she said, stirring the coffee pot with a little spoon. "They're probably bombs exploding near Section Seventeen."

"Is it happening every night?"

"Yes." Ameena poured a cup. "You still like the foam, right?"

"You know me." Shamil grabbed the foamy cup and brought it closer to his lips, hoping that cardamom-scented steam would flush away the anxiety those thunders stirred. "Were there any bombs in the city?"

"Don't be silly," Ameena said, pouring herself half a cup, a habit she'd embraced after hitting her fifties. "No sugar, just the way you like it."

"To think we'd be at war." Shamil took a bitter sip. A gentle wind blew through the balcony's spearmint plants, lifting some of their dried-up leaves and landing them in his lap.

"All bad dreams come to an end," Ameena said, brushing away the leaves that fell closer to her.

"What if this one doesn't? Would you leave?"

"And abandon our lives here? Impossible."

"I thought I was your life," Shamil teased, wishing to hear her say it once more.

She put her cup down and looked at him. "And I thought I was yours until you left."

"You know why I had to."

"You ran away," she frowned, her words opening the wounds of the past. "You could've reconciled with Laila. Instead, you took the easy way out."

"I couldn't force her to love me, Mum."

"But, what if she changed? What if she loves you now?"

"Then she would have said it," Shamil said before another thunder, louder than the others, startled him. Ameena was unphased. "How are you not startled by this?"

"Say nothing shall afflict us but what the almighty has ordained for us," she recited, her conviction as strong as the coffee she had made. "Anyway, I can't expect to change your mind about staying as much as I don't expect you to change my mind about leaving."

"There's a difference between leaving to a place where one can be happy and staying where one's life is in danger."

"Ar-Raqqah is calm; it's not like the other cities."

"Unbelievable," Shamil sighed as he looked at the empty street where one of the doves flew down and sang. The chilly breeze was getting warmer as the bakeries lit their rack ovens and sun rays cracked their way across city buildings. "I look around us now, and it all seems so peaceful, yet I can't shake off this grip on my chest that's keeping me from enjoying this precious moment with you, Mum, and this is really upsetting me."

"It's all written, Son," she said with a comforting smile.

Was it really up to fate? His mother's words lingered in the air like the scent of the spearmint plants around them, and Shamil couldn't help but feel a sense of resignation weighing down his shoulders.

He moved his cup of coffee around the saucer, tracing patterns in the foam. Ameena had always found comfort in fate, in the idea that everything was predetermined and out of our control. On the other hand, Shamil had to be in control. He couldn't leave things to chance.

Lifting his head, he looked into Ameena's hazel eyes, glimmering with the faint reflection of the sun's rays.

She hadn't aged a day in the five years he'd been away, his beautiful mother, and he couldn't imagine leaving her behind.

"Mum, if something were to happen to you, it would scar me forever," he choked.

"Don't be silly." She turned her gaze away from him for a second, undoubtedly hiding her tears, before she wiped her face with her sleeve. "Your life is still ahead of you. Besides, death is inevitable, and we're all getting on that bus eventually."

"As late as possible, inshallah," he said, pulling his chair closer to embrace her. She gave him a brief hug as he kissed her head.

"As soon as it is written, Habibi."

"Promise me, if the rebels take the city, you won't stay here."

"They'll never take the city," she shrugged, reaching for his cup. "See, you hardly touched your coffee, and now it's cold."

"Promise me!"

She looked at him, his cup still in her hand. "Fine, I promise, if Allah wills it, and there is no other way, we'll come with you," she said, lifting some weight off of his chest. "Now, sit well while I pour you a new cup."

"I don't mind it cold."

"Well, I do," Ameena poured the cold coffee back into the pot, then put his cup back in front of him, empty. "Your friend Alaa liked his coffee cold as well. Such a good man he was."

"Was?" Shamil said, flipping his empty cup like Ameena had done hers.

"One second." She picked up her flipped coffee cup and squinted as she tried to make sense of it. "Hmm." She frowned and put the cup back down.

"What did you see?"

"Nothing exciting, maybe a better reading on yours," she said, picking Shamil's up. "He used to visit us every week," she continued as she carefully read Shamil's fortune. "He used to say Zain needed his father, and I used to tell him that we all needed Zain's father. Then the protests began, and he disappeared."

"Well, I'm here now," Shamil said, aware of the burden his absence had placed on the ones he loved. "And Alaa could be in Aleppo somewhere."

She kept on turning his cup around in her hand, and his patience ran short. When she finally looked back at him, concern had filled her eyes.

"What did you see?"

"Don't worry about Alaa. It's all rumours."

"Let me," Shamil said, grabbed the cup from Ameena's hand, and traced the patterns of coffee ground inside it. What did she see, and why couldn't he, with all his analytical prowess, see it?

"Oh, good, you're up early," Mudhar said, joining them on the balcony. "Jassim wants to see you."

Shamil put his cup down. He knew he had to pay Jassim back for securing his arrival to the city and for getting Zain out of prison; still, he wasn't looking forward to that meeting. Jassim was the kind of man who did favours only to collect favours in return; it didn't matter if the same blood coursed through their veins.

"What about Nadia?" Ameena interjected. "She'll stop talking to me, I swear, if we don't have lunch at hers."

"We'll have dinner at Nadia's. Jassim is more important."

"Jassim can wait, Baba," Shamil forced a smile— the news about Alaa had him flustered. "Coffee?"

"Your father doesn't have coffee," Ameena said, covering the coffee pot with a saucer.

"Well, if you allowed me to have coffee, I would have had it," Mudhar said, pulling a chair to sit next to her.

"All right, can you two not argue, please?" Shamil said.

"We're not arguing; this is normal," Mudhar said, putting his arm around Ameena's shoulders. She nudged him gently but then laughed it off and leaned back towards him, resting her head on his shoulder. "This is how she expresses her love by keeping me on my toes."

"Speaking of love, who is 'K'?" Ameena asked, her eyes as curious as ever.

"Let the man have his privacy," Mudhar said.

"Why does everyone think 'k' is a lover? Why not a hashish dealer, for example?" Shamil sighed. His parents seemed more concerned about his romantic pursuits, or rather, the lack thereof, than the looming threats that surrounded them.

"Well, who is it then?" Ameena insisted.

"Mum, come on-" Shamil began before the balcony fence rattled as another distant blast echoed through the city.

"Dear God." he ducked instinctively, shaken as his parents looked at him with amusement. How were they not afraid? Were they that brave or that oblivious? "You two think this is funny?"

"You'll get used to it, Son," Mudhar said with his annoying confidence. "It's been like this for almost a year now, and nothing has happened."

"Bombs, Dad, Bombs. Don't you hear them?" Shamil asked, pointing his hand at the empty street, his blood beginning to boil. "Soldiers in every corner of the city, smoke-filled streets, people getting shot, and you say nothing has happened?"

"And where would you have us go?" Mudhar asked, almost mockingly, as he always did when trying to win the debate on serious matters.

"More importantly, how?" Ameena added. "I don't have a passport."

He hadn't thought about it before—why only the men in his family carried passports. It was a societal norm so deeply entrenched that it had never bothered him, not until now. Living abroad had changed that. Watching others, women and men alike, move freely with their passports in hand, he'd begun to see the cracks in his own culture.

"You take your wife and son and leave; we'll be ok," Mudhar said.

"I'll sort everything out. And Mum, you promised when the time comes, you'll leave," Shamil said firmly.

"Jassim first, then passports," Mudhar concluded, looking at Ameena shaking her head at him before she got up. "Are you making breakfast?"

"Let Jassim make you breakfast," Ameena said, stepping into the kitchen. She was no doubt upset that she had to reschedule with her sister Nadia.

"I am not that hungry. I can wait," Shamil said, glancing at his apartment building to see a hooded man standing by the entrance. He hadn't noticed him coming into their street or left the building's gate open. Someone must have opened it for him.

"Who's that man?" Shamil asked before Zain emerged from the building, holding a large sports backpack.

Chapter 13: The Rebel

"Zain!" Shamil's voice sliced through the stillness, drawing Zain's attention as he handed the hooded man the backpack he was carrying. With a nod, the man turned and disappeared into the distance.

"I'm heading up," Zain said, but Shamil couldn't let it slide. He needed to know what was concealed within that backpack.

Shamil sprang up, accidentally crashing the coffee table into Mudhar's lap. "Sorry!" He moved to assist, but Ameena motioned for him to proceed.

"Don't make a scene," Mudhar grumbled, coffee staining his clothes from the waist down.

Shamil hurried toward the stairs, only to find Zain blocking his path.

"What?" Zain's smile appeared strained. "That was Waleed, my trainer."

It was a lie, undoubtedly.

"What did you give him?" Shamil stared at him, his temples throbbing with frustration.

"I returned his elastic bands."

"A whole bag of bands?"

"We can go ask him if you like."

"Okay, let's do it."

Zain's face flushed as he pulled out his mobile phone. "I'm calling him now, and you can search his bag."

"We're having breakfast now," Mudhar interjected, joining them on the stairs. "Go to the balcony and help set the table with your grandmother."

Zain nodded, rushing into his grandparents' house as if nothing had happened.

"This was completely unnecessary," Mudhar said, crossing his arms.

"He was acting all shady; I couldn't simply ignore it," Shamil waved his hand in frustration.

"That was his trainer, Waleed; I recognised him," Mudhar said, stepping closer to Shamil. "You just have to create problems where there are none."

Shamil bit his tongue. He knew Zain's transaction with Waleed wasn't as innocent as Zain wanted them to believe, but he didn't want to aggravate things any further. "I'll join you in a moment," he said to Mudhar, retreating downstairs to the courtyard where the rock fountain was. He needed a minute by himself to gather his thoughts and calm his nerves.

Seating himself by its edge, he immersed his hands in its cold water. Despite always being filled to the brim, that ancient fountain never overflowed unless disturbed. He splashed his face several times before kneeling by its edge and submerging his head beneath its icy surface. Holding his breath for as long as he could, he waited until he could no longer hear his heart pounding before he lifted his head from the frigid water, wiped his face dry, and went upstairs to join the others.

Ameena had already filled the balcony coffee table with an array of Syrian delicacies—cheese, olives, omelette, bread, jam, and more—items Shamil had yearned to savour with his family for years. But the magic was lost. The first bite felt forced, clinging to the walls of his oesophagus, refusing to go down. The bites that followed felt routine, devoid of the joy and comfort he had so deeply missed.

With effort, he rose from the table and went to the kitchen, Laila following him closely.

Quietly, she closed the balcony door behind her. "Are you okay?" She stood nearby.

"Yeah, I'm just jetlagged," Shamil said, not wanting to burden her with his worries.

"We're not in a rush to do anything today. Just go back to bed."

"I still need to get the passports."

"That, too, can wait," she said, filling a glass of water. She murmured a silent prayer, her breath soft as she blew over the rim before she handed him the glass. "This will help calm you down, inshallah."

Shamil's gaze lingered on the curve of her lips, his eyes tracing their movement before he finally lifted the glass and drank. The cool water eased the bitterness that had gathered at the back of his throat. He set the glass aside, his thoughts shifting to the looming uncertainty. If the rebels seized the city before he had Laila and Zain's passports, he would have no choice but to resort to smuggling them out. For that to work, he realised, he would need to bring Laila into the plan sooner rather than later. "I need you to pack yours and Zain's essentials. Documents, degrees, certificates, anything lightweight that you can carry in a bag."

"What did you hear?" she stepped closer.

"I have been speaking to a smuggler — he suggested we cross the border into Iraqi Kurdistan."

"A smuggler?!" Laila recoiled as if Shamil's words had threatened her.

Glancing around to ensure no one else was within earshot, Shamil leaned closer to Laila. "Don't panic; it's just in case things escalate here," he muttered, almost ashamed to admit it. "I have to do something, Laila. There were at least ten explosions overnight."

"Not this!" she said in a hushed tone, but Shamil gestured for her to stop as Mudhar approached the kitchen.

"What are the love birds plotting?" Mudhar quirked a thick black eyebrow.

"We're registering Laila and Zain for passports today," Shamil responded.

"I'm already dreading it," Laila chimed in, directing her gaze at Mudhar. "Queue and all."

"I'm not getting a passport," Zain said as he entered the kitchen, holding the breakfast tray.

Laila and Shamil exchanged a glance.

"Not even for a new laptop?" Laila teased, and Zain hesitated.

Laila had once suggested bribing Zain with electronics and other expensive gadgets—after all, he was a teenager. But Shamil disagreed, hoping his son would honour his requests out of respect. He was wrong.

"Price range?" Zain asked.

"Unlimited," Shamil said, building upon the momentum Laila had initiated.

Zain regarded Shamil sceptically. "If you buy me the laptop I want, I will apply for a passport, but that doesn't mean I'm agreeing to leave. Deal?"

"But you'll leave if the fighting reaches the city?" Shamil asked.

"Nothing will happen to the city, Baba. Our opposition is peaceful."

"And if violence is the only way left for the opposition?" Shamil asked, and Zain went silent, seemingly unable to comprehend that the opposition he'd been cheering for could ever turn violent.

"Obviously, if it's not safe here, we'll all leave. I'm not stupid," Zain said.

"We can go to the shop right now, then," Shamil affirmed.

"And Jassim?" Mudhar asked.

"He'll have to wait," Shamil brushed it off.

Quickly downing a cup of cold tea, Shamil got changed, and in less than forty minutes, they were at one of the many electronics shops Zain had suggested. By the time it was eleven, Shamil had already inhaled two cups of coffee, and Zain still hadn't decided on a laptop.

"The new brand I want won't be available until next week," Zain complained, leaving the last shop.

"There are other options," Shamil said.

"They sucked," Zain shrugged, checking his phone discreetly. He frowned, typing something. "All right, I'm going to the gym."

"Walk with me," Shamil said, not believing him. "Consider it a warm-up before your session."

"It's an hour's walk!"

"So? That's three hundred calories, give or take."

"I'm bulking up, not slimming."

"Come on, I haven't seen the city in years," Shamil pleaded. "We'll walk to Al-Rasheed Park, and you can go to the gym from there."

Zain sighed. "Okay, but we're fast-walking."

"I'll even race you," Shamil gestured with his hand, and Zain led the way.

It wasn't particularly cloudy that day, but whenever a stray cloud drifted in front of the sun, the temperature plummeted dramatically, and Shamil felt the cold sting deep in his bones.

Syrian winters were as treacherous as its summers— a sunny day could turn into a blizzard in seconds.

"We'll go through the Statue Square. It's faster that way," Zain said, zipping his jacket.

Shamil nodded, looking at a queue of men in front of a packed notary office. A small boy wearing a thick black jacket and carrying a large thermos caught his eye. His left arm was loaded with a tower of white plastic cups, and steam seeped through his red nose and dark blue Thermos. Strolling alongside the queueing men, the boy offered them some hot tea. Few bothered to buy, their arms tightly crossed as they tried to conserve warmth in the cold air. But the boy carried on, smiling innocently amongst a swarm of frustrated men.

Shamil's heart ached, unable to take his eyes off of him.

"Lots of children work," Zain said, seemingly indifferent.

"It doesn't make it right."

"When the regime falls, it will all become better."

"Will the queues become shorter, and people get richer overnight? Will that boy's parents suddenly begin to care about him?"

"It's.. Maybe. Ugh, can we just walk faster?"

Shamil let out a sigh, observing the young boy who seemed to have abandoned his sales efforts. "Hey, Boy," he motioned to the boy, who hurried over to them. "How many cups do you have in your Thermos?"

"Plenty," the boy replied, retrieving an empty plastic cup from his side pack. "Have one, Uncle? It's delicious."

"How much for all of it?"

"Really?" The boy's face lit up with surprise as he began to count on his fingers. After pausing twice, he sighed, scratched his head, and then turned back to Shamil. "What's three times forty-nine?"

"One hundred and forty-seven," Zain answered before Shamil could respond.

"My mom said the Thermos can fill fifty-five cups. I sold five and spilt one," the boy explained.

"I'll pay you for fifty cups, so I owe you one hundred and fifty Liras," Shamil offered.

"We have tea at home, you know," Zain interjected.

"It's not for us," Shamil said, handing the boy one hundred and fifty Liras. "See that queue?" He pointed at the men. "I want you to pour them a cup each. Do that, and I'll give you another one hundred and fifty."

Zain crossed his arms tightly over his chest, his foot tapping rapidly against the floor.

"One hundred and fifty more?" the boy exclaimed as he counted the money.

"Yes," Shamil confirmed, handing him the remaining amount, trusting the boy would complete the task.

"May Allah reward you for each lira a thousand times, Uncle," the boy's smile widened, revealing his dry, round cheeks. He tucked the money into his trousers and dashed toward the men.

"Do you feel less guilty now?" Zain said.

Shamil's face flushed. While he had bought the tea out of guilt, his son's comment still embarrassed him.

"These are the same people you are trying to help. I'm giving them tea, something they want, while you're trying to give them a revolution, something that you want them to want."

"If they had freedom, they wouldn't have had to queue in the cold to start with."

"All I'm saying is not everything is black and white."

"Come on, not again," Zain sighed, turning his back to the queue. "Can we at least walk and talk?"

Shamil hastened his pace, and for a few moments, silence reigned between them. How could he convey to his son the harsh realities of revolutions? Was it even a revolution taking place in Syria? And if so, did they believe they could succeed? No amount of activism, peaceful or otherwise, could dismantle the Syrian regime. Al-Baath party had engineered it to endure organised armed uprisings, capable of decimating entire cities regardless of who lived in them—a truth Shamil knew intimately. His days serving in the Army, and later under Jassim's arm, had shown him that the only thing the regime had held sacred was its own survival.

Passing through the Statue Square, Shamil lifted his gaze to the statue of Hafiz Al-Assad, the former president of Syria. "It feels so much smaller now."

"It looks the same to me," Zain said, observing the statue with disdain.

"You see that?" Shamil pointed at a little green pushcart by the northern entrance to the square with two large trays of cooked lamb heads on it.

A short, round woman stood behind it, selling brain sandwiches.

"Alaa used to bring us there, me and your mum, and we couldn't stomach it."

"Yeah, Uncle Alaa eats everything; he once tried to feed me a cow's eye," Zain grimaced.

"Or even a sautéd goat's testicle."

Zain gagged. "I'd rather die than eat that."

Shamil smiled before his phone vibrated with a message from 'K'.

Your fakes will be with me tomorrow. And you're in luck; I can get you out in two days at no extra cost. The road is very safe. Cash only.

Shamil slowed his pace, reading the message one more time. He could agree to K's offer, and he could be safe abroad with his family, ridding himself of all that worrying and pretence. In no time, he could be back in his room in London with Zain and Laila by his side. Small as it was, Shamil was never anxious in that room, and he didn't have to worry about bombs or rebels or government operatives disrupting his life. Yet, something about pursuing that option didn't feel right. It sounded too easy to be true. Besides, things weren't as bad as the news reports Shamil had researched before leaving London, and life seemed almost normal in Ar-Raqqah city.

I'm not in a rush to leave. I'll pay you the rest of the money when we meet, say in two weeks?

Shamil hit the send button.

"Is that Mama?" Zain asked.

"It's.... a friend from work," Shamil stammered, putting his phone away in his pocket. "This square used to be full of marchers, but now there's hardly anyone here," he changed the topic.

"She said you used to hate the regime marches."

"I didn't hate them, but I didn't like them either."

"You were forced to participate, isn't that slavery?"

"We all participated, and that made us feel equal in a way."

"Seriously?" Zain turned to face him. "Innocents are dying every day, and you're here praising slavery marches?" he raised his voice.

"It's not like that," Shamil said, glancing up at the sky, where a thick blanket of heavy clouds obscured the sun, and distant rumbles alarmed the square park visitors to pick their bags up and head out. Luckily, Shamil had his sturdy black umbrella with him—all those rainy days in London had taught him never to go anywhere without it. "Come," he gestured to Zain to take shelter beside him as the clouds began to pour.

Zain pulled his jacket's hoodie on top of his head. "It's just rain."

"You'll get wet," Shamil said before a strong gust of a drowning wind almost wrestled the umbrella out of his hand.

"It's a storm, Baba," Zain said. "We're bound to get wet."

Shamil frowned, holding the umbrella closer, his phone vibrating with another message from 'K': **Suit yourself, Hakim. FYI, there's talk about a large protest hitting the streets. If I were you, I would leave ASAP.**

Reading that message, Shamil felt a sinking certainty in his heart—Zain was lying to him. He knew about the protest. Perhaps it was why Zain had met that man in the morning. Had he provided supplies for the protest, or worse, were there weapons in that bag?

Shamil looked around him, ensuring no one was nearby. The park lay deserted— only fools would have lingered in that downpour. "Zain, I can put up with your online presence, but not the protests."

"Seriously? Now?" Zain said.

"I know about tomorrow's protest."

"We must speak for the people."

"You will, once we're abroad. I have contacts, I," Shamil began before he was interrupted.

"You lie!" Zain raised his voice. "All you do is lie."

"Son.."

"You're just like Jassim. I showed you people getting killed, and you still support the killers."

"Why do you think I quit SAFI then?"

"Because you're weak," Zain was now shouting, his eyes raging with anger. "Instead of standing up to Jassim, you ran away and left us."

"I'm weak because of you!" Shamil shouted, his frustration getting the best of him. "I can't let anything happen to you, or to your mum, or to my parents. I won't allow it."

"Nothing will happen to me."

"It has already happened."

"It won't happen again," Zain said, facing Shamil, the rain assaulting them from every angle. "Now, can we please just go home? You're soaking wet."

"You said it, it's just rain," Shamil muttered. His son's concern for his well-being tugged at his heart, but he couldn't shake the turmoil inside of him. He removed his glasses, brushing away the water droplets that clung to them.

His futile attempts only smeared the lenses, distorting his view even further.

"Fine, you stay here if you want; I'm going," Zain said, striding away.

Shamil grew increasingly frustrated, not knowing what to say. He would never disobey his father, Mudhar, despite how much he had disagreed with him, and he certainly would never turn his back and walk away from his father the way Zain just did. Still, Shamil felt he deserved it; he had no right to demand Zain's respect when he had been away from him all these years. He would fix it once they were all in the UK. Once there, he would rebuild his connection with Zain—he had to.

Trailing his son by a few metres, he soon found them both back in the apartment. It had been a long day, and Shamil needed to rest. He dragged his bare, cold feet to the living room, the television murmuring the news in the background. And before he knew it, weariness overtook him, plunging him into a dreamless sleep on the sofa.

Chapter 14: What The Heart Wants

Laila gazed into the gaping maw of a blue travel bag spread out on her bed. What essentials should she pack? Everything she laid her eyes on seemed essential. Zain's birth certificate, his school records, his clothes, hers, her degrees, her cherished golden jewellery, the kohl eyeliner passed down from her late mother, the photo albums capturing their family's happy moments, the blue dress she'd worn the night before. She hadn't even had a chance to wash it properly, but she packed it anyway.

Smugglers? For goodness's sake, what had gotten into Shamil? Resorting to such extremes. And how many bags was she allowed to carry anyway? He didn't specify, and Laila couldn't just guess and waste her time packing and unpacking. Would it have harmed him to consult her beforehand? Resorting to smugglers and uncertain routes, Was it even safe?

She knew they had to leave, but Shamil's decision was uncharacteristically reckless.

She unlatched the windows in her bedroom, letting in a cool breeze. The flurry of packing and searching had left her perspiring as though she were enduring the most intense of hot flashes. The whole thing was rushed. She wiped her forehead dry as she sat on her ottoman, facing the blue bag, now full, on her bed. Gathering her wavy black hair with one hand and lifting it to expose her sweaty neck to some air, she fanned herself with the other hand, scanning her surroundings for things to pack.

A photo of Shamil holding little Zain's hand, with a birthday cake adorned with a single candle, caught her eye. She couldn't recall the last time she had seen Shamil laugh as genuinely as he did in that photo. It was all her fault. If only she hadn't confessed her true feelings to him on that very day, perhaps things would have turned out differently. But telling him was the only way; it would have killed her otherwise, pretending to love him when she hadn't. Not the way she loved him now.

Wiping away a small smudge, she softly traced her fingers over the photo, lingering on Shamil's face, before carefully tucking it away. She tied her hair up, zipped the blue bag shut, and pushed it under her bed.

Shamil's plan was risky, and she didn't have to go through with it; he would never force her. She could ask him to wait a few weeks until their passports were legally procured; in fact, she would do just that, and he would have to accept it. She just had to show him things weren't as bad as they seemed.

It was almost lunchtime, and Laila hadn't cooked anything—Ameena had asked her not to. She could still bake some biscuits without angering her mother-in-law, especially since she was going to follow her instructions to the letter. She'd learned her lesson.

Taking a little paper with the recipe for chocolate biscuits, Laila entered her kitchen and retrieved the butter. Step one was melting it. By step five, her bedroom window was straining against the violent wind, and by step nine, Zain had returned home, with Shamil following closely behind.

"Grandma made biscuits?" Zain stood by the kitchen door, his eyes beaming and almost drooling.

He was as damp as the towels he often left on the bathroom floor, his nose red and wet.

"Shoes!" Laila complained, pointing a butter-laced spatula at him.

He rolled his eyes. "I'm hungry!" he said, taking off his shoes and revealing even wetter socks.

Laila sighed. No matter how often she scolded him, he was always messy. "Well, until you wipe the floor dry, you're not getting any."

"Fine," he replied, tossing his socks in the laundry basket. "Where's the mop?"

"Here," A barefooted Shamil handed it to him. "Tea?" he offered Laila.

"Get changed, I'll make you some," she said, reaching for the kitchen cupboard. "Chamomile?"

"With extra sugar."

An odd request as he'd always preferred his tea without sugar— to savour the natural sweetness of the herbs, he'd often claimed, a sentiment Laila would disagree with. To Laila, sugar never detracted from the natural sweetness of things— if anything, it accentuated it. Shamil must have been exhausted.

She slid the tray of cookies into the oven, set the timer for thirty minutes, and then carried two cups of extra sweet chamomile tea into the living room. Shamil couldn't have fallen asleep that quickly, yet there he was, sprawled face-down on the sofa, the remote control dangling from his hand as the news droned on the TV.

Gently, she placed the teacups on the coffee table and tiptoed toward the bedroom. There, she fetched a thin grey blanket.

The apartment wasn't freezing, but Shamil always woke up with a migraine if he slept without cover, and she wasn't about to let that happen. She needed him to have a clear head for when she would tell him that his plan was 'unwise.'

Carefully unfolding the blanket, she draped it over his pale, cold-stricken feet and tucked it snugly around his shoulders before settling on the floor beside the sofa.

She surveyed his tired face, counting the unfamiliar lines and shadows beneath his eyes that made him appear older than his years. In her mind, she ran her fingers through his black hair, brushing it away from his forehead. She trailed her touch down the side of his face, tracing the contours of his trimmed beard, his cheeks, and his lips. If it were possible, she would have pressed a kiss against them, a kiss that could ease his burdens and her own. When they decided to separate all those years ago, the first few months were fraught with difficulty. Boundaries were drawn, only to be tested and redrawn, an exhausting cycle that eventually gave way to a fragile balance. Over time, they learned to coexist like two best friends raising a child together. Yet, there were moments when the closeness between them felt too familiar, almost natural. In those instances, she would catch herself leaning in, reminded of their separation, and quietly pull back, creating the distance she knew had to remain.

Reaching for the remote in his hand, the ring on his finger caught her attention. It was still there, half buried into his skin as if it'd never shifted from its place. He was still hers. She still had a chance.

"Leave it," Shamil said, barely opening an eye.

"I knew you were awake," Laila playfully pushed his shoulder. "Your tea is getting cold."

Shamil groaned, sitting himself up as if his joints were creaking. "I like it cold," he said, cracking his neck with effort. "We need a new sofa."

"You need vitamins," Laila said, sitting on the sofa beside him. "And some moisturisers, or else those lines would become permanent." she pointed at his face.

"The sofa lines?" Shamil checked his reflection on his mobile. "You do know they're just pressure marks, yeah?"

Laila narrowed her eyes at him; he needn't mansplain what a sofa line was.

He smiled, grabbing his cup and gulping half of it before he coughed vigorously. "Wrong pipe," he squealed.

"I'll get some water."

Laila got up with haste, and Shamil grabbed her arm, clearing his throat. "I forgot about the sugar."

"You wanted it," Laila said, sitting down beside him. "And you chugged it down as if you were being chased. You don't have to rush everything."

Shamil tapped his chest, coughing. "I was thirsty."

"Ask for water then."

"The tea seemed reasonable."

"And you choked on it."

"Laila..." Shamil said, his tired brown eyes looking into hers for sympathy.

"Ugh," she sighed, sitting back on the sofa beside him. "Get your feet up," she added, grabbing a small pillow from behind the sofa, where the radiator was, and putting it on her lap.

"They're cold," he hesitantly turned to his side on the sofa and lifted his feet near the pillow, looking confused. "What're we doing?"

"You'll see," she said, adjusting the warm pillow underneath his feet.

"Oh my," Shamil said, burying his hands under his armpits.

"I haven't even started," Laila smiled as she ran her hands against his freezing toes, gently rubbing each until they were as soft and warm as the chocolate chip cookie dough she'd been kneading.

"Should I be paying you for this?" Shamil threw another one of his ill-timed jokes, smiling awkwardly.

"Just, shhh," Laila interrupted, and he made a 'sealed lips' sign with his hand.

They sat there, not talking for a few minutes, news of a burning world streaming on their TV as their bodies exchanged heat. Laila's gaze was focused on Shamil's feet as they slowly regained their colour, and she could see him from the corner of her eyes, looking at her and only at her.

"He hates me," Shamil's voice broke the peace.

"No child hates their father," Laila said, knowing that Zain's feelings weren't hatred but anger and longing at once.

"You hate yours."

Laila's hands paused as she glared at Shamil. Was he, for real, comparing the two? "Are you also a pimp?"

"I'm sorry," Shamil leaned forward, putting his hand on Laila's shoulder. "I shouldn't have mentioned him."

She pulled her shoulder away. "Don't," she frowned, her hands denying his feet their caring touch.

"It was a stupid comment; I'm sorry," he continued apologising, sitting up closer to her.

"I'm fine," she replied, averting her gaze as an unexpected wave of tears threatened to overwhelm her.

She hated her father; it wasn't a secret. In fact, she hadn't spoken to him a word since she got married, despite Shamil's many attempts to reconcile them. He was the reason she rushed into marrying Shamil, the reason she never pursued university, and the reason her neglected mother passed away alone. She hadn't visited him once, not even after he'd almost died in an accident, and had never regretted it. Still, why did Shamil's words hurt that bad?

"Laila…" Shamil said softly, and her chest tightened. "Come on, he's not worth your tears."

He shuffled closer to her, running his hand down her shoulder, her arm, her elbow, a pattern all too familiar to her. Was he?

"No!" she exclaimed, her finger pointed at him in warning. She could see the glint in his eye that signalled his intention to tickle her. It was his usual tactic, which he had employed countless times when he was in trouble. And more often than not, it had worked—Laila could never hold out for more than a few seconds before dissolving into helpless laughter. But not this time. She wasn't going to let him win that easily.

"What?" he said, innocently raising his hands before he sneakily brought one down to tickle her waist.

She knew he was going to do it. She hated it. She'd always hated it, yet somehow, at that time, she also wanted it.

"This!" she pushed his hand away.

He smiled, attempting to tickle her again. "I'm not doing anything."

She grabbed his hand. "You're such a child sometimes."

"Am I now?" He reached for her back with his other hand, where he knew she was most ticklish.

She curved her back as an intense wave of electricity pulsed through her chest, causing her to laugh. "Sham!" she squeaked, pushing his hand again before turning to face him. Swiftly, her fingers landed on the side of his neck, a little below his earlobe, and he recoiled instantly, pulling away from her and onto his back on the sofa.

"I'll stop. I'll stop," he shouted as she got on top of him, prodding him with her tickles wherever she knew he'd crack. "Laila, I'll stop!" he laughed, a loud and genuine laugh, one she had missed immensely.

He held her hands firmly as she sat on his lap, her hair cascading slowly onto his face, her breath matched his, and so did their heartbeats. Looking into his kind brown eyes, it was as if he longed for her as much as she had longed for him.

He smiled at her, a forced, half-warranted smile. He'd often given her one when his lips said what was not in his heart.

"Truce?" he said, dispersing the magic.

She could have kissed him right there and then. Oh, how she wished she could. Instead, she nodded, getting off his lap as he released her hands.

"Are you finished playing? I need to come in," Zain said from behind the living room's partially closed door.

Laila got off Shamil's lap, quickly fixing her hair as if not wanting to be caught doing the forbidden. "Of course you can," she said, gathering the pillows that had fallen on the floor.

"Where's my camera?" Zain said, frantically searching the TV stand.

Laila peered outside the window. The lights were still on, which reassured her, yet she couldn't help but wonder why Zain was so nervous. Was there going to be a protest nearby? "Amr has it," she said.

"You gave it to him?"

"You said he could borrow it."

"Not all the time!"

"Call him, maybe?" Shamil interjected.

"I need it now," Zain groaned, stomping his foot on his way out of the living room.

"Should we be worried?" Shamil asked, looking at Laila, and she almost said it all.

The phone call she'd overheard, the chats she'd had with Zain, the fact that whenever Zain held his camera, a protest was either happening or about to happen. Everything she'd been suppressing at the tip of her tongue would have been out in the open, and her chest would feel so much lighter.

But how would Shamil react?

He was already plotting to venture with smugglers on risky roads, and Laila didn't wish to add to his worries. Who knew what else he would do?

"I'll talk to him," Laila said, following Zain into his bedroom. And before she could catch a word, he was gone.

Chapter 15: Face Masks and Gasoline

The lights flickered off, casting the apartment into darkness. The murmurs from the streets outside grew louder. The front door slammed shut. A protest was brewing.

"Zain!" Shamil shouted as he sprang from the sofa.

"I'll get him," Laila grabbed her Abaya.

"Stay here," Shamil said, slipping into his trainers and bolting downstairs. The cacophony of roaring men now drowned out all other sounds, and the last thing he wanted was for Laila to be caught in the chaos on the streets.

Turning a corner, he could only catch glimpses of Zain, flocks of chaotic crowds separating them. How did they all gather that fast?

"Wait!" Shamil yelled in Zain's direction, his voice hoarse and strained as stabbing pain spread across his chest.

"The people want to end the regime," the platoon of masked men roared. "God, Syria, Freedom."

Bashing stationary cars and painting over traffic lights, the masked men's rage was palpable, and so was their thirst for violence. Shop owners hastily closed their stores, even with customers still inside; only fools would risk getting caught in that commotion. It was a scene straight out of the videos Shamil had seen on the internet, but only now were they both caught up in it. He scanned every face around him, every waist and every shoulder strap.

Surely, Jassim had his informant infiltrate the protest, taking note of who did what. He would deal with that later; finding Zain was all he could think of.

The wailing of sirens pierced the air, blending with the chaotic voices outside and inside Shamil's mind. Every clip of protests in Syria he had seen had ended in police shooting at civilians, and he didn't want to witness that first-hand. He didn't want to believe it.

Bulldozing through the throngs of people, Shamil ignored those who fell in his wake—his only focus was finding his son. Finally, he spotted Zain's scarf, and he sprinted faster, but he couldn't catch up.

"Fuck!" Shamil cursed, frustration boiling over as smoke billowed from burning tyres.

Then it dawned on him: Zain's obsession with his camera and the photos he had shown Shamil. Most were captured from elevated angles, far higher than any ladder or platform could reach. Zain must have been on one of the rooftops overlooking Al-Naim Square, and the tall building opposite Shamil had to be it; there were no other accessible buildings in sight.

He slammed shut the entrance behind him, ensuring no one could follow, then mentally mapped out potential escape routes as he made his way to the roof. Zain better be on it, and if he wasn't, Shamil could at least scan the area from above, looking for him.

He pushed the rooftop gate open, and a surge of relief flooded through him—Zain was there.

"Why did you come?" Zain's voice was almost unrecognisable behind a keffiyeh and a black hat. Beside him, a masked companion set up a tripod.

Shamil grabbed Zain's arm. "You're going to get us killed, I swear it."

Zain shrugged him off, unwrapping his scarf with urgency. "Cover your face!"

"I'm not covering anything— we're going home right now."

"We can't now," Zain said, pressing the scarf into Shamil's hand. "You'll get us exposed!"

His masked companion added, "Please, Uncle, cover your face."

Shamil half-wrapped the smoke-filled scarf around his face and peered cautiously around the rooftop, then at the sky above. He couldn't see any drones hovering around, nor were there any nearby rooftops high enough for someone to take a shot at them. It was safer to stay where they were than to risk getting arrested or shot at on the streets.

"Baba, keep low," Zain said, crouching by the tripod. His nerves seemed unshakable as he pointed his camera through gaps in the roof fence.

Cursing under his breath, Shamil hunkered down behind Zain, watching his city erupt in rebellion. The grim reality awaiting those who dared to speak out was all too familiar to him. He had witnessed it firsthand during his time in the military and later under Jassim's command. The dungeons, where SAFI usually kept their prisoners, could always accommodate more. It was only a matter of time before that awful fate again became a reality.

He braced himself for the impending brutality of Jassim's security forces, crouching behind his son, expecting the worst.

Zain remained calm and composed as he expertly framed his shots.

He adjusted his focus with precision, eyes scanning the neighbourhood with calculated intensity. He had positioned Mirrors strategically to reflect multiple angles as if creating his own surveillance network. He aimed his camera at the reflections, zooming in for the perfect shot, anticipating the protesters' movements. Amr, Zain's friend, followed his instructions, moving around that dark roof with ease, undoubtedly familiar with it beforehand.

Moments later, the lights flickered back, and the protesters scattered frantically, their whistles piercing the air with urgency as police units flooded the area.

"There's a window at the end of the fourth floor's corridor. We can use it to enter the adjacent building," Shamil said. "In case the police come looking."

"We'll use that, uncle," Amr said, pointing at a bent metal bar attached to a large diesel tank. "We'll dangle down the vents if we need to."

"Focus!" Zain nudged Amr, who grunted and resumed recording the arrival of the police.

Shamil looked through Zain's mirrors at the police cars arriving at Al-Naim Square, and to his bewilderment, they seemed rather indifferent to the chaos unfolding around them. They traversed the streets with an unhurried pace, their batons poised but unused, as rioters disappeared in narrow streets and side alleys. It was as if they all were merely going through the motions, participating in a theatrical performance. Yelling empty threats, they strolled around the square for a few minutes before returning to their vehicles.

That was it.

No shots were fired. No arrests were made. No civilians were throwing stones at soldiers. None of the anticipated turmoil materialised. It didn't make any sense to Shamil. Was this all part of some elaborate simulation? He began to question his own perceptions, unsure of what to believe.

"I got amazing footage," Zain jumped with excitement, high-fiving Amr before turning to Shamil, his hand held up.

It took Shamil a few seconds before he high-fived back, still processing what had happened. It couldn't have been just for show; something was off. He scrolled to Laila's number to let her know he had found Zain, and as he hit the dial, loud bursts of Kalashnikovs filled the air.

Ducking with haste, he pulled Zain down with him as Amr threw himself towards the diesel tank.

"Not there!" Shamil gestured to Amr to get away from the diesel tank, fearing a stray bullet would cause it to explode, and Amr crawled away.

Five rounds were fired, Shamil quickly estimated, all from the same direction where the police were.

"Did they shoot someone?" Amr asked, his face pale.

"They can't," Zain quickly interjected.

"The shots were in the air," Shamil said, checking through one of the fence gaps to see whether the police had left. Luckily, no dead bodies or injured civilians were anywhere to be seen. "They don't seem to have arrested anyone."

"It's always like this," Zain scoffed, dusting himself up. "Jassim's orders."

"Yeah, he's stupid," Amr mocked as he deconstructed the tripod. "As if we would ever stop protesting."

Shamil's lips parted, but no words came out. Jassim was many things but never stupid.

"Let's—" Shamil's words were cut off by a sharp metallic screech, followed by a thud and sparks flying nearby. His instincts screamed danger. What was shot up into the air was bound to fall back. He hurried Zain and Amr into the stairway as pain shot through his left leg, warmth seeping through his joggers.

"Shit, that was close," Zain said, his voice strained with nervous tension, and Amr chuckled, seemingly uncaring of what had just happened.

"You think this is a joke?" Shamil's rage boiled over. That stray bullet could have easily ended their lives in an instant. The diesel tank could have exploded, sending shrapnel slicing through them. They could have been maimed or scarred for life. "You worry too much, Uncle," Amr retorted, his tone flippant. "And you don't worry enough," Shamil's gaze bore into Amr's. "Do your parents approve of this?"

"Baba, no one was injured," Zain interjected.

"It's people like you that kill revolutions," Amr smirked.

Shamil clenched his right fist so hard that barely any blood was left in it. If Amr were older, he might have struck him, but now was not the time for it— adrenaline had corrupted them all.

"We're done here," Shamil grabbed Zain's arm and pushed him towards the stairs. "Home. Now."

Exiting the building, Shamil linked arms with Zain as they hurried through the now well-lit streets.

Shops were reopening, and people wandered about, laughing and chatting as if nothing had happened. The city's residents had become desensitised, treating the upheaval as a ritual—one some participated in while others merely observed. It was a seemingly peaceful ritual here, yet in other cities, it had turned violent and bloody.

Shamil wasn't going to wait for it. He kept a firm grip on Zain until they were safely back in the apartment. With Laila there to keep watch over their son, he slipped into the bathroom and locked the door behind him. Inspecting the cut on his leg, he noted it was minor but realised how much worse it could have been. He retrieved the first-aid kit and sat on the edge of the bathtub, methodically suturing the wound himself. He then buried the bloodstained joggers at the bottom of the laundry basket. Zain didn't need to see them and feel the weight of guilt. It wasn't his fault—Shamil should have been more vigilant.

Scrolling to K's number, he quickly typed a message. **I need the passports tomorrow. I believe the protest has passed.**

The answer was instant. **You'll get what pleases you tomorrow, Doc.**

T Hashem

A Status Report

Syrian Arab Republic

Syrian Air Force Intelligence - Aljazeera Branch

Urgent Addendum to the Field Report - December 22nd, 2012

It is imperative to notify you that two additional groups of smugglers have been neutralised and their leaders apprehended. Despite this, numerous other rogue factions are persisting near the Turkish border. Our sources indicate that Islamist elements have infiltrated these factions, potentially leading to a consolidation under an Islamist banner. We have also received intelligence indicating the presence of armed terrorists disguised as civilians during the forthcoming protests in Ar-Raqqah city. Although a significant assault on the city is not anticipated, the presence of armed individuals poses a substantial threat to both participants and observers. In adherence to the commands of Colonel Jassim Al-Sayed, Head of SAFI, firearms will not be utilised to disperse the protests. However, it is assessed that in the event of terrorist aggression against our personnel or civilians, our forces will be compelled to respond. While every effort will be made to minimise civilian casualties, it is recommended that our response to any hostile actions be prompt and decisive to deter further aggression.

Long live Syria, proud and free, and victory to the leader of our nation.

Copies to: Colonel Jassim Al-Sayed's Office. General Saleem Masri's Office. Archives.

The Syrian Dandelion

Chapter 16: The Root and The Branches

"Get in the car, NOW," Mudhar said, turning the key in the ignition as the engine.

Shamil slipped into the passenger seat, his eyes darting to his phone—still nothing. Frustration mounted as he scrolled through useless screens. He had tried everything: restarting the device, connecting to Wi-Fi, and even switching to the laptop and PC back at home. Nothing worked. No emails, no updates, no signal. It felt as though he had been completely severed from the digital world, and the one person who could have commanded it was Jassim.

"We could have had breakfast," Shamil muttered, his stomach growling. All he had managed since last night was a cup of coffee Laila had made.

"We'll eat at Jassim's," Mudhar said, snapping his seat belt into place and shooting Zain a stern look. "You better behave yourself."

"Why do I have to come?" Zain said.

"You're not leaving my side," Shamil answered, closing the door behind Zain before settling into his seat.

"Your mum picked this, but we'll say you brought it from London, all right?" Mudhar handed over a folded piece of dark blue silk, richly ornamented with golden threads—a present fit for a king.

"Why not just say Grandma picked it?" Zain asked, slumped into the back seat, his headphones dangling around his neck.

"So that your father looks foolish for not bringing Jassim anything from London?" Mudhar scoffed.

"I'm just saying he'll know it's from Grandma."

Mudhar said nothing as he drove away. He was never one to mince words, but his silence was even more unsettling. What did Jassim want that was so urgent? Had someone reported them to the police for the protest? Had Zain done something online overnight? It didn't seem possible— Zain had been asleep each time Shamil checked on him. And why wasn't the phone connecting to any network? It wasn't adding up.

"Here, put this on." Mudhar handed Shamil a grey tie.

"So, now it's a job interview," Shamil said.

Mudhar wasn't amused. "You argue for the sake of arguing, you know that right?" he said, turning onto a concealed avenue that connected Jassim's mansion to the main street.

Shamil wrapped the tie around his neck, a bit too tight for comfort, and glanced out the window at Jassim's grand estate. Two sorrowful peacocks, confined in their tiny cages by the gates, greeted them with broken, mud-stained feathers and missing crowns. Even if someone were to set them free, there was a haunting stillness in their eyes, as though the desire to escape had been extinguished long ago.

The garden surrounding the villa was impeccably maintained, but the mouldy fountains, barely functioning, told a different story. Security cameras dotted the perimeter, their lenses reflecting a cold, unblinking vigilance. Guards stood at every entrance, their Kalashnikovs ready.

"The colonel wants to talk to the adults only," one of the guards said to Mudhar, gesturing towards the guest room. "The young man stays in the waiting hall."

"Grandpa?" Zain looked at Mudhar.

"Surely Jassim would want to see his grand-nephew," Mudhar argued, but the guard remained firm.

Laying a hand on Zain's shoulder, Shamil pulled him away. "Shout for me if you have to, okay?" he whispered, and Zain shrugged as if Shamil's words carried no significance. He slipped on his headphones as the guard led him into the waiting hall, Shamil's vigilant gaze never wavering. Whatever Jassim demanded from him, Shamil resolved to feign compliance, nod and smile as he always had, and proceed with his intentions once they departed.

Inside the guest room, the scent of cigars and rose water filled the air as Jassim sat on his silver-embroidered sofa throne, grinning. Shamil surveyed the corner cameras—they were all switched off—whatever Jassim had planned for them, he certainly didn't want a record of it. Sealed folders lay atop an ivory-lined glass table in the centre of the room, and paintings of the Al-Baath Gods hung on every wall, their eyes following Shamil with an eerie gaze.

"Hakim, you bring light into this house," Jassim cheered, rising to shake Mudhar's hand.

"The light is yours, Cousin," Mudhar replied, approaching him.

Hugging Mudhar, Jassim glared at Shamil with damningly dark eyes. "Our little doctor," he said. "I almost didn't recognise you with that shaggy beard."

Shamil scratched his stubble. Barely covering his chin, calling a beard was a stretch. He reached out and grasped Jassim's hand, matching his tight grip in a test of endurance. "I would shave, but Laila prefers it like this," he joked, forcing a smile as Jassim's grip tightened, reaffirming his dominance.

"We should have found you a new one a long time ago," Jassim sneered. "That woman broke you."

Shamil pursed his lips, feeling blood rush to his face and sweat form in his armpits. He would have had little say in the matter if Jassim decided to marry him off to someone else with his father's blessing. He had almost forgotten how much Jassim and his father looked alike until he saw them sitting beside each other: the same thinning, short, black-dyed hair, hawkish noses and prominent chins. Despite the weight Jassim had put on, his sharp-edged face remained as menacing as ever. "Congratulations on the promotion."

"You call this a promotion?" Jassim scoffed.

"He means that the city needed people like you," Mudhar explained, looking comfortable in his seat next to Jassim. "Someone has to keep control of things around here, no?"

"You flatter me, Cousin," Jassim said, turning his attention to Shamil. "So, our Little Doctor, our Pride. Tell your father what you have been up to. Or would you rather I tell him instead?"

Shamil frowned, taken aback by Jassim's words.

"Kareem? That lowlife criminal?" Jassim ridiculed, exposing Shamil's plan. "Our 'pride' here has been plotting an escape with a group of criminals," Jassim continued. "He would have gotten all of you killed with his idiotic plan."

"Sham?" Mudhar exclaimed.

"I would never..." Shamil tried to speak.

"Did I finish talking?" Jassim interrupted, wagging his cigar at him before turning to Mudhar. "Cousin, did it look like I finished?"

"I don't know what to say," Mudhar answered.

"One assumes that after I got your son out of prison and you safely to your mother's lap, you would come to me the moment your feet touched the ground to express your gratitude," Jassim continued. "Instead, you've been conspiring with criminals."

"I didn't come here to be insulted," Shamil erupted from the chair, his face flushed with heat, only to be met by a raging roar.

"Sit down!" Jassim's voice echoed through the guest room. His veins were engorged like dark brown snakes slithering up his neck.

Mudhar quickly intervened, laying his hand on Jassim's thigh as if to tame his rage. "Son, sit down," he asked Shamil.

"Sit. Down." Jassim insisted, and Shamil clenched his fist, his eyes briefly breaking contact with Jassim to glance over the folders left on the table. They must have carried items that Shamil knew would be damaging to him, and he better sit down and take Jassim's insults if he were to learn what was in them. Letting out a loud exhale, he resigned back into his chair.

"We are family, something you seem to have forgotten." Jassim leaned back, a smirk tugged at the corner of his lips.

"You're the root, and we're the branches, cousin," Mudhar said.

"Indeed, Uncle," Shamil said, almost choking on it. Jassim's ego needed constant stroking as if being the head of their family and their richest weren't enough.

"You know, we're looking at this all wrong." Jassim put out his cigar. "At first, your father and I thought a night in solitary would teach Zain a lesson, and he would stop all his nonsense protesting. But, as you can already see, nothing can deter that brat from protesting. Then I went through the intelligence report again, and I saw an excellent opportunity."

Shamil glared at Mudhar in shock. Was he in on it? Zain's arrest and humiliation, and God knows what else was done to him in the solitary cell, were with his blessing? How could he?

"Leave Zain out of this," Shamil said pre-emptively, knowing what Jassim was about to ask.

"It's remarkable, really, how this has worked," Jassim said. "I mean, talk about trapping rats, right cousin?"

"Jassim brought up a sensitive matter at our house, within earshot of Zain," Mudhar said, with less confidence than his twin.

"Instantly, Zain relayed that intel to the rebels, and they acted upon it," Jassim continued, looking at Shamil as if waiting for him to celebrate or congratulate him on his brilliant idea. "And then we did it again. Guess what happened?"

"You can't be serious," Shamil growled. "You have thousands of informants, and you want to add my son to your pool of expendables?"

"Nothing will happen to him," Jassim dismissed Shamil's fear with a wave. "Besides, he was, well, still is, in direct contact with some rebel leaders."

"Under a fake name," Mudhar interjected as if this tiny detail would soften the blow.

"Particularly with that fool they call The Syrian Dandelion. The only Syrian thing about him will be the bullet I plant in his skull," Jassim said, disgust evident on his face. "He's rather fond of your son, you know, almost fatherly," he added, his eyes drilling into Shamil's, seeking to provoke.

"You're mad, I swear," Shamil snapped, his voice rising. "You sent your son to his death, and now you're about to send mine?"

"My son is a hero," Jassim thundered. "Unlike your brat who has tarnished our family's honour."

"My son's life is worth our entire family's honour."

"Is this how we raise our children now?" Jassim turned to Mudhar. "Disrespecting their elders?"

"London has corrupted him."

"What do you call those that conspire against their government and aid their enemies? There used to be a name for this," Jassim's eyes bored into Mudhar, demanding an answer.

"Traitors."

"Zain doesn't know what he's doing," Shamil pleaded. "Let me take him with me, and this whole thing will be over."

"Yeah, yeah." Jassim tossed a folder to Shamil's side of the table without a word. The name tag read 'Zain'. "You should be able to check your emails now," he said, tapping Mudhar's arm to join him for dinner. Mudhar complied, leaving Shamil alone in that folder.

Shamil's fingers fumbled as he loosened his collar; there were so many glaring signs—what an idiot Shamil was to think Jassim was above spying on him. The missed calls from unknown numbers and the passing echoes he assumed were network glitches—of course, he spied on him. His emails were all marked as read, even the ones received minutes ago. Shamil would check what was sent from his accounts later, but now Zain was the priority.

Flipping through the folder, each page Shamil turned seemed to tighten the noose around his neck. He leaned forward, his elbows digging into his knees; the room seemed to close around him. Zain wasn't only an informant now but a target for the rebels when they realised his intel was a trap. The pages of Zain's file were littered with messages from numerous accounts: The Syrian Eagle, The Syrian Rebel, Aleppo's Lion, and others claiming leadership in the rebel ranks. They sought exclusive photos, intelligence, and even his true identity. They seemed to trust him, thinking he was a high-ranking government official in disguise, with the information Zain had been able to procure for them. Zain had been cautious enough not ever to use his real name nor reveal his location. But if SAFI were onto him, then surely the rebels wouldn't be that far behind.

Going over thousands of messages, confusion was beginning to take over Shamil. Every other supposed rebel leader had asked something of Zain, except for The Syrian Dandelion. He had guided Zain, checked up on him almost every day, and never asked him for intel. Zain had volunteered that information despite being warned not to endanger himself.

It was painfully evident how he looked after his son, 'almost fatherly' - Jassim's words gnawed at Shamil's mind like a parasite. He must have known who Zain was; why else would he care that much?

How had Shamil let this happen?

His innocent child had been used as a pawn by both the rebels and Jassim, each seeking to exploit him for leverage. The weight of this revelation was almost too much to bear, and Shamil's anger towards himself grew greater.

Why Zain? A question he needed to answer before he could negotiate a way out with Jassim. Yes, Zain had somehow managed to infiltrate the opposition ranks online and gain their trust, his large online following playing a big part in it. Still, any savvy informant could replicate his online persona and influence within months. Was Jassim so desperate for a win that he would use whatever means available? Or was he genuinely trying to cleanse their family's name?

There was no point dwelling on it, though. The damage had already been done, and regrets wouldn't change anything.

As the sun set, recitals from a nearby mosque filled the mansion halls, blending with the lingering scent of rose water and Jassim's cigar. The atmosphere felt heavy and oppressive, as if Shamil was at a funeral or awaiting one. Soon, Jassim returned, his belt straining against his protruding stomach, with Mudhar clinging to his arm. It was time for answers.

Chapter 17: Power Balance

Jassim turned on the air conditioning to dispel the scent of rose water that filled the guest room. He had instructed the guards to sprinkle some in celebration of his cherished lieutenant's return, not expecting it to turn the room into a madras, reeking of mullahs and sheikhs. He loosened his belt, his stomach now full, and strode towards Shamil with Mudhar hooked to his arm.

"Quite something, isn't it?" Jassim prodded, sitting opposite him. He had meticulously studied the file before he sent in his response to General Saleem, the head of Section Seventeen, claiming that Zain was working for him and that he had commissioned the leaked intel. What else could he do? Arrest his own flesh and blood for real this time, to be tortured and maimed? Admit that his grand-nephew was a traitor? Such an admission would embolden his adversaries, exposing his failure to control even his close family. He couldn't afford that; too many livelihoods depended on him maintaining his status. Zain's actions had forced Jassim's hands, and he had to make the best out of an outrageous situation.

Shamil held up a page. "This is from yesterday."

"He never stopped," Jassim said.

"The rebels are going to take the city, aren't they?" Shamil asked, closing the folder.

"Nonsense," Jassim scoffed, the very notion almost making him chuckle. The only way the rebels could take the city was if he and Saleem agreed to vacate their posts, a plan they had previously entertained.

"The blasts are getting louder. Your guards are abandoning their posts..."

"It's all planned."

"The protests are growing larger," Shamil continued. "You're losing control of-"

"I can end it all with one signature," Jassim interrupted, confident in the military's capability to wipe out the rebels should they get his clearance. The only reason he hadn't done so yet was the collateral damage the civilians would suffer.

"You can't even arrest a rebel leader with a fake name. For all you know, he's one of your own lieutenants, knowing your every move. Is this why you're so desperate to use a teenager?"

"I'm offering you a chance to clear your son's name."

"And turn him into a target for the rebels?"

"The rebels' days are numbered," Jassim snapped, slamming his hand onto the table. He had had enough of Shamil's insolence. "You think I need you or your little brat? If not for our family's honour, I would have let him rot in a prison cell, just like every other traitor."

"You know where this is heading. You just don't want to be the one pulling the trigger," Shamil pressed.

Jassim exhaled deeply as he glared into Shamil's eyes. Finally, he could see the fire of determination in them. This was the man he had trained alongside his son Adil, the one he had hoped would remain his left arm after losing his right. "You see it now, don't you?"

"All I see is Bloodshed?"

"It's avoidable."

"It's inevitable."

"I will prevent it," Jassim said, leaning closer to Shamil, but he stopped short of telling him that only he could carry his family's legacy forward.

"If you don't need us, let us go," Shamil said, his tone subdued. The fire in his eyes faded, and with it, Jassim's pride in him. "You have Zain's online accounts. Use them however you want."

"Do you know how hard it was for me to get to where I am today?" Jassim asked, his tone softer this time.

"I promise you; Zain won't be a problem; I'll even change his name once we're abroad to spare you the headache," Shamil answered.

"You would abandon our family's name?" Jassim leaned back, his stomach turning at the sight of his once-proud protege crumbling before him. Zain's accounts held no value to him; it was Shamil's presence that he wanted, their only heir. But not like that. That weak man wasn't the cunning lieutenant he had trained alongside his son. "You may leave if you choose to. Go back to that shithole hospital where they treat you as their servant. But I swear on Adil's soul, I will disown you and will treat you and your son the same way I treat every other traitor."

"Cousin, no need for this," Mudhar intervened, just as Jassim knew he would.

Mudhar never had the backbone to deliver such a punishment—he had always been lenient with Zain and Shamil.

It surprised Jassim that he had agreed to have Zain arrested — even brief as it was. Perhaps Mudhar's longing to have Shamil return from London had eclipsed his concern for his grandson, and that's why he had agreed.

"Al-Sayed don't harbour traitors," Jassim said.

"Just give us two days, I promise, you'll hear what pleases you," Mudhar said before he turned his attention to Shamil. "Apologise to your uncle."

"No need," Jassim interrupted before turning his gaze to Shamil. "Actions speak louder."

"We'll see." Shamil got up, extending his hand.

Grasping it, Jassim pulled him closer. "You owe this to Adil."

Shamil nodded, withdrawing his hand as he signalled for Mudhar to get up.

Resigning back in his seat, Jassim watched them leave before he grabbed Zain's file and set it ablaze in the bin beside him.

"Tawfeeq!" he called, and in seconds, his informant Tawfeeq was stomping a salute in front of him. "You'll be his shadow, understood?"

"Yes, Sir," Tawfeeq stomped another salute before bolting after Shamil.

What a shameful situation it was, having to spy on his own flesh and blood, but it was necessary; any honourable man would do it to protect his family.

Jassim lit another cigar and took a deep pull as he closed his eyes. He held the smoke inside his lungs until his head spun, and his conflicting thoughts rapidly converged into one pressing desire: to exhale.

Chapter 18: Fathers

Shamil scurried across the waiting hall to where Zain was seated, grabbing his arm and leading him out of the mansion and into Mudhar's car. He prayed for the strength to keep his anger in check—his son was in even greater peril than he had initially anticipated. His father was complicit, and there was no clear path out of this nightmare.

First things first, the spying had to stop.

Snatching Zain's phone, Shamil removed the SIM card and smashed it to pieces.

"Why?" Zain squeaked.

"They're spying on you," Shamil said, checking the side mirror for any followers. "Drop me off at the Peasant's Market," He instructed Mudhar, too enraged to face him directly. The market was the only place Shamil felt confident he could lose any tails.

As they arrived, Shamil tossed his jacket and tie into the car, swapped his leather shoes for Zain's trainers, and unbuttoned his shirt. "He doesn't leave your sight until I'm back," he said to Mudhar, slamming the door shut before Mudhar could argue against it.

Ruffling his hair, Shamil plunged into the throngs of people crowding the market's narrow alleys. He quickened his pace, darting through a spice shop on one side and emerging from a fabrics shop on the other. Vehicles couldn't pass through where he was heading, not even small bicycles. He zigzagged through the maze of stalls until he was confident no one was following him. Exiting the market, he hailed a taxi and directed it to a phone shop several kilometres away.

He paid in cash for three new phones and SIM cards, all registered under fictitious names. With that task completed, Shamil took a different taxi back home. As he turned a corner to his street, his attention quickly shifted to a pickup car he didn't recognise parked in front of Mudhar's clinic. Standing outside, Mudhar raised his voice, arguing with a young man, and Shamil quickened his pace, trying to catch up to the conversation.

The young man's face twisted in anguish as he pointed at a woman slumped in the backseat of his car. Her skin was a sickly shade of blue, the colour of asphyxiation, and her lips were tinged with the same deep hue. She gasped for air, each breath a struggle as her body fought against the lack of oxygen.

Shamil jumped into the back of the car without hesitation and helped support the woman up straight. The sound of her chest crackling and throat gurgling left little room for doubt—he had seen enough patients in respiratory failure to know that Mudhar's clinic wasn't equipped to address her ailment.

"Please help her," the young man cried as a group of Shamil's neighbours gathered around him.

"She needs oxygen," Shamil replied, rolling the woman's Abaya into a pillow that supported her neck before he leapt out of the car. "We don't keep oxygen in the clinic. You must take her to the hospital now," he repeated what Mudhar had already said.

"Can you at least give her an injection? They always work."

Shamil glanced at the woman. Her condition wasn't worsening, but it wasn't improving either.

He considered riding in the back with her, escorting her and her distressed son to the hospital. But that would have been the extent of the help he could provide—something her son didn't seem to understand. Shamil's presence at the hospital wouldn't have changed the woman's fate, and he couldn't leave Zain unattended any longer.

"She needs a hospital, NOW," Shamil said, shutting the car's backdoor.

The young man cursed under his breath as he got back into the driver's seat. "May God never forgive you, Animals," he muttered before his tyres screeched against the pavement as he drove away.

"There's no winning with these people," one of the neighbours commented.

"They just don't get it," Mudhar replied, looking as flushed as when he had a hypertensive crisis in the past.

Shamil hurried Mudhar into the clinic, closing the door firmly behind them and drawing the curtains. The sight of that sickly woman had already drawn too much attention to their street. People would judge Mudhar no matter what—whether he chose to treat her or not. People always judged, especially when they didn't understand the reasons behind someone's actions.

Dimming the lights in Mudhar's office, Shamil helped him to his chair. He watched as Mudhar took a few deep breaths, his hands trembling slightly.

"That woman is going to die, and her son will blame me for it." Mudhar rubbed his temples vigorously as if his blood pressure needed another trigger.

"You're not an intensivist. What could you have done?" Shamil asked, trying to calm him down. Despite still being angry with him, he wouldn't want his father to fall ill. Mudhar was rather sensitive to fluctuations in his blood pressure.

"I don't know." Mudhar let out a long exhale as Shamil sat across from him, a cluttered wooden desk separating them. "Anyway, Jassim expects an answer in two days."

"I'm not going to do it," Shamil asserted, grabbing Mudhar's stethoscope off of the desk. The earpiece was hanging loose, and it had been bothering him the moment he noticed it.

"He will disown you."

"So what?" Shamil interjected, "He can keep the inheritance. I saved enough money for all of us to live abroad."

"As beggars?"

"As refugees."

"Same shit."

"For just a few months."

Mudhar grimaced. "Why on Earth would I go back to scavenging for food?"

"Jassim is delusional; the fighting will hit the city. There's no other way," Shamil grunted, his anger building. "Someday, somehow, a rogue rebel will shoot at an officer in the city, and the police will return fire. Once blood is shed, there will be no turning back. And now Zain is caught in the middle of this situation; I can't just sit back on my ass and do nothing."

"You've been sitting on your ass for years," Mudhar snapped, hitting Shamil where it hurt. "I'm more his father than you ever were."

"This is rich coming from you."

"I was a good father; I never abandoned you."

"You were never around; your money was," Shamil tossed the stethoscope onto the desk, unfixed. And what a great father you are to Zain, allowing Jassim to use him like that. How could you?"

"Zain put us in that situation. What was I supposed to do?"

"Be stricter with him? You sure know how to."

"So that he buggers off like you did?" Mudhar asked, tears now forming at the corners of his eyes. A sight Shamil never thought was possible. "All Jassim speaks about is his dead son. How he misses him, how he wishes he could be in the same room with him, how they could go hunting, camping, and how none of that was possible because his son was dead, and then here's me, my son alive yet I still couldn't talk to him, hug him, smell his shirt or do anything with him."

"Baba…"

"No, you don't get to sit here and tell me what a father should or shouldn't do," Mudhar interrupted. "When Jassim told me we could get you back and clear Zain's name at the same time, I answered yes. There was no other answer. I wanted you back."

"Baba, I know I shouldn't have left," Shamil softened his tone. "But right now, I need to get Zain out of this situation. The only way he can be safe is abroad."

Mudhar adjusted his chair forward. "And how are you planning to do this?" he asked, wiping his face.

"I'll show you." Shamil grabbed a pen and an empty prescription paper.

"I'll take him tomorrow to Uncle Mezar's cottage in Jazra village and keep him there away from the internet and the protests," Shamil explained as he drew a map of their area, pinpointing the locations of the roadblocks he had confirmed and the wilderness paths used by shepherds in the countryside, ones he'd used on hunting trips with Jassim and Adil in the past. "When the rebels invade Ar-Raqqah, tens of thousands of people will flee the fighting, and there will be safe corridors for civilians to use. We'll use that commotion to travel East to..."

"This is ridiculous," Mudhar interrupted, attempting to take the pen out of Shamil's hand. "Your 'plan' depends on the rebels taking the city, which won't happen."

"Just listen." Shamil pulled his hand away. "Let's assume the rebels fail, and Ar-Raqqah remains safe; what harm would hiding Zain for a few weeks bring?"

"You're going to anger Jassim with this; I say we just do as he asked," Mudhar said, snatching the paper Shamil had drawn his plan on and shoving it down the drawer. "You're so obsessed with leaving; it's not like any of us was ever harmed."

"What's this then?" Shamil pulled his trousers up and ripped off the bandage, revealing his wound.

144

Mudhar's face went pale. "How?"

"A stray bullet from last night," Shamil said, discarding the bandage. "It hit a few feet away from a large diesel tank."

"Who sutured it?" Mudhar asked, his forehead glistening with sweat, a sign Shamil could not ignore.

Quickly, he reclined Mudhar's chair, lifting his legs onto the desk. When the colour returned to Mudhar's face, and his pulse normalised, Shamil left his side and got him a glass of water.

"The new medicine is stronger than I thought," Mudhar said.

"You're just dehydrated," Shamil said, pouring him another glass of water. "We'll continue this later."

Mudhar nodded. "You go home; I'll follow you in a bit."

"Baba."

"Go. I'm fine."

Hesitantly, Shamil left the clinic, casting one last glance at Mudhar to ensure he was all right. Shamil had always seen his father as an indestructible man of boundless powers. When Shamil was a teenager, Mudhar shielded him from political, racial, and religious divides, highlighting only the beauty their little city of Ar-Raqqah possessed.

In fact, Shamil had been so oblivious to Syrian party politics that he almost got Mudhar interrogated and perhaps even jailed in 1993.

"I want nothing to do with politics," Shamil had declared, refusing to sign the pledge of allegiance to the Al-Baath party at his high school's initiation ceremony.

"Are you crazy?" Alaa, his best friend, had whispered, his head down as he signed the pledge. "You must sign it."

The pale principal seemed unsure how to respond. What Shamil had done was unprecedented — no one dared say no. Had he not owed a favour to Mudhar, he would have unleashed severe consequences on Shamil and his family. Instead, the principal had clamped a rough hand over Shamil's mouth and dragged him to his office.

Shamil still remembered the smell of urine on the principal's fingers, the disgust he felt, unable to spit or swallow.

"You asked me to stay out of politics," Shamil had protested when Mudhar arrived, trying to justify his unforgivable action. There were few times in Shamil's life when he saw fear in his father's eyes, and this was one of them.

"What I meant was politics against the Al-Baath party, Son. We're all Al-Bath's children," Mudhar had said, signing the pledge on Shamil's behalf with the principal as their witness.

That's when Shamil realised his father wasn't the Superman he believed him to be and that their way of life came with a demeaning price — a price the teenage Shamil wasn't yet brave enough to denounce.

Mudhar had always been protective of Shamil but rarely showed his true feelings. "Emotions are weakness," he would often preach, with his twin, Jassim, patting him on the shoulder in approval. Shamil, on the other hand, was a very emotional young man, something he both blamed and thanked his mother, Ameena, for. Seeing him on the verge of tears weighed heavily on Shamil's heart, but what Mudhar did was unacceptable. Nothing justified using Zain, no matter how well-intentioned it was.

Entering his parents' courtyard, Shamil ensured his trousers weren't stained with blood before he announced his presence. There, Zain, Ameenah, and Laila were having dinner by the rock fountain. Steam floating from the hot rice and lamb stew had Shamil's stomach juices flowing rampant, but he couldn't bring himself to eat.

"Where's your father," Ameena asked, quickly grabbing a plate and filling it with rice, no doubt sensing how hungry Shamil was.

"You can't use your old phone," Shamil said, sitting next to Zain and handing him one of the new phones. "Sign into your Facebook account using this one and change your email and the associated phone number."

Zain looked at him, sceptic. "And this one isn't bugged?" he asked, food flying from his mouth.

"Change your password, email, and number now," Shamil insisted, and Zain snatched the new phone, his face turning red as he examined it. He reset the new phone a couple of times before he logged onto his Facebook account and frantically changed his details.

"Bugged?" Laila asked.

"What's going on?" Ameena followed.

"Just give me a second," Shamil addressed both of them before turning his attention back to Zain. "You must charge the battery full before you can use it."

"Where's its charger?" Zain asked, removing a sticker from the back of his old phone and posting it onto the back of the new one.

"Give me," Shamil threw his hand in front of him. "I'll plug it in while you reset your old phone."

Zain hesitated, holding onto his new phone.

"I'll do it in front of you, here; I'll plug it in the downstairs kitchen and leave it there!" Shamil reassured him, and he nodded, handing over his new phone.

In the kitchen, Shamil checked that he was out of Zain's field of vision before he swapped Zain's new phone with the other one he'd bought, ensuring the transfer of the sticker. He then dropped it off to the ground, where Zain could see it crash.

"Shit," Shamil grunted, collecting the phone, Zain bolting towards him.

"You broke it?" Zain snatched his now-swapped new phone.

"It's a minor scratch," Shamil said. If it doesn't work, you can take your sticker, and I'll get you a new one."

Zain turned the phone on to a welcoming screen. "Come on, it needs setting up all over again."

"No harm was done. Stop crying," Ameena intervened. "It still looks way better than your old, cracked phone."

"You don't get it," Zain complained, grabbing his bag and walking into the kitchen, where the charger was hooked up.

"He'll be fine," Laila reassured Shamil, undoubtedly sensing how stressed he was. Not that she'd know the real reason why he'd been stressed.

Locking himself in the toilet, Shamil pulled the phone Zain had logged in on and ensured his accounts were still active before he switched it off and hid it in his trousers safe pockets. The last thing he'd imagined was to spy on his son, but he had no other choice if he were to ensure his son remained safe until he secured a route out of Ar-Raqqah. He would come clean with Zain once they were abroad, hoping that he would forgive him.

"Shamil, there's a commotion outside the clinic," Ameena's voice reverberated behind the toilet's closed door. Shamil exited with urgency and darted towards his parents' front door, where loud cries of a man echoed through the courtyard's corridors.

"You killed my mother," a man's voice screeched in agony, followed by a loud blast.

Chapter 19: The Doctor is God

When the deafening echo of the blast reached Shamil's ears, panic surged through his veins, thrusting him toward the clinic. Thoughts of the worst-case scenario flooded his mind — and he burst outside, his eyes fixed on the young man holding a single-barrel shotgun aimed at his father. In that timeless moment, Shamil swiftly scanned for any visible injuries. Mudhar's chest remained unharmed, his face and head intact, and his limbs seemed untouched—except for his left arm, where blood was pouring down.

Instinct took over, and Shamil's legs thrust him toward the young man, who was frantically attempting to reload his weapon. Shamil's hands moved faster. He leapt at the young man, seizing the shotgun as he violently tackled him to the ground, and with a practised motion, Shamil's thumb located the lever, swiftly flipping it and activating the release mechanism. In an instant, the shotgun sprang open, breaking apart with a familiar click. Shamil then flung the handle aside as a surge of primal fury fuelled his every move.

"When you strike your enemy, do it with enough force to incapacitate, yet not enough to end their life," Jassim's teachings echoed in Shamil's mind, remnants of the lessons ingrained in him during his youth. "Break their limbs, shatter their bones, disfigure their faces, but ensure they understand that their survival was a conscious choice on your part."

Unleashing a barrage of punches, Shamil repeatedly battered the young man's arms as he desperately shielded his face. But as Shamil's fists connected with the man's bloodied countenance for the third time, an invisible barrier halted his assault. He found himself perched atop his victim, panting with his fist suspended in mid-air, refusing to complete its intended target: the grieving face of another human.

The heft of his anger gradually subsided, yielding to a growing sense of guilt. The young man's mother had just passed away; who could blame him for seeking vengeance?

Shamil turned his gaze back to his father, witnessing him rise with Zain's support. This reassured him that, as he had expected, his injuries weren't fatal. Then, his attention shifted back to the young man beneath him.

Gripping his shirt, he hoisted him upright. "You will return home, gather your belongings, and vanish," Shamil said, his voice trembling with rage. "You shot the cousin of Colonel Jassim, so pack up whatever shit you possess and vanish, or he will end you."

"You could have saved her," the young man sobbed, casting accusing eyes upon Mudhar, who was getting in the car with Zain.

Shamil seized his anguished face in his hands, compelling him to meet his gaze. "You're wrong; nothing here could have saved her," he uttered as he foolishly scrutinised the wounds his fists had inflicted. How had he allowed himself to mar that young man's face so brutally and yet, paradoxically, concern himself with his well-being?

The bruises his fists had left on him could heal in time, but if Jassim were to find him, those bruises would become a child's play in comparison. "I'm letting you go this time to honour your mother. Otherwise, I swear I would have broken both your arms before I handed you to Jassim myself."

"I called the police, Hakim," Abu Rhadi, one of the neighbours, said, emerging from his shop. He had witnessed the entire incident, and he couldn't have intervened sooner— not with his severe limp.

"Find out where this man resides, and get him a taxi there," Shamil asked the neighbour.

"Hakim?" Abu Rhadi objected. "He shot your father,"

Shamil was well aware of that; still, who knew what he would have done had anything happened to his mother, Ameena? He would have lost his mind as well.

"He wasn't thinking," Shamil released his grip on the young man, gathering the pieces of his shotgun and tossing them into the backseat of Mudhar's car. The young man took a step back and collapsed onto the pavement, covering his face with both hands as he sobbed.

"Abu Radhi, please, talk to his family and have him hide for a while. If Jassim finds him…" Shamil pleaded with Abu Radhi, his voice cracking with his rapid heartbeats.

"As you see fit, Hakim," Abu Radhi nodded, then shuffled towards the grieving young man.

Sitting in the back of Mudhar's car, the dismembered shotgun at his feet, all Shamil could envision was the young man's bloodied face.

He had acted in self-defence, preventing him from loading another shell into his weapon, so why was guilt gnawing at him?

He couldn't have saved that woman, and neither could Mudhar; that was an undeniable truth. Yet, if only he had accompanied her to the hospital, perhaps her son wouldn't have held them responsible.

Closing his eyes, Shamil pressed his hands firmly against his forehead as if attempting to reset his mind. He had to shake off these thoughts— distractions were a luxury he couldn't afford.

As soon as Zain pulled over at Dar Al Shifa Hospital, two nurses and a doctor hurried to assist Mudhar, helping him onto a well-equipped trolley. They swiftly manoeuvred him through the wide automatic gates into a spacious reception and then into the lifts. Shamil lingered behind Zain as there wasn't enough space for them on the lift, anxiously waiting for it to descend. His brain faltered, and he found himself spacing out, thinking how lucky they were the young man had missed his target. Distant memories carried him to the confines of his father's clinic, where an extraordinary piece of art, meticulously crafted from ancient copper, adorned a prominent spot on the wall. A magnificent display of blown-out sculptures depicted Babylonian lions locked in a fierce struggle, their jaws clamped around each other's throats. And atop this glorious scene, a healer triumphantly mounted the battling beasts, embodying a sense of unyielding power and dominance. Engraved at its bottom in a beautiful Arabic calligraphy, 'The Doctor is God'.

"He'll be ok, right?" Zain's voice snapped Shamil back.

"He will. They were minor injuries," Shamil replied, pressing the lift call button yet again as it seemed to have been stuck on the fifth floor. "Let's take the stairs," he suggested, and Zain followed.

On the fifth floor, the hospital's manager guided them into his office, where refreshments awaited them. "Dr Mudhar asked that you two await him here," the manager said before leaving the office.

"Typical," Shamil scoffed, resting his back against the comfortable black-leather sofa. Mudhar had always refused to be treated by Shamil or any of his relatives, for that matter. He held a firm belief that mistakes were bound to happen in medicine and that it was best not to hold your dear ones responsible for any lasting pains resulting from being misdiagnosed or mistreated.

"He's always like that," Zain said, grabbing a glass of freshly squeezed juice the manager had left for them on the table.

"I used to think of him as a God," Shamil said, the copper painting not leaving his imagination. "When I was ten or eleven, everything he did impressed me," Shamil continued as Zain listened. "The healer of the city, their beloved, who wouldn't charge the poor for his services."

"He still doesn't charge them," Zain commented, his drink sitting still in his hands. "I don't know why he wouldn't see that sick woman or even you; you could have helped, no?"

Shamil nodded, not sure at this point whether, indeed, he could have helped.

"When I was your age, there were times when your grandfather would ask the patients to head to the hospital, instead of treating them himself, and that would confuse me. I mean, it just didn't make sense to me," Shamil said, looking at his hands, traces of blood still stained them. "Then I became a doctor myself, and I, too, discovered the reality of our limitations. It humbled me - I had misjudged your grandfather."

"I never thought of it that way," Zain began, a smile almost visiting the corner of his lips before he went silent. Shamil's bruised knuckles trapped his glare. "Did it hurt?"

"Him more than me," Shamil said, feeling the urge to hide his hands in shame.

His eyes downcast, Zain whispered, "You scared me."

"I knew what I was doing, Son. He couldn't have hurt me."

"No, I mean YOU scared me," he confessed, his gaze averted. "I thought you were going to kill him."

"I had to do it. I.." Shamil tried to explain himself.

"I know. I know," Zain quickly interjected, the words tumbling from his lips. "I just thought maybe you could have restrained him and handed him over to the police."

"They would have shown him no mercy; Jassim would have ensured it," Shamil countered, a bitter taste accompanying his words. "But, yeah, in an ideal world, I would have restrained him."

"Wouldn't you want to live in that world?" Zain's gaze met Shamil's, seeking answers.

Silent and full of shame, Shamil looked into his son's hopeful brown eyes and saw an undeterred will to do whatever it took to make that mirage of an ideal world a reality. An overwhelming desire to do what's right and help those in need, one that Shamil was all too familiar with when he was his age. A desire that had Shamil entrapped in a loveless marriage with Laila when he had offered to save her from her father. A desire that took away his happiness, and he wasn't going to let it take away his son's.

Chapter 20: Headlock

Laila pressed her forehead harder against the soft fabric of her praying rug. "You're closest to God when you're prostrating," her mother used to say when teaching her how to pray. Now, Laila needed to be very close to God, pleading fervently for Mudhar's safety. She had never seen that much blood before, except during Eid Al Adha, when the blood of sacrificed sheep and cows flooded the streets. Blood always smelled the same, regardless of its source: repulsively metallic.

Finishing her prayer, she glanced at Ameena, who was weeping, her forehead pressed against her own rug. Laila didn't want to disturb her— she knew Ameena would want to be left alone. The house needed tidying up anyway—soon relatives, friends, colleagues, neighbours, perhaps even the entire city, would wish to visit Mudhar and check on him. Not only was he Jassim's cousin, he was also one of the city's best doctors.

Pulling the edges of her dress and tying them around her waist, Laila quickly vacuumed the thick wool carpets, wiped the tables, hung the curtains, and set out the guest cutlery by the kitchen stall, ready for when the visitors arrived. Everything had to be perfect— the last thing she needed was an unwanted comment from her mother-in-law.

"Ameena! Ameena!" a woman's cry echoed through the stairwell and into the front door. It was Nadia, Ameena's sister. "My God, daughter, is he alive? Is he okay?" Nadia asked, hands clutching her chest as if to help her breathe. Poor woman—two flights of stairs were enough to take her breath away.

"He's fine, auntie," Laila said, helping Nadia take off her abaya.

"How is he fine? His arm's gone," Ameena sobbed, rushing to hug her sister.

Laila stepped back, fairly certain Mudhar's arm was intact— Shamil hadn't seemed overly concerned when they left for the hospital. Ameena had always been prone to drama, and Laila wasn't about to apologise for her misstep.

"Oh, Merciful," Nadia whispered, hugging her weeping sister and kissing her head. "He's a man— he'll be all right."

"Inshallah," Ameena nodded, pulling away. "Would you lock my head? It's going to explode."

"Of course, sweetie," Nadia gestured to Laila, who quickly removed her headscarf and handed it to Nadia.

She never understood this whole 'headlocking' thing. How could tightening a headscarf against someone's temples ease their pain? If anything, these scarves were so tight that their hair barely had any space to breathe when they wore them.

She wouldn't dwell on it. If headlocking was going to ease Ameena's pain, then Laila would have done it herself. But now, since the expert carer was here, Laila needn't intervene.

"Can you use this as a lock?" Laila handed Nadia a spoon.

"Of course," Nadia grabbed the spoon and inserted it into the knot she'd made with the headscarf before tightening it around Ameena's temples. "Is this good?" she asked Ameena.

"God bless you," Ameena tapped Nadia's hand to stop.

"How sweet is your coffee, Auntie?" Laila asked.

"As sweet as you are," Nadia smiled, securing the spoon in place. She had Ameena's face, if Ameena had slept less and eaten more: a kind face with a hint of sadness. She even wore the same clothes as Ameena, not because they shared the same taste, but because whenever Ameena had worn a dress enough times, or it had suffered minor damage, she would then pass it on to Nadia to wear.

Laila nodded, getting up to make the coffee just as police sirens filled their street. Men's voices barked at the neighbours to get back into their houses, leaving little doubt: Jassim had arrived. Untying the knot she'd made around her waist, Laila released her grey-striped dress and rolled down her sleeves. She grabbed a spare headscarf from the coat hanger by the main door before opening it to find Jassim standing there.

"Is she decent?" he asked, no salutations or regards, not like Laila was expecting any.

"Nadia's locking her head," Laila said, half closing the door, not wanting him to see her hair. "I'll open the guest room's door for you."

"She can lock mine next," he wiped his boots on the doormat before turning to face the entrance to the guest room.

Laila fixed her headscarf, then paced towards the guest room where Jassim had already let himself in— the door must have been open. He couldn't have been there for more than seconds, yet the smell of burnt vanilla, the only thing Laila could stand about him, had already filled the room. "Coffee?" she offered.

"Bitter," he answered, taking his boots off before he settled on the sofa. "Tell the women that he's okay."

"Alhamdulillah," Laila said, grabbing two pillows and stepping closer to him. "For your back."

He leaned forward, looking away from her, as she placed one pillow behind his back and another at his side. She didn't expect a "Thank you"—that wasn't something Jassim did, nor did Mudhar or any other old man for that matter. It was women who cooked, cleaned and tidied up for men, who even locked their heads whenever they wanted. It was a blessing that Shamil hadn't turned out like them, and for that, Laila had Ameena to thank.

"Have you seen it?" Jassim asked.

"We were inside."

"How many men were there?"

"Just the one."

"And your husband couldn't catch him?"

"Uncle's wound took priority."

"I see." Jassim took his phone out and dialled a number, glaring at Laila as the call went through. "Any problems with the lamb?" he spoke into his phone. "Turn up the heat then."

Laila forced a smile, retreating into the living room. He had no further use for her. She could never tell whether his contempt was personal or simply how he treated everyone, being a colonel and all. He had smiled at her in the past, praised her looks, and even called her the bride of the Euphrates, as he had adorned her with golden necklaces and thick bracelets and, at times, made her feel cherished.

That was until his son Adil passed away.

It was as if whatever joy had resided in him, little as it was, died with his son. He had become a shell of a man, consumed with slogans of honour and martyrdom as if they were the only things defining his entire existence.

She wasn't bothered by his behaviour—if anything, she pitied him. Who knew what she'd become if she lost Zain? She couldn't imagine it.

"Was it your idea?" Jassim's voice rose, sharp and demanding. Was he speaking to her? Laila turned to face him.

"I..." she began, but Jassim cut her off.

"The smugglers, was it you who rushed him?"

Heat flushed Laila's face. She had known Jassim would eventually discover Shamil's desperate plan. She had naively hoped it would be after they had reached safety abroad. But for him to think she had pushed Shamil into risking their lives—she hadn't anticipated that.

"Shamil does what he wants; he's the man of the house," she said, trying to deflect and not wanting to engage Jassim any further.

"Is he now?" Jassim scoffed, his piercing eyes fixed on her. "Well, you better convince him to stay, or else he won't have a house to be a man of."

Laila sealed her lips, swallowing the retort that burned her tongue. She wished she could tell him to take his fortune to his grave—she didn't want any of it. Instead, she said what was expected of her, "We'll only do what you and Uncle see fit."

Closing the guest room's wall divider behind her, Laila rushed into the kitchen, her hands quivering with rage.

If she had stayed any longer, she would have broken down in tears, and she wasn't going to give Jassim the satisfaction of seeing her crumble or, worse, pity her.

"Ignore him," Nadia said, joining her in the kitchen. She had undoubtedly overheard Laila's conversation with Jassim. "I swear, he'll go up in flames if he smiles. Such are the devils."

"I'm more at ease with him frowning," Laila said, grabbing the coffee jazzve. "At least you know what he's thinking when he frowns."

"I say we put salt in his coffee," Nadia nodded at the saltshaker, her tone leaving little doubt she had done it before.

Laila instinctively pulled the jazzve away from Nadia. "Auntie will kill us!"

"Oh, don't you worry about her," Nadia said, handing the cardamom-scented coffee bag to Laila. "She's being overly dramatic."

"She's just worried about Uncle's hand."

"Pfft," Nadia waved her hand dismissively. "When my husband served in the military, a grenade went off a few metres behind him. I have a photo of him with shrapnel wounds all over his thighs and cute little butt cheeks, and his smile couldn't have been any wider."

Laila resisted a chuckle. Despite Nadia's humour, she couldn't shake the image of Mudhar's bloodied hand from her mind. "Auntie, he could have died."

"When it's our time, it's our time," Nadia lit the gas. "Now, let's make some coffee, or else Mr. Frownie will have a fit."

Chapter 21: A Gentle Pressure

Shamil helped Mudhar out of the car, his wounded left hand secured in a plaster cast. Fortunately, the injuries weren't severe, and Mudhar was expected to recover within a month.

"May harm never find your way," Jassim murmured, embracing Mudhar and kissing his forehead before guiding him into the guest room. "The dog who did this will be at your feet."

"No need for it, Cousin," Mudhar said, settling Jassim next to him. "Had you seen how Sham confronted that man, you would have been proud."

Shamil glanced at his bruised knuckles. Jassim had trained him well, and he would have wanted Shamil to finish what he had started.

"Yet, he let him escape," Jassim sneered, spitting on the floor. "Proud, my ass. Adil would have broken arms and pulled out teeth first."

"May God have mercy on Adil's soul," Mudhar said, gesturing for Shamil to go to the living room. He must have wanted him to reassure Ameena. "He was such a brave man."

"More man than you will ever be," Jassim glared at Shamil with accusing eyes. He had never forgiven him for his son's death, making it painfully clear whenever Adil's name came up.

Shamil had loved Adil, but he wasn't going to let Jassim abuse him any longer. "You're going to insult me in my own house?" Shamil snapped.

"I do as I please," Jassim rose from his seat, eyes blood-red, hand twitching. If Shamil had been one of his subordinates, he would have felt the sting of Jassim's palm by now. "You would have had nothing—no house, no clinic, no cars—if it hadn't been for me."

"Look at you, smothering us with your kindness," Nadia mocked, opening the room divider as Laila trailed her, coffee in hand. "How would we ever survive without you?"

She glanced at Shamil as if both saluting and reproaching him. She'd never worn a hijab, nor would she ever do it; her long, wavy grey hair cascaded in voluminous waves down past her shoulders, adding to her elegance and wisdom. She paced toward Mudhar as fast as her inflamed knees allowed, reciting a silent prayer before blowing on her hand and running it over Mudhar's cast. "May this be the end of all your ailments."

"What about your ailments?" Jassim asked, adjusting himself to face her. "Should I say a prayer for you?"

"You'll have to say a thousand," Nadia smiled, her fierce hazel eyes meeting Jassim's. "Such is the blessing of old age you and I enjoy."

Jassim grunted, the reminder of his age not sitting well with him. "We're not the same."

"Son, go get your mother," Mudhar said to Shamil, his eyes conveying what his tongue couldn't: Nadia and Jassim shouldn't be left alone together for long without buffers.

Of all their relatives, Nadia and her husband were the only ones to refuse Jassim's favours.

They believed his fortune was tainted with blood, and they wanted no part of it—not when God was already testing them by not giving them children. They didn't want to anger Him further should a miracle ever happen.

Pressing a gentle kiss onto Ameena's forehead, Shamil unlocked the headscarf that had suffocated her scalp. She was married to a doctor and a mother to another; still, she'd rather instead tie a cloth around her head than take a simple tablet. He helped her choose an appropriate attire befitting Jassim's presence. Even during her worst illnesses, Ameena had always dressed well for the occasion.

"This could have been it," Ameena said, her voice trembling. "We could have lost him."

"Spare us the mention of such evil, Auntie," Laila interjected, entering the room with a cup of chamomile tea. "Uncle has seen far worse, and God has always shielded him."

"This was a mere gunshot. What will you do when rockets begin to rain upon us?" Shamil said, reminding them of the reality they had been refusing to accept.

"Now isn't the time for such thoughts," Ameena replied.

"These are facts, Mama."

"Where's Zain?" Laila asked.

"He went home," Shamil said, fighting the urge to check Zain's messages now that he had access to them. Laila shouldn't see that. "He wanted to fix his laptop in the apartment."

"I would keep that laptop broken," Nadia remarked, joining them. "It brought us nothing but trouble."

"If only it were that simple, Auntie," Shamil said, stepping closer to her for a hug.

She raised her hand to stop him. "I'm upset with you."

"Auntie.."

"You've called me Mama so many times, I foolishly believed it," Nadia's voice cracked. Then not only did you leave me and your family, but you didn't come to say hi when you returned, as if I weren't fifteen minutes away from here."

Shamil reached for her hand, laid a soft kiss on it, and then placed it on his head. "I'm sorry, Mama," he said, well aware of the consequences of calling her that in front of Ameena. Still, she was precious to him, and he owed her an apology.

Nadia pulled him closer, laying a kiss on his forehead. "Habibi, you're forgiven."

"Good, we cleared that up," Ameena said, undoubtedly jealous of her sister's affection for Shamil. "Sham, what did Jassim tell you?"

Shamil glanced at Nadia, her eyes brimming with curiosity. As much as he loved her, he still dreaded discussing Jassim's revelations in her presence. She would undoubtedly amplify everything, and the gossip would never end.

"I'm handling it," he replied, striving to reveal as little as possible without lying to her. "For now, let's focus on Father's recovery."

"For all his faults, we are fortunate to have Jassim safeguarding the city," Nadia remarked.

"Poor young soul, Adil. He would have been your age by now," she added.

"Indeed," Shamil forced a smile, not feeling exceptionally fortunate nor wanting to discuss Adil any further. "I'm going to check on Zain."

As he turned the key in the lock, opening the door to his apartment, the world around him seemed to spin in dizzying circles. He felt lightheaded, and for a brief second, darkness eclipsed his vision. Leaning against the wall, he pressed his head against its cold surface and closed his eyes for a moment. His thoughts drifted to the busy emergency department of a distant London hospital, of all places, where he had once worked. Memories flooded his mind, recalling a time when dizziness had overwhelmed him there as well. The attending consultant had kindly intervened with a gentle touch of concern as he had ushered Shamil aside, saying, "I understand your need to treat everyone, but how can you assist others if you neglect your well-being?"

He had offered Shamil a steaming cup of hot chocolate, and together, they sought refuge in the staff room, momentarily escaping the relentless demands of the Emergency Department. Shamil recalled the exhaustion that had weighed upon his weary frame and how that small respite had fortified him, carrying him through the remainder of his shift.

The evening Mudhar was shot had been marked by insistent vigilance, and Shamil's body, fuelled only by the meagre remnants of coffee he'd had that morning, protested its deprivation.

Inside the kitchen, Shamil grabbed the sugar pot and let two spoonfuls melt their way through his tongue into his bloodstream. A glass of cold water washed the remaining sweetness down, and a splash of cold water zapped him awake.

He had planned to speak to Zain about the rebels, but his near collapse had signalled him to choose a less sensitive topic—a distraction of some sort.

Standing by Zain's door, Shamil looked at him sitting at his desk, his laptop sprawled upside down before him, a screwdriver poised against its underbelly. A smile of comfort found its way into Shamil's heart— his boy was safe, and he was there with him.

"How bad is it?" Shamil asked.

"This stupid screw won't come off," Zain grunted, failing to loosen the screw at the centre.

Shamil pushed the clothes scattered across the floor, clearing a path for himself. Then he grabbed a chair and sat next to Zain, putting his hand in front of him. "Here, let me show you a trick."

Zain hesitantly handed the screwdriver, perhaps doubting Shamil's ability to fix anything. "It's impossible, don't bother."

"Just watch," Shamil said, meticulously wiping the tip of the screwdriver before blowing a gentle breath into the stubborn screw's aperture. With care, he inserted the screwdriver, applying gentle pressure as he tapped the end until it nestled securely. "It's not just about force— it's about knowing where to apply it."

Testing his technique, Shamil twisted the screwdriver, pleased to see it loosening. "Now it's your turn," he said as he handed it back to Zain.

Zain grasped the screwdriver and turned it carefully, his eyes locked on the task. A smile spread across his face as he sighed in relief when the screw finally gave way.

"Now, let's see what we have here," Shamil said as he lifted the laptop's bottom lid, revealing its interior.

"I have dropped it a couple of times," Zain said, bending the neck of his desk's lamp for better lighting.

"There's Nothing that can't be fixed," Shamil said, disconnecting the hard drive and handing it to Zain. "Give it a wipe."

Zain nodded, grabbing a clean tissue, and the sound of one of Jassim's guards scolding a passerby raised. "I wish we weren't related to him."

"He believes he's protecting us," Shamil said.

"By spying on us?"

"If it weren't him, someone else would, Son. We would both be in jail, you for your actions, and me for being your father."

"So, we should just be silent and take the abuse?"

"If we want to escape this, then yes," Shamil answered, wishing the conversation remained about fixing a broken laptop rather than fixing a fractured nation.

"And where's the honour in that?" Zain retorted.

"More honourable than this fake Syrian Dandelion. He's directing violence while sitting comfortably abroad," Shamil said, slipping momentarily, his facade faltering. Zain's shocked gaze met his, and in that instant, he knew he had to rectify his misstep.

"Him and other rebels, The Eagle, The Rooster, they all lie."

"You singled him out," Zain squinted.

"Father mentioned him," Shamil cleared his throat. "Do you know who he is?"

"He keeps it private."

"So, he could be anyone. Even Jassim could be The Syrian Dandelion, tricking you and your friends."

"Now, that's just silly," Zain scoffed, but he paused, his eyes spacing out momentarily as if, for a fleeting moment, Shamil's suggestion was plausible. He shook his head. "He can't be. He even warns me because I'm Jassim's relative."

"Is he threatening you?"

"No, not like that. He's a good friend..." Zain began before he bit his lip. "Okay, never mind. Let's see if this works," he changed the topic, switching his laptop on.

Yet, just as the words hung on the precipice of Shamil's lips, poised to spill further questions, a simultaneous vibration rattled both their phones, and neither of them reached to answer as they stared at each other.

"Loading screen, this is promising," Shamil uttered, a facade of eagerness masking the burning curiosity to uncover the message that had just arrived. "I'll get some water," he got up and retreated to the corridor, drawing his phone from his pocket. It bore a message from The Syrian Dandelion, one he couldn't yet fully explore in fear of Zain finding out it was marked read before he did.

"Zain, it's Grandpa," Shamil said loudly, extinguishing the screen's glow with a tap. "He wants us to join them for dinner."

"All right…" Zain said, but before he could finish, a loud blast sent the window shields flying as the ground shook underneath them.

Chapter 22: The Doctor

In a fraction of a second, Shamil found himself inside Zain's room, shielding him as the ground shook violently. Picture frames crashed to the floor, and flakes of dust and paint poured down from the ceiling like confetti in a nightmarish celebration.

Shamil quickly confirmed that neither was injured. He kept a firm grip on Zain and guided him into the corridor, where he believed their chances of survival would be higher should another blast devastate the building.

Car alarms erupted throughout the neighbourhood, echoing through the streets like a frenzied flock of birds. Holding Zain close, Shamil's mind stretched each minute into an eternity.

The cacophony outside intensified with the distant voices of Jassim's guards speaking of Jassim's house being hit.

He pulled Zain, descending the stairs to where Jassim's guards had gathered. Through the whirlwind of commotion, his eyes briefly captured a glimpse of Jassim as he hurriedly disappeared into his fortified black Mercedes, his guards leaping into their jeeps.

Fragmented remnants of shattered wood and shards of glass now carpeted the street, and wisps of smoke curled skyward, rising ominously from the direction of Jassim's grand mansion.

"Sham," Ameena called from the balcony, her golden hair flying around her face. The shock of the blast had caused her to forget to wear her hijab.

In no time, Shamil and Zain were with her and the rest, trying to make sense of what had just happened.

"A suicide bomber hit the guesthouse," Mudhar explained, holding onto the landline phone, Nadia by his side. "They must have thought that Jassim was there."

"Should we head to the bunker in case another bomb hits?" Laila asked, looking at Shamil.

"Or, go to Nadia's house?" Ameena interjected.

Frustration welled up within Shamil, threatening to spill over. "I warned you about this," he said, trying not to raise his voice. "I knew this would happen."

"Calm down, now, we didn't get hurt," Mudhar said, handing the phone to Nadia.

"Sure, let's wait until we do, okay?" Shamil retorted.

"Baba, it wasn't the opposition," Zain said, as if it mattered who'd blown up their city—bombs did not discriminate. "They just posted online that this wasn't them."

Shamil glared at him. "We were in that guesthouse six hours ago. What if…" he trailed off, his voice fading away, overcome by the images of what could have happened had they stayed longer at Jassim's.

"Can someone take me back home?" Nadia interjected, her complexion drained of colour. "Mazen isn't answering."

"We shouldn't make rash decisions," Mudhar said, seemingly ignoring Nadia's plea.

"We'll wait and see what God shows us," Ameena added as if God hadn't already shown them enough.

"Show us what?" Shamil said before Nadia's distress erupted into tears.

"Take me home, please," she raised her voice, short of a scream.

Swiftly enfolding her in a protective embrace and planting a light kiss on her head, Shamil volunteered. "I will take you, Auntie."

As Shamil made his way towards the front door, Nadia hooked to his arm, the incessant ringing of the house bell had Shamil curse at whoever was behind it. As he swung open the door, a familiar figure stood before him—it was Nizar, the guard who had accompanied him on the journey from Aleppo to Ar-Raqqah.

"Jassim wants you at the hospital immediately," Nizar said with an authoritative tone.

"I'm busy now," Shamil frowned at him. As if Jassim bossing him around in person hadn't been humiliating enough, now he's authorised his minions to do so on his behalf. Shamil wasn't going to have it.

"This isn't a request," Nizar sneered, smugness lurking in his eyes. Behind him, another armed figure emerged from the idling jeep. There was no mistaking it; had Shamil resisted them any further, they would have dragged him.

"Let me grab my jacket," Shamil said, stepping back inside and attempting to close the front door.

Nizar instantly obstructed the door with a well-placed foot. "Fast as a thunder," he commanded.

Shamil left the door as is, escorting Nadia back inside his parents' house.

"I will have them drop you off first," he said to her, then called for Laila to grab him a jacket.

When she arrived holding one of Mudhar's jackets, he pulled her aside. "Zain never leaves your sight, okay?" he warned. "Not to go to the gym, nor friends, nor even to the shop at the corner. He must stay home until I return."

Laila nodded, brushing her hand against his arm before she ran her fingers across to his, offering him momentary solace. "Please do what Jassim says. We can't afford to anger him now."

Shamil reciprocated her gesture, his fingers delicately intertwining with hers. "We'll have to wait a little bit longer."

"I know," she murmured, her gaze momentarily tracing his lips before retreating. Did she long for him as much as he longed for her, or was it fear of the unknown that had her seeking refuge in his eyes?

Shamil stood there puzzled, and just as quickly as the moment had emerged, it dissipated, and Laila averted her gaze, releasing her hold on his hand.

Oh, how hopelessly in love with her he was still; every fleeting touch had him yearning for more. Once he finished appeasing Jassim, he would find a way to take her and Zain abroad. There, he could set her free and unburden his soul from the guilt that had been crushing him.

Sitting in the back of Jassim's escort's jeep, their smoke suffocating him once more, Shamil scanned the roads to the national hospital. Police had barricaded every entrance, allowing only the passage of ambulances.

They confined the patients to the ambulances, awaiting clearance, before they would let them in.

Inside the emergency department, chaos reigned. The waiting area had transformed into a makeshift triage zone, littered with trolleys lined up like broken soldiers, each armed with first aid supplies. Frantic police officers and nurses scurried about, their hands laden with saline bags, gauze, and suturing kits.

Amidst the turmoil, Jassim's guard guided Shamil towards the surgical emergencies unit, where Jassim himself stood at the epicentre, overseeing the chaotic first aid efforts. He didn't possess any medical expertise—he simply needed to show that he was in control.

Six injured men lay in various states of consciousness within the unit. Three were awake and responsive, two displayed severe visible injuries, and one young man sat on the floor, clutching his head before his complexion turned deathly pale. Reacting swiftly, Shamil rushed to his side, assisting him in lying down.

"Elevate his legs," he instructed, lowering the man's head gently onto the floor with the help of a guard. His scalp was intact, his face unbruised, but his shirt and trousers were covered in dust and debris. There were no bone fragments, no specks of blood—only the unsettling signs of internal distress. His breathing grew laboured, and cold sweat slicked his neck. "He's going into shock. I need immediate access."

The worries that had consumed Shamil on his journey to the hospital were eclipsed by a compulsion to preserve the lives of the wounded. Swiftly, he ripped open the young man's shirt, his eyes searching for any visible wounds that could account for the critical state of shock.

No external injuries marred the surface, yet the bruised expanse of his lower abdomen hinted at a deeper, more insidious source—internal bleeding.

"Ayman, are those O neg?" Shamil urgently called out to Ayman, one of the nurses he'd worked with in the past. He had just entered the unit carrying a large box of blood bags.

Ayman tossed him two bags. "All O negative," he confirmed before bolting away.

Immediately, Shamil inserted two cannulas into the man's arms while a medical student prepared the connection tubes and fed them into the cannulas.

"What spaces do we have?" Shamil asked a nurse, hoping for a coherent response.

"Spaces?" he replied, appearing disoriented.

Shamil turned to face Jassim. "I need one guard to head to the operating theatres and another to the resuscitation bay. We must determine the number of available spaces, anaesthetists, nurses, and doctors. Now!"

"You heard him," Jassim commanded, gesturing for two guards to dart away.

Shamil rose to his feet and approached Ayman, who had returned with a box of sterile gauze. "Can you handle this one?" Shamil pointed at one of the injured men.

"On it," Ayman nodded, swiftly attending to his patient's shredded thigh with haemostatic gauze. He had it under control.

Moving to the next injured man, Shamil noted multiple minor puncture wounds peppering his chest.

Despite the severity of the wounds, the man's breathing remained steady, and the medical student attending to him appeared competent enough to manage the situation. Satisfied with their capability, Shamil left them to their task.

The remaining three patients suffered from non-fatal limb injuries, a relief as Shamil didn't have enough hands to treat them all. Instructing a nurse to attend to them and keep him informed of any developments, Shamil pivoted sharply as a guard delivered urgent news.

"They have one theatre slot available, Sir," the guard reported. "Mr. Haji insists they can only accommodate one patient."

Without hesitation, Shamil seized an empty trolley and loaded the shocked man onto it. As they raced outside the unit towards the operating theatres, Jassim's hand closed around Shamil's arm, a rare display of concern flickering in his eyes.

"This is what I'm trying to prevent," Jassim said in a low voice. "You can't let him die."

Shamil wrenched his arm free. "Then pray he won't."

If only life and death were his to command, Shamil wouldn't have had sleepless nights haunted by the faces of all those who died on his shifts despite his best efforts. It never got easier; he just had to learn how to live with it and enjoy the little victories whenever someone survived.

"I need a minute," the theatre nurse gasped, sweat pouring down his face, dark stains marking his scrubs' underarms.

They had just finished operating on a patient and hadn't had time to sanitise the place. Blood splattered the green-tiled floor. Gauze and instruments lay scattered across every visible surface.

Shamil couldn't waste any time. He grabbed two theatre sheets and threw them over the soiled bed, swiftly covering them with a waterproof sheet. The injured man's blood pressure was dangerously low; it would have killed him before any iatrogenic infection would. "We're moving him now," Shamil directed the nurses, with Mr. Haji at his side.

Three gruelling hours later, the young man had undergone extensive surgery, yet, against all odds, his heart continued to beat.

"He survives?" Ayman greeted Shamil in the surgical unit.

"For now," Shamil replied wearily, sinking into the seat next to Ayman, their shoulders touching. "It's been too long, my friend."

"I thought I'd never see your tired face again," Ayman turned to Shamil, his face lit up with a broad, gleaming smile. "Are you here to stay?"

"Not for long," Shamil admitted, casting a sombre eye over the familiar surroundings. Five years had passed since he last set foot in this dismal pit, and he had hoped never to return to its stench of faux leather beds and rusty metal fixtures or its grimy dark-green curtains that swept the floor. He then looked back at Ayman, looking polished in his usual attire: a black shirt peeking from under a half-buttoned white coat, highlighting his abundant chest hair.

His meticulously polished black shoes matched the sheen of his heavily oiled hair, a style he had championed since the mid-1990s.

"Jassim dragged me here," Shamil said, still wondering whether Jassim had summoned him to the hospital to guilt him into joining his fight against the rebels or because they genuinely needed doctors.

"He's one scary bastard," Ayman muttered, thrusting his phone toward Shamil, where a live broadcast of Jassim played out.

"Today's heinous act will not go unpunished," in the video, Jassim spoke into a bunch of microphones set on his desk. "I will capture every single one of you and will crush your windpipes with my hand." He gestured as if holding someone's neck before squeezing the life out of it. "You are nothing but cowards hiding behind your mask. Well, I will tear down those masks one by one until everyone sees your ugly faces."

Shamil pressed pause. He knew what Jassim was capable of and didn't need a reminder.

"Don't do that," Ayman grunted, resuming the video. "We need to see this."

Shamil sighed, glancing back at the mobile screen. A guard entered the video frame beside Jassim, gripping a masked young man with his hands bound in front of him. The resemblance to Zain was uncanny, as if Jassim had deliberately chosen him to provoke Shamil and illustrate the potential fate awaiting his son should he dare to defy him.

"We've had our eye on this traitor for some time now; still, out of mercy, we didn't arrest or charge him with anything. He's a university student. I thought we would give him a chance to open his eyes and realise his actions were wrong on his own, and he goes and does what? He records today's bomber moments before he cowardly blew himself up, then he posted the video online, gloating and praising the rebels." Jassim gestured with his hand to the guard, who pushed the masked young man closer to Jassim and then unmasked him. "For his acts, I promise you, he will be spending the rest of his youth rotting in prison instead of graduating from his university. And this goes for..."

Shamil switched off Ayman's phone— he had seen enough.

"Shit's getting real, man," Ayman remarked, tucking his phone into his white coat. "Soon, the police will start using live ammo."

"Jassim wouldn't allow it," Shamil replied, checking the time on his phone. It was forty minutes past midnight, and he needed to get back home— he'd left Zain unattended for too long.

"Just because you two share the same blood doesn't mean he's like you," Ayman said, patting Shamil's shoulder before standing up. "Now, let's see how large the queue is outside."

"The queue?" Shamil sighed, recalling that Jassim's entourage had barred entry to the hospital until they finished with the blast victims, leaving dozens of patients stranded outside. "I can't stay," he added, glancing at the emergency department packed beyond capacity, the air thick with an unpleasant odour.

"You can lie down a bit if you're tired," Ayman said, an unfamiliar look of disappointment on his face.

"Unless you came here to treat your people only, then vanish?"

Whether Shamil liked it or not, Jassim's guards were undeniably 'his' people—the inevitable burden of being related to a colonel. Despite all the charity Shamil had done, the free consultations his father had offered, and the intel his son had provided to the rebels, when it came down to it, he and his family would always be judged alongside Jassim and his associates. On any other day, Shamil would have lingered until the last patient was seen. But today was different— he couldn't leave his rebel son alone.

"How did you manage before I arrived? Just continue doing that," Shamil murmured in shame.

Ayman crossed his arms, his gaze sweeping over the dozens of patients queued behind him. "Does it look like we're coping?"

"I haven't eaten anything," Shamil said.

"I'll get you some food."

"I'm not even sure I'm licensed for this; I don't want trouble."

"There's literally still blood on your shirt from the soldiers; you can't pick and choose who you break the law for."

Shamil looked away, unable to distinguish if the knot in his stomach was from hunger or self-loathing. "Come on, Ayman, I'm just one doctor. You can manage without me."

"All we've had this entire week was one doctor," Ayman said with a bitter laugh, scratching his neck before resting a hand on Shamil's shoulder. "You know what, just go home."

"I'm sorry," Shamil said, hastening his pace as if he needed fresh air before he suffocated.

It pained him more than he had ever imagined possible, having to say no. He had always been a yes man, believing in kindness and the idea that what goes around comes around. Anyone could ask him for a favour on the very first day they met, and Shamil would try his best to deliver, expecting nothing in return. The sad reality was that his kindness was often seen as a weakness to exploit, and he had to learn to live with the angst of saying no rather than the disappointments that followed a yes.

What could he have done?

His family needed him. A suicide bomber had just hit their city, and at any second, the rebels could take over. Leaving was the only logical option, but he still couldn't do it.

Standing in the parking lot, Shamil opened Zain's Facebook on his phone, scrolling for new messages. He hoped to find something so alarming that it would force him to leave the hospital, easing his conscience. But there was nothing. Zain had erased all his messages, leaving just one last status update: "I won't be using this account again. Our revolution will go on without me until victory."

Did Zain know Shamil had his login information? Or had he indeed quit his online persona out of fear of consequences? Either way, this wasn't the outcome Shamil had wanted.

He called Laila, hoping her voice would drown out the cries of the ill he'd left behind.

"You're late. Is everything okay?" Laila asked.

"Yeah, I couldn't leave any sooner," Shamil replied, stretching his left shoulder, where a chronic pain had flared up.

"How many were there?

"Too many," Shamil said, falling silent as he listened to her breathing on the other end. "Listen, has Zain gone outside at all?"

"He's been in his room playing games all evening. Why?"

"Laila," he hesitated, not wanting to upset her. "The hospital is full of patients."

"Are you taking a taxi back?"

"They don't have enough doctors tonight."

"Have you eaten?"

"I have to help."

"Sham, you..." Laila began, then exhaled deeply, and Shamil heard all the unspoken words that followed. He could tell she wanted him to come home and rest; she had always complained that he wasn't looking after himself. But leaving the hospital would have undoubtedly given him a restless night and an unforgiving conscience. He had to help. "Make sure you eat something, anything."

"I will," he reassured her.

Pacing back towards the surgical emergencies unit, Shamil felt his steps lighter and more purposeful. The queue was as long as when he left, but it was still manageable.

"Do you have any pills on you? My shoulder is killing me," he asked Ayman.

"Always," Ayman said, grinning as he handed Shamil a tramadol pill. "We're gonna be up till the morning prayer, inshallah," he added, grabbing a zaatar wrap from under the desk. "Take a half."

Shamil washed down the bitter pill with a sip of water and motioned for the guards to let in another patient. He then split the wrap and took a large bite, settling a score with it.

"Better than your wife's cooking, eh?" Ayman joked. Shamil nodded, his hunger amplifying the deliciousness of olive oil, spice, and bread.

With his stomach finally full, Shamil focused on what he did best. An endless line of patients awaited his and Ayman's care. Morning prayer and sunrise passed unnoticed, and as the day shift started, Shamil's aching body surrendered to an unexpected slumber in the private examination room, only to wake up to the loud barks of men arguing.

Chapter 23: A Mortal with a Stethoscope

"No! You can't bring her back next week," Ayman argued with an old man outside the private examination room, his raised voice jolting Shamil awake.

In a panic, Shamil slid off the bed, his face wet with drool, and squinted against the bright sun rays burning his eyes. He checked his pockets—phone, wallet, keys—they were all where he had left them. How was it already quarter past three in the afternoon? He had barely closed his eyes.

"Listen, you take her now; she fucking dies, all right?" Ayman continued, and Shamil, now fully awake, started following the conversation. "Do as you wish," Ayman said, shutting the door behind him and cursing under his breath as he tossed a tray of soiled forceps into the autoclave.

"The network is down?" Shamil asked, checking his mobile phone.

"Yeah, since morning," Ayman said, turning the autoclave on. "Your wife called the unit; I said you were sleeping."

Shamil grunted, pulling his shoes from underneath the bed and quickly slipping them on. He shouldn't have slept at the hospital; he couldn't even remember when or how he had fallen asleep.

"I need a favour," Ayman said in front of Shamil. My brother was arrested three months ago; they say now he's with SAFI."

"What was he arrested for?" Shamil asked; the sooner he could sort out Ayman's request, the sooner he could leave.

"He was caught treating the rebels from his home."

"I'll see what I can do," Shamil said, saving the details on his phone. Securing Ayman's brother's release would certainly deepen Shamil's debt to Jassim, and Jassim might even refuse it. The least Shamil could do was check if the brother was alive and well and whether he could be freed. "This stays between us, okay?" he added, patting Ayman's shoulder, only to hear Shareef, one of the hospital guards, stomp his feet into the unit.

"Unless you're dying, leave now," Shareef shouted. "We're closing. Quickly now. Get off your asses."

"What's going on?" Shamil mouthed, looking at Ayman.

"Nothing good from the sound of it," Ayman said as they both dashed out of the private examination room.

Shareef pushed the patients and their families into the waiting area, and another police officer led them to the rear exit via the Outpatient Department. Two military vehicles blocked the Emergency Department's entrance, preventing anyone from getting inside or leaving.

"Why are you closing the department?" Shamil asked, glancing at his mobile to see if the network was back. It wasn't.

"We need all staff on standby," Shareef said, pushing the last patient out of the unit.

"The hooligans are broadcasting live protests around the city. It's not looking good for Colonel Jassim," he whispered, tucking his hands under his armpits.

Shamil didn't wait to hear any further information. He'd already seen the outcome play in his mind, one that Zain mustn't be in. Within seconds, his feet propelled him towards the operator's office, hoping the landlines were still running. That was the fastest way he could check on Zain's whereabouts, a voice in his heart screaming at him that his son was one of the protesters.

Storming the operator's office, Shamil grabbed the closest phone to him, but it wasn't working. "I need a line," he said.

"Here, use this one," the operator, looking startled, handed him a headset, and Shamil's fingers quickly dialled the numbers.

"Where's Zain?" Shamil said breathlessly as soon as Laila picked up.

"He went to the gym an hour ago."

"I said don't let him go!" Shamil couldn't hold back. "What were you thinking?"

"Uncle intervened; what was I supposed to say?"

"There's a large protest in the city. I'll go to the gym to look for him and bring him back. Keep calling him. Tell Father." Shamil blurted into the headset, handing it back to the operator, and did not wait to hear what Laila was still saying.

The gym was a ten-minute walk from the hospital, five if he ran— and Shamil ran as fast as his limbs could, only to be stopped by a uniformed thick man he didn't recognise.

He raised his fat arm to block Shamil's path and furrowed his eyebrows so tight he could have held a knife with them to point it at him.

"Who is this?" the uniformed man said, looking back at Shareef, the hospital policeman, approaching him from behind.

"He's the surgical doctor, Sir," Shareef said, slowing down his pace.

"Why aren't you in your unit?" the uniformed man asked Shamil.

"I'm leaving," Shamil said, pushing his way through the man's heavy arm. He had no time for whatever petty powerplay that man had displayed. Zain needed him.

"You'll sit like a dog in your unit; I say otherwise, understand?" he squealed, grabbing Shamil's arm.

"And who exactly are you?" Shamil said, looking at the man's shoulder, three stars and an eagle. Not good.

"I'm your mother's fucker if you don't do as I say," he shouted.

"General, he didn't mean it that way, sir. He's one of ours," Shareef intervened, stepping between Shamil and that rabid man. "He is Colonel Jassim's nephew."

"SAFI's Jassim?" the general grinned, glaring at a silent Shamil.

"Yes, Sir," Shamil said, biting his tongue and taking advantage of Shareef's timely intervention. Even Jassim would have had trouble justifying his actions had he chosen to ignore that general's requests.

"No one leaves the hospital until I stand you down," the general said, waving them to leave.

"Yes, sir," Shamil and Shareef submitted, pacing back towards the surgical unit.

"Who exactly are you?" Ayman raised his tone, repeating Shamil's words as he and Shareef entered the unit. "Are you insane?"

"Not now, Ayman," Shamil checked his phone, but there was still no network.

"Show some diplomacy, Hakim," Shareef interjected as if Shamil didn't already know that. "There's no joking with these people."

"I wasn't thinking, all right?" Shamil said, looking outside the unit's windows where more soldiers had gathered. "My wife cut her hand pretty badly, and I lost it."

"I would have gotten you out, but General Saleem is a menace; he takes things very personally," Shareef said, glaring at Saleem's entourage before he turned to face Ayman. "Perhaps you could charm him."

Ayman spat in disgust. " I'd rather beat my cock with a cactus."

Shareef let out a low chuckle, shaking his head. "One day, you might have no choice, my friend," he said, his voice dripping with cynicism as he walked away toward a group of three young soldiers huddled nearby.

"Disgusting pigs," Ayman said quietly, glancing at Shareef and the soldiers before he pulled Shamil to the side. "Is it your son?" he whispered.

"He said he's at the gym, but I know he isn't," Shamil dialled again. "Fuck this network."

"I would sneak you out, but not before the shit-barrel leaves. We need to wait for the right moment."

Shamil nodded, wishing he hadn't stayed overnight and had just gone home to where he could keep an eye on Zain. He wouldn't have been stuck at the hospital, disconnected from the outside world, while his son could be seconds away from being shot at. He regretted snapping at Laila; it wasn't her fault. It was he who had yet again abandoned them.

"Why are the soldiers here in the hospital? It's not like anyone is planning to attack us here," Shamil asked as more armed soldiers flooded the hospital.

"These fools aren't here to protect us. They're here to arrest anyone that gets injured at the protest," Ayman said, frowning at the soldiers, then spitting his chewing gum on the floor. "At least if your son gets hurt, God forbid, and they bring him here, we can stop them from arresting him."

"Just shut it," Shamil said, walking away from Ayman and inside the private examination room.

He locked the door behind him and inspected the window's edges for vulnerabilities. During his time in that department, he and other nurses often barricaded themselves in that small room when a drunk patient or an enraged relative posed a threat. It was their refuge until the police arrived. Even back then, Shamil had always considered escape routes, and the window was his only way out.

Climbing onto the bed, he applied pressure to the lower edge, trying to loosen it just enough to slip through without drawing attention. The window was less than a metre high, so he wouldn't have to jump far.

He planned to sneak through the back exit, catch the first taxi, and find Zain wherever he was.

The plan seemed to be working. Yet, as he managed to dislodge part of the window, a distant burst of gunfire echoed through the hospital walls, followed by a loud bang. Shamil couldn't wait any longer. He kicked the window with all his strength, the sound of gunshots blending with the thuds of his feet. With a final, powerful kick, the metallic window frame crashed down, taking the shattered glass with it. Without hesitation, he leapt out of the window, Ayman's voice trailing after him.

"Take the keys," Ayman shouted, holding them out. "My motorcycle is the red one!"

Grabbing them, Shamil dashed towards the parking lot. Frantic police officers rushed past him, bumping into him without a second glance— bigger things were happening, and more significant events were about to unfold. He quickly spotted Ayman's bike—it was a striking red, impossible to miss. With a flick, he started the engine and sped through the hospital's rear gates, the guards looking confused about whom to let in and whom to let out.

The gym was only minutes away, but he couldn't afford to waste any time—he was certain Zain had lied. Following the direction where the gunshots had been loudest seemed logical, but now there were no more shots to be heard. He had to stop and ask passersby, hoping some would point him in the right direction.

Parking by the entrance to Al-Rashid Park, Shamil pulled out his phone, Zain's name filling the screen.

He hadn't felt it vibrating and had almost missed the call.

"They shot at us, Baba," Zain cried, his voice almost drowned out by the storm of chanting in the background.

"Are you hurt?" Shamil pressed the phone harder against his ear. "Where are you?"

"They shot Amr. He's bleeding. I need your help, Baba."

"Are you out on the street? Is anyone coming after you?"

"I'm at Amr's house. He's bleeding from his chest, Baba. Please save him," Zain's voice was rising in panic as the chanting grew angrier. It was getting harder to hear him. "He's coughing up blood. Oh God, he's dying, right? Baba, is he dying?"

"Zain, listen to me," Shamil yelled into the phone. "Take a towel or any fabric, fold it like the baby towels your mum makes, and press it hard on the wound, okay? Don't leave Amr's house. Don't hang up. I'm coming to get you now."

Shamil put the call on speaker, slipped it in his shirt pocket where he could still hear it, and sped off on the motorcycle toward Al-Mansur Street, where he knew Amr lived. Throughout his journey he heard Zain's pleas and the loud cries surrounding him. He listened to those around him call for vengeance while others wanted to burn the city down. Shamil had treated enough injuries to know that Amr's were fatal unless they got him to a hospital and that applying pressure wouldn't change the outcome, but he needed to give Zain something to do to keep him from falling apart.

Standing idle in the face of death was a burden his son didn't deserve to carry, not that young.

Traffic lights were on, but no one was paying attention. Everyone drove manically, trying to get to their families as police cars congregated around official guest houses and government buildings, undoubtedly preparing for any potential backlash.

Entering Al-Mansur, where Amr's house was, it felt like stepping into the aftermath of a coup. Angry mobs roamed the streets, instructing shop owners to lower their rolling shutters and blocking car paths with burning tyres and chopped wood. Armed with thick wooden bats, they bashed the fronts of pro-regime shops and overturned the few police cars they had captured. As Shamil turned a corner, heading toward where he believed Amr's house to be, a group of men stopped him, demanding he turn back. They didn't recognize him — he wasn't one of their own.

"I'm a doctor," Shamil yelled, hearing the distant cries of women mourning Amr. "I'm here to help."

The men let him through, and he soon found Amr's house — the one with the largest crowd and the loudest screams.

"Make way for the doctor," shouted one of the men behind Shamil as he struggled to push through the angry crowd blockading the front door. Few responded. They needed a miracle, not a mere mortal with a stethoscope.

Shamil had only met Amr once, on a rooftop—a fleeting encounter. Yet, seeing him lying on the floor, choking on his blood, brought tears to his eyes.

Amr's father cradled his head, whispering the Shahada into his ear, desperate to ensure his son's clear path to heaven. But Amr struggled to whisper it back. How could a father bear the thought of his son departing life without reciting the Shahada? Death seemed unbearably senseless.

Zain sat beside Amr, pressing a blood-soaked towel against his motionless chest. He knew his friend was gone but couldn't let go.

"He's a martyr now," Shamil whispered into Zain's ear, laying a hand on his shoulder and helping him up.

What else could he say or do? It was too late to save Amr but not too late to save Zain.

"We were unarmed, Baba, I swear," Zain cried.

"I know. It's not your fault," Shamil said, hugging him close. "We need to leave right now before the police arrive."

"This man is Jassim's relative," a man shouted, pointing at Shamil. "Why are these criminals here?"

"Seize them!" another shouted. Shamil instinctively shielded Zain, his eyes scanning the chaotic scene. It was helpless.

"Fuck Jassim," Zain said, glaring at the accuser.

"Brother, I just want my son," Shamil said to Amr's father.

"And I want mine," the father replied, defiant. "Your family destroyed us."

"There's no God but Allah," the crowd chanted, closing in on Shamil and Zain. The very air they breathed seemed to run short.

"I'll bring you his shooter," Shamil shouted, trying to hold back the rage of the crowd. "I'll bring you his shooter, and you can exact your vengeance however you like."

"We'll burn them all," an angry voice shouted. "One man is not enough."

"They'll kill us all," Shamil shouted back. "The army will kill all of us, my son included," he said, pointing at Zain.

"His son was in jail," a young voice intervened.

"And his father is a good doctor," another added.

"We're not your enemy," Shamil pleaded, holding Amr's father's arm. He hoped that he could reason with him, father to father, and if not, at least he had bought himself some time, hoping Jassim would send someone in to get them. "Brother, use me. Let's end this together."

"I want Qasas, justice," the father said. "You bring us whoever did this."

"I promise you, we'll do that," Shamil said.

"And I want a funeral," the father added, his voice cracking. "I won't bury my son in secret like a criminal."

"He's a martyr and will be treated with dignity," Shamil said, knowing he'd over-promised Amr's father; still, he would have said anything to get himself and his son out of there. "But I must go now; the police can't find us here."

Amr's father raised his hand, and the sea of onlookers parted, forming a narrow path for Shamil and Zain to escape.

As they moved, some men patted Zain's shoulder, offering their condolences and gratitude. Others, however, shot him with venomous glares as if blaming him for Amr's tragic death.

They reached Ayman's red bike, its mirrors now shattered and the footstands charred. Shamil ripped the blood-soaked towel from Zain's hand and hurled it into a burning tyre. He swung his leg over the bike, and Zain latched on behind him, resting his head on Shamil's back.

The engine roared to life, and Shamil tore through the labyrinth of roadblocks with the single, desperate objective of getting Zain home.

Chapter 24: Mothers' Prayers

Standing guard on the balcony, Laila recited verses of the Quran she had memorised, her voice tremoring with each word. It was a desperate plea for divine protection over Zain, one she had seldom needed. She clung to the hope that those sacred verses would form an invisible shield around him, guarding him from all harm until he returned home.

Her heart pounded against her ribs as if someone was punching her from the inside. How had she allowed Zain to leave? She wanted to dash out into the chaotic streets to search for him, but Mudhar's stern warning echoed in her mind. "Our women don't roam the streets aimlessly; we're not without honour," he had warned her with his usual commanding tone. Ameena had reinforced this sentiment, dragging Laila back into the house when she tried to leave.

Now, the balcony was her only refuge, the sole place where she could breathe. Inside, the walls felt like they were closing in, suffocating her with each passing second of uncertainty.

"Anything?" Ameena asked, joining Laila on the balcony.

Laila shook her head, unwilling to speak. The words on her tongue were only going to cause pain.

"You couldn't have stopped him," Ameena added, pulling up a chair.

"Uncle made me let him go," Laila snapped. "And you said nothing."

"Had you insisted, he wouldn't have let him."

Laila scoffed. As if defying Mudhar was ever an option. She was already walking a fine line, trying to balance her duties as a mother and a wife, all while knowing that Mudhar and Jassim could easily have Shamil marry another woman and cast her aside as a servant to the family. "You're right; it's always my fault," she said bitterly, leaving the balcony and entering her in-law's kitchen.

For seventeen years, Laila had lived with them, cherished as the wife of their only son and the mother of their only grandson, yet often felt like a prisoner. She barely had a say in anything—everything she did had to fit an expectation. Not that there was much she would have objected to, but simply knowing she could have objected would have made her feel equal.

If anything happened to her boy, she didn't know whether she would ever forgive any of them, Shamil included. Why did he have to stay at the hospital? Why wasn't his son his only concern? Wasn't he the one warning her about how dangerous it was to leave Zain alone? Why couldn't he be there, supporting her as she challenged Mudhar?

"He's here," Ameena's voice made Laila's heart pound even harder. She ran down the stairs, her hijab slipping off and hanging by a clip onto her shoulder.

"There's blood on you," Laila said, frantically examining Zain for injuries, his tearful eyes avoiding hers, his lips sealed. "Why is there blood on him?" she shouted, looking at Shamil for answers.

"It's not his," Shamil said, grabbing her hijab before it fell onto the floor. "Go inside, now."

"Are you hurt?" Laila asked Zain, holding his face between her hands, a cold expression covering it.

"Get inside!" Shamil insisted, grabbing her arm firmly like he'd never done before and pulling her with Zain inside his parents' courtyard. Zain, covered in blood, had attracted the unwelcome attention of prying eyes. "Don't wait for it to dry out," he instructed Zain before turning his attention to Mudhar. "We need to talk to Jassim."

Laila guided Zain into the ground floor bathroom, her mind torn between checking for injuries and understanding what had happened. She helped him sit on the edge of the bathtub, her eyes carefully scanning his body for any signs of harm. Her fingers trembled as she brushed his hair away from his forehead, looking for cuts or bruises. Finding none, she felt a brief wave of relief as the muffled sounds of Shamil and the others arguing echoed from the courtyard.

"Landlines are off; I've tried again," Mudhar said, loud enough for all to hear.

"We hide him at Aunt Nadia's and wait a day or two to see how the situation unfolds," Shamil suggested. "God knows how many people recorded him today; his face will be all over the news."

"So much blood," stammered Zain, shivering as Laila gently washed his hands, chest, and neck. "Is this how cheap Amr's life was?" he wept, staring at the red water swirling down the drain.

Laila's chest tightened, the raw metallic smell suffocating her as she watched her broken son. "He is a martyr now," she tried to console him. His continued sobbing was her answer.

"They didn't stop shooting. We shouted, we said we're unarmed, we're peaceful, and they continued to shoot at us," Zain continued, wiping his face. "They saw him bleeding on the floor, and they shot him again, Mama. Why?" Laila had no answers— life hadn't prepared her for such conversations.

"There will be a judgement day," she said, echoing her mother's words whenever she had questioned life's injustices.

"When? Where was God when Amr got shot? What did he do wrong to deserve to die?"

"He was protecting you. My prayers kept you safe."

"And Amr's mum didn't pray for him?" he asked, looking her in the eyes, breaking her heart.

Laila knew Amr's mother had prayed for him, just like every other anguished mother did as they waited to hear about their missing children. Why God chose to answer her prayer and not others wasn't something she was prepared to question. She wouldn't dare ask God why.

Rubbing away the last remnants of soap on Zain's shoulder, tears blurred Laila's vision. She pulled him in for a tight embrace, hoping to shield him from the harshness of a world she couldn't fully explain.

"They deserve this regime," Zain groaned. "Especially those that stood there watching us get chased and ratted out. These traitors don't deserve freedom."

"I told you it's pointless," Laila pulled away." You almost got killed today. Is that what you want?"

"I would have become a martyr," Zain muttered.

"I don't want you to become a martyr," Laila said, her tone rising. "You'll just be another number soon to be forgotten and an eternal torment for me."

"I have to avenge him."

"You'll stay at Auntie Nadia's house until things calm down. If you try to leave her house, I swear to the Almighty, I will hand you to the police myself," Laila's voice rose, firm and resolute. She's had enough of Zain's stubbornness, and pandering for him had almost gotten him killed. No more. "I would rather see you alive in prison than bleeding to death in my lap."

"Are we good?" Shamil intervened, entering the bathroom. Laila bit her lip, looking at him with a mix of uncertainty and pain. How could they ever be good again? Was it even possible for them to leave now that death was at their doorstep?

Drying himself off, Zain nodded in silence as he got dressed. He then reached for his phone, switched it off, and handed it over to Laila. "I don't want to see or read anything. I just want this to end," he said, pulling his hoodie over his head and heading into the courtyard.

"I'll drop him off at Auntie Nadia's house," Shamil said, following after him.

"I'm going too," Laila interjected firmly before anyone could object. Tending to Mudhar and Ameena's needs wasn't her priority — her son was.

Shamil turned to face her, his tired eyes now reassuring her that he was there for them. "Are the bags ready?"

"Yes," Laila replied hastily, though she knew they weren't. She had wanted to discuss it with him, but the opportunity never arose. "Just give me an hour."

"Don't rush it," Shamil said softly, reaching for her hand and gently wiping away a speck of blood that had somehow transferred onto her skin. "I'll drop him off now and head to Jassim, then I'll come pick you up."

"I'll take a taxi to Auntie's when I'm ready," Laila said, not wanting to wait too long before she joined her son. Who knew how much time Shamil would spend with Jassim?

"Okay, just be careful," Shamil said with a bitter smile. Laila waited to see Zain get in the car with Shamil before she could bolt to her apartment. She had to know Zain was on his way to safety first before she could busy herself with packing their bags.

Watching Mudhar's car get smaller as Shamil drove away, Laila's mind drifted into swirling darkness. What if that was it? What if they were late, and that was the moment they got stuck? What if.

"Are you okay?" Ameena said, joining Laila in the street.

Laila held her composure; It wasn't the time to be weak. "I don't know what I would have done if they hurt him," she said, unable to look Ameena in the eye.

Ameena drew her into her arms and recited, "Say nothing shall afflict us but what God has ordained for us; he is our lord, and upon him may the believers rely."

"Blessed be," Laila said, surrendering to her warmth and wishing she was a child once again, embracing her late mother without a sliver of worry in her burdened heart. She grew up too fast and assumed the role of a parent. Oh, how simple she thought they had it.

"Come inside, daughter," Mudhar said with a soft tone. "I'll make us some tea," he offered, something he'd only done when his guilt overwhelmed him.

"In a second, Uncle, I need to pack," Laila said, wiping her face as she let go of Ameena.

For seventeen years, she had been their daughter, seeking solace on their shoulders when she couldn't contain her emotions, all the while understanding that despite not having the freedom she desired, her life could have ended up a lot worse.

Chapter 25: Next to God's Throne

Jassim yanked open the drawer and grabbed his pistol. He checked the chamber and slammed the magazine into place before slipping it into the holster strapped to his chest. It had been over a decade since he last fired a shot—he hadn't needed to. Now, his aim had to be sharp. With a target on his head, he knew he had to shoot first if it came to that.

The rebels blamed him for the death of that teenager, Amr. The regime held him accountable for the ensuing riots, expecting him to crush the uprising with an iron fist. His rivals in the military were circling, eager to see him fail and seize the opportunity to oust him in disgrace. After all, he was an outsider—a Sunni man who had risen through the ranks, defeating his Alawite rivals with his ruthlessness and intelligence. His tribal roots and connections made him a threat to the very foundation of the regime, but it also made him an invaluable ally.

God knows he had tried his best to spare Ar-Raqqah from the bloodshed that ravaged other Syrian cities. He had strengthened relations with tribal leaders, fortified his forces' positions within the city, and infiltrated every aspect of public life with informants. If a fly on a wall were to flip one wing before the other, Jassim would have known about it. How one stupid mistake jeopardised it all was beyond his comprehension. His instructions were crystal clear: never shoot at civilians. Still, it happened, and he was certain the culprit wasn't one of his own.

It was only a matter of time before he discovered who was responsible for that unforgivable act, and retribution would soon follow.

The intercom on his desk rang incessantly, and Jassim finally pressed the answer button.

"Sir, General Saleem is here for you," the voice on the intercom said.

Before Jassim could respond, the door to his office was pushed open.

"What's the matter, Colonel, keeping me waiting like that? I was going to get upset," General Saleem said, peacocking into Jassim's office. His face, smug as ever, held a grin Jassim was all too familiar with—a grin that relished in his opponent's failure.

"You speak as if we dare make you wait, General," Jassim replied, leaving his desk to greet him. "A few calls had to be made; you know how it is."

"Is that so?" Saleem tapped Jassim's shoulder. "Close the door," he added, sitting in Jassim's chair, his uniform straining against his bulky torso.

Jassim smirked, taking his time as he paced to the door to shut it. He knew Saleem and the others would taunt him for the way he had managed the protests without lethal force; he just didn't expect it to happen so soon. "You look rather ecstatic," Jassim said, sitting opposite Saleem.

"Well, it was inevitable, wasn't it?" Saleem quickly answered, his gloating smile barely contained. "It's time we intervened."

"It's all under control."

"Of course, you'd say that."

"Two days, and all will be back to how it was."

"Nonsense," Saleem interrupted, grabbing one of Jassim's cigarettes and fiddling with it. "Units three and seven will deploy around the statue square and the city council."

"And if riots were to approach?" Jassim asked, already knowing the answer.

"Then we would do what's necessary," Saleem said, biting a piece of the cigar and then spitting it in Jassim's direction. "I saw your nephew this evening right before he hysterically smashed through a window at the hospital," he added. "I would save face and retire now, you know, before your family disgraces you even further. First, a manic son, and now a mental nephew. People will talk."

Jassim erupted, staring Saleem down. "Get the fuck out of my office."

"We're doing this now?" Saleem tossed the cigarette onto the table.

Jassim reached for his pistol. "You have ten seconds. On the eleventh, your brain will be splattered on this wall."

"You'll learn your place soon enough," Saleem said, getting up.

"My place is next to God's throne, you imbecile!" Jassim pulled the pistol and pointed it at Saleem. Despite Jassim being a rank below him, neither Saleem nor anyone else could begin to imagine what Jassim would be capable of if he ever chose to challenge them. "Threatening me in my office? Out! Now!"

Saleem stomped out, his congested face as if a grenade seconds before it exploded. Despite Jassim being a rank below him, neither Saleem nor anyone else could begin to imagine what Jassim would be capable of if he ever chose to challenge them.

Slamming the door behind him, Jassim stormed back to his desk, violently sweeping Saleem's litter off it, crashing an ashtray in the process. He snatched the sheepskin that lay atop his chair and hurled it to the ground. Saleem's filth had no place near him.

Units three and seven were inexperienced in riot control. If Saleem thought deploying them into the city would quell the protests and impress higher-ups, then he didn't understand the rebels as intimately as Jassim did.

"Summon Nizar to my office, NOW!" Jassim barked into the intercom.

"Yes, sir," the voice at the other end responded. "Uh, sir, your nephew is here. He insists on seeing you."

"Send him in."

Jassim hung up, unstrapping the chest holster and tossing it onto his desk. Despite its lightness, it felt surprisingly heavy, as if its mere presence constricted his every breath.

He leaned back in his chair, observing as Shamil barged in. His glasses were smudged, hiding his sunken eyes. His shirt was crumpled and damp as if it had been chewed on by a dog, and sweat gleamed on his forehead.

"Sit," Jassim gestured before Shamil could speak.

"They shot at Zain."

"Sit," Jassim insisted, but Shamil remained standing.

"A few inches more, and they would have killed him too."

"It was an accident."

"Five times, they shot the boy," Shamil slammed his hands on Jassim's desk. "In the chest, over and over."

"They will pay for their insubordination," Jassim softened his tone. "Now sit. Let's talk."

Shamil hesitated, his eyes momentarily fixated on Jassim's pistol.

"It's yours if you want it," Jassim pushed the pistol towards Shamil.

"I never want it," Shamil pushed it away, then settled into a chair. "Jassim, it's bad. They almost lynched us, and I had to lie my way out of it."

"Your son shouldn't have been there," Jassim said, not revealing to Shamil that while he knew Zain's location, he couldn't have intervened in time. His informants were outnumbered, and any attempt at rescue would likely have ended with Shamil and Zain harmed.

"I screwed up, I know," Shamil tapped his head vigorously. "I should have been at home."

"He needs to lay low for a few days."

"There are videos of Zain online, cradling a bloodied Amr. He'll be all over the news now."

"I'm already on it," Jassim pulled a tissue and handed it to Shamil. "The idiots who fired the shots will be handed over for Qasas."

Shamil wiped his face with Jassim's tissue. "I promised them a funeral."

"They'll have a public prayer, followed by a funeral. I've already instructed the police to clear their posts between Al Fawaz Mosque and Al Baya graveyard tomorrow morning and until mid-day."

Shamil lowered his head, and a bitter smile of realisation ran across it. "Your men were there."

"Some were, yes."

"The ones that backed us up?"

"It was getting dangerous."

"Shareef, too?"

"Let's not waste time here," Jassim leaned forward. "They're not your allies; I am. You think if the rebels enter the city, they'll let you or your son go unpunished?" Jassim asked, and Shamil remained silent. "Your parents as well; you're all Al Sayeds and will always be treated as such."

"I'll get them all out before that happens." Shamil shook his head, refusing to accept what was blindingly obvious.

"You'll get them all killed," Jassim retorted, his voice rising.

"Well, help me," Shamil pleaded, defeat in his eyes. "Get us escorted to the border before any of us get hurt."

211

"And then what? Let your son humiliate our family even further?" Jassim asked, and Shamil fell silent. "The second that brat crosses the border, he'll post videos of himself and brag about how he helped the rebels."

"So, you'd rather see him die here?"

"Nothing will happen to him. I've got it all under control."

"He was inches away from your men's bullets. Jassim. I'm not like you— I won't survive losing my son," Shamil said, and Jassim felt the acidity climb up his throat. Despite everything he had done, the man he had been proud of was now nothing but a weakling, begging him for an escape. Invoking Adil's memory like that—how dare he? Jassim would not waste another breath on Shamil, not when things in the city were about to get messier.

"Go home to your wife," Jassim gestured for Shamil to leave, the very sight of him now turning his stomach. "I'll keep your father updated."

"I.."

"Now!"

Shamil nodded, struggling to get up, then dragged his feet to the door. He paused for a moment, his eyes fixed on the corner where a deer Adil had taxidermied stood tall—a silent testament to a hunt they had once shared. "I'm sorry about Adil; I should have been there for him," he said, looking back at Jassim as if Jassim's son was a mere afterthought.

"Just go," Jassim gestured, and Shamil followed his command.

Once gone, Nizar entered, closing the door behind him, an amused look on his face.

"Was he in solitary?" Nizar mocked.

"One of his own making," Jassim replied, lighting a cigarette. It had been too long since he'd had one that day, and it was time. "How's the mare?"

"Ready for mounting."

"I want the video to be disgustingly damning."

"Boss, when have I ever failed you?" Nizar answered, the smugness in his words reassuring Jassim.

Why couldn't Shamil be like him?

"Good," Jassim took a deep pull before he blew it in Nizar's direction. "Anything of interest at the clinic?"

"Oh, yes," Nizar snatched a piece of paper out of his pocket. "This was in Mudhar's drawer."

Jassim unfolded the wrinkled paper, revealing a hand-drawn map of Ar-Raqqah's exit routes. It included rough estimations of roadblocks and other paths through the wilderness. The handwriting was unmistakable—elongated K's and fat-bellied L's. It was clearly Shamil's work. Jassim scoffed, his lips curling in disdain, and without a second thought, he crumpled the paper and tossed it into the bin. Shamil was still plotting an escape, and Jassim had to crush those futile plans for good. He wouldn't allow Shamil to remain the fragile husk he had become. A weakling—what other word could capture him? Good men didn't abandon their country in its hour of greatest need; such betrayals were the fault lines along which nations collapsed. Honour would become a forgotten artefact, as useless as an unworn medal. Why was Jassim the only one who understood this? Had he been blind, failing to recognise Shamil's cowardice for what it truly was? Or—no. Perhaps the blame lay elsewhere. Perhaps it was Laila's doing. Nothing fractures the very being of a man quite like the neglect of a woman he loves.

Once Amr's funeral was over, Jassim would crack down on every rebel sympathiser in the city. Every illegal clinic that treated the rebels and every relative of those who conspired against the state.

Shamil was either with him or with the rebels, and he would have to choose: rejoin SAFI and work with Jassim, ensuring his legacy is passed down to his family, or risk having Zain get arrested. For real, this time. "At the funeral tomorrow, I want our men to rile up the passersby. Let as many people as possible participate and shame those that don't."

"Consider it done, Boss," Nizar reached for a cigarette. "May I?"

Jassim handed him the packet.

"Boss, pardon my ignorance, but wouldn't that make us look bad? You know, allowing a large funeral for a traitor?" Nizar asked.

"A necessary evil," Jassim lit Nizar's cigarette, and Nizar patted his hand. "I'm thinking five thousand would participate, six maximum, and I want our men to then direct them to the Statue Square."

"I see," Nizar blew a heavy cloud of smoke. "It will be chaotic, Boss."

"And it won't be blamed on us."

Chapter 26: The Chase

Returning to his apartment, Shamil felt an agonising cramp shoot down his thigh, one he often had whenever his stress levels were too high for his body to handle. He stopped at the northern entrance to Al-Rashid Park, where two magnificent statues of the Lions of Babylon stood sentinel, their black stone forms as mysterious to Shamil as they had always been. He clambered up the base of one of the lions and nestled between its rock-hard paws, leaning his back against its majestic chest as he waited out that paralysing cramp. As a child, he had climbed on the lions' backs, imagining himself a conqueror, but now it seemed a foolish fancy. He knew he should go home, but his feet hesitated—returning to an empty house held little appeal. The traffic lights around him still flickered, though no one paid them any mind; the absence of police had left the laws unobserved. It was nearly midnight, a time when, even on ordinary days, the streets were deserted. Still, a young man trudged by, pushing a wooden trolley with a large pot of boiled corn cobs perched on top. The usual plume of steam was missing, yet the sweet scent of corn drifted towards Shamil. It did nothing to rouse his appetite, but it did stir memories of simpler times.

He could almost hear the roar of Adil's jeep as it tore across the countryside south of the Euphrates, their last trip together. Adil was behind the steering wheel that day, and Shamil clung to the side, a hunting rifle thrust out the window, his eyes fixed on a flock of ducks flapping ahead of them. The landscape, a streak of green and gold, was covered by a rolling carpet of feathers lifting off in perfect synchrony.

"Slow down! I need a steadier aim," Shamil shouted over the howling wind and rumbling engine.

Adil grinned, his brown eyes as intense as his father's. "Take the shot, you wuss."

The jeep hurtled faster, the ground beneath them a blur. Shamil squinted against the wind, his grip tightening as he took aim. With a swift squeeze of the trigger, the rifle blasted, sending a single shot echoing across the open land. A small duck spiralled down, landing with a soft thud in the grass.

"Seriously?" Adil laughed. "It's as small as your dick."

"Still bigger than yours," Shamil shook his head, a smile tugged at the corner of his lip despite his frustration.

"I know where we'll go," Adil's eyes lit up with the thrill of the hunt. He turned the jeep around and sped up towards the sanctuary by the Al-Assad Lake, which no civilian was allowed to enter without a special invitation from the mayor or a special clearance from another high-ranking official.

As they approached the gate, Adil waved at the guards. "I'm here for the hunt."

The guards, clearly accustomed to Adil's presence, nodded and let them through without any questions.

The sanctuary was unlike anything Shamil had ever seen. Vibrant birds flitted between the trees, their vivid colours making him question his senses. Impossibly large rabbits darted in and out of the underbrush while oversized lizards lay on sun-warmed rocks, their presence both mesmerising and unnerving.

Adil's laughter rang out as he pointed out a particularly large lizard, tracking the birds with its eyes and even frowning at them.

"He's got your angry look!" Adil chuckled.

Shamil's gaze wandered, absorbing the serene beauty of his surroundings. It was a glimpse of untouched wilderness right next to the usual, mostly dry hills and valleys he was accustomed to. It was another trophy reserved exclusively for the regime and its allies, serving as an unattainable aspiration for ordinary citizens.

"Now we're talking," Adil said, his voice dropping to a low, focused tone. His keen eyes had spotted a deer grazing in a nearby clearing. "Bet you I can take it down with a single shot."

"You'll get us in trouble," Shamil started, and Adil shushed him as he took aim, his focus unyielding. The sound of the rifle echoed through the reserve, but the shot missed. The deer, though injured, bounded into the thick brush, leaving a trail of blood.

"You missed from this distance?" Shamil teased.

"Fuck off," Adil's face flushed red as he reloaded his rifle.

They followed the trail, moving through the undergrowth stealthily as if they were on a military ambush. After some time, they found the deer, alarmed and ready to skip away, a reasonable distance separating them. Shamil steadied his aim, going for the kill as it felt inhumane to leave that deer to suffer its injury. His heart thudded as he took the final shot, the deer collapsing with a quiet cry.

Within seconds, Shamil raced towards the fallen creature, his breath hitching in his throat, with Adil close behind. The deer's wide, tear-brimmed eyes locked with his, asking him, "Why."

Kneeling beside it, Shamil tenderly closed its eyes as it took its final breath. He ran his hand across its belly, soft and undisturbed, suggesting it hadn't been carrying young.

"Forgive me," Shamil murmured, his voice barely audible.

"Nice shot," Adil said.

Shamil looked at him. "She was suffering."

"Come, we'll find another for me."

Shamil frowned at the idea. They didn't even need to shoot that deer. Who was going to eat it, anyway? While Mudhar had a taste for roasted wild ducks, the only reason Shamil kept going on the hunting trips was to bring him more. A deer, much larger prey, was something neither of them wanted. Both Shamil's and Adil's families had enough meat in their fridges for weeks, and Nadia would rather eat eggshells than a deer.

"I saw a fox near the edge of the reserve. Now, that's a challenge," Shamil suggested, though he hadn't seen any. He just wanted Adil out of the sanctuary and back into the jeep.

Adil was quick to agree; he wasn't one to run away from a challenge. Leaving the sanctuary, the search for the fox became a wild chase. The jeep sped through the rugged terrain, Adil's focus unrelenting. Shamil knew they were unlikely to find anything, but Adil's determination only grew stronger.

And then a fox appeared, darting across a small pond, Adil's excitement palpable.

"Is that the one?" Adil yelled, gripping the wheel with renewed intensity.

"Yes," Shamil said, not knowing what else to say. It's late now, though, so let's just head home."

"No fucking way," Adil snarled, ignoring Shamil's protests. He drove recklessly, skimming the edge of the pond, narrowly missing the fox on several occasions. The thirst for the kill was visible on Adil's now demon-red face. He cursed and sped up, seemingly abandoning the idea of shooting the fox and opting to run it over instead. The fox's evasiveness only fuelled his rage, and when it managed to cross the pond, he seethed with fury. The fox sauntered on the other side, almost taunting Adil, daring him to drive through the pond. Without hesitation, Adil hit the gas, plunging the jeep into the muddy water. The wheels churned helplessly, and the vehicle became hopelessly stuck in the thick, slippery muck.

"Stop! Stop!" Shamil shouted at Adil, grabbing the steering wheel. "You'll dig us deeper."

"Motherfucker!" Adil yelled back, slamming his hands against the wheel as the engine sputtered and died. "I'll fucking kill it."

Adil's fury was nothing new. Losing was a concept he couldn't tolerate. Once he set his mind on something, he pursued it ruthlessly, regardless of the cost.

Shamil pushed the door open against the mud, the jeep now half-buried. He trudged to the dry edge of the pond while Adil remained stubbornly in the driver's seat, refusing to soil his boots.

"I'm calling father," Shamil said, scrolling through his contacts for Mudhar's number.

"No!" Adil shouted, poking his head out the window. "He'll tell on us, and I don't need that headache now."

"We need help getting the car out."

"Well, call someone else."

Shamil sighed and dialled Alaa's number instead. An hour later, the sun had dipped below the horizon, and still, there was no sign of Alaa.

"Call him again," Adil said, his mouth full of sweet corn from a cob Shamil had handed him.

"My battery is dead. You call him," Shamil replied, unwrapping a sandwich.

"I don't have any reception," Adil muttered, tossing his nibbled cob out the window and licking his fingers. It was as if the raging beast who had been chasing a fox had transformed into a petulant child.

"You can't keep losing your shit like that," Shamil said, glancing at Adil.

"Just let it go," Adil snapped, his gaze fixed ahead as if still hunting for the elusive fox in his mind.

"I'm just saying—"

"Let it fucking go!"

Shamil fell silent, and they both waited for Alaa in the gathering darkness. Those words lingered as the last Shamil remembered Adil saying. He hadn't seen or spoken to him since. A week later, Shamil left for London, and two years after that, Adil was martyred. Shamil often wondered if Adil had gone too far again, chasing an enemy that taunted him.

Would he have stayed alive if Shamil had been by his side, holding the steering wheel just as he did with the jeep, preventing him from digging himself an even deeper grave? Was leaving Adil another sin he had to atone for?

Shamil pushed the thought aside—it offered no answers, only a dull ache of futility. His cramps had eased, but the cold night pressed closer, and rest was now essential if he was to figure out how to keep his family safe in the coming days.

He leapt down from the lion statue, his boots striking the ground with a muted thud. For a moment, he lingered, gazing up at its frozen majesty. The lion's unyielding stare seemed to carry a message—courage, perhaps, or the kind of certainty that only Ameena's faith could match.

He nodded to it, a silent farewell, not out of reverence but as if acknowledging an old comrade. Then, without another glance, he turned and began the walk back home. The streets were silent, and darkness clung to every corner, so dense that Shamil could barely make out where his feet landed with each step. Even so, he refused to use the flash on his mobile; a beam of light would turn him into a target, a glowing invitation to anyone lurking in the shadows. He'd seen enough victims during his time at The National Hospital before leaving for London to know how these things ended.

Why is he slowing down? Shamil darted the alleyways, looking for an escape should the motorcycle rider who slowed down behind him approach any further. He moved quickly, his hands buried in his coat—not for warmth, but for the reassurance of the sharpened pencil hidden inside.

If that man, whoever he was, ambushed him, he wouldn't hesitate. He'd stab first before he would be stabbed.

The man's motorcycle roared, and Shamil stepped closer to the fence of the building he was walking by before he turned back to see who it was. He would jump the fence if he needed to, but hoped he wouldn't. In seconds, the motorcycle zoomed past Shamil, and he could catch a glimpse of the man's face, a black scarf obscuring it.

Chapter 27: No Honourable Woman

Frantically packing the bags, Laila grabbed what she could, not what she needed. Clothes were thrown haphazardly, documents crammed into folders without order, and cherished mementoes stuffed into pockets and corners. She just wanted the bags full before she could leave for Nadia's house.

Zain had left his laptop on, his Facebook feed filled with terrifying images from that day, and Laila couldn't help but click on the video that kept on nesting at the top of the newsfeed. Her son was inches away from death, something her mind couldn't process. It didn't seem possible; God would not have allowed it. God would never allow it.

Trying to close that horrific video, Laila's hand trembled, accidentally dropping the mouse onto the floor. She bent down in a rush, reaching under Zain's bed to retrieve it, when her fingers brushed against a plastic box. Inside was a pack of cigarettes, the sight of which made her stomach turn. Zain, her Zain, had been smoking. How had she been blind to it? Tears welled up in her eyes as she collapsed onto the floor, clutching the pack to her chest. He had lied to her again, and she had failed as a mother. She didn't know her son as well as she thought she did, and that broke her as much as seeing him covered in blood did. He had almost died; she couldn't shake that thought out of her head, and the longer it remained there, the darker her thoughts got. Was it all her fault?

Gathering herself, Laila tossed the pack of cigarettes inside Zain's top drawer, pretending she hadn't seen it. She slipped into her silver-embroidered abaya and hurried downstairs, searching for a taxi. At the corner of the street, a group of young men loitered, some of whom she recognised. She gestured for Shadi, their neighbour's son, and he came running.

"I need a taxi," she said, hoping he would fetch one for her from Al-Naim Square. He shrugged, telling her that he had barely seen any taxis that evening; no one dared drive for fear of being stopped by the police.

"You can't go out this late, Auntie," Shadi insisted, causing Laila to frown. It was infuriating that even the neighbour's son felt he had a say in what she could or couldn't do.

Inside her in-laws' house, Laila called all the taxi companies she knew, but no one answered.

"Uncle," she turned to Mudhar for help. "I can't find any taxis. Could you drive me to Nadia's?"

"Don't you see his arm?" Ameena interjected, though Laila had seen him drive with one hand before, and his left arm was injured, not his right one.

"We will wait for Shamil," Mudhar said, lying on the sofa, the television remote in his hand as he flipped through the news channels.

"I can walk there," Laila began, and before she could finish, Mudhar was sitting up, glaring at her, his face as threatening as Jassim's.

"Have you hit your head or something?" he said, a vein popping on his forehead. "No honourable woman of ours walks the streets this late."

Ameena glared at her in silence, and Laila's tears threatened to fall.

Once again, she found herself unable to do anything, imprisoned without shackles. She could sneak out and walk to Nadia's house, but had she done so, she would have upset all the men in her life, including perhaps even her son Zain, who would question how on earth his mother walked all that distance without a male companion.

No honourable woman indeed.

Entering her apartment, she slammed the door shut and forcefully pulled down her hijab, letting it hang loose around her shoulders. She grabbed the pack of cigarettes out of Zain's drawer, snatched the corridor's carpet with her, and threw it on the balcony. More than often, she felt she was being punished for sins she hadn't committed; she might as well start committing them so that her punishments felt justified.

She sat on the carpet, her hair uncovered, and grabbed one of Zain's cigarettes. Lighting it, she took a deep drag, feeling the bitterness smear her tongue. Her hands trembled as she ran them through her hair, her mind suffering a thousand worries. Would her life have been different had she not married Shamil? It was supposed to be a solution, a way out of a life she didn't want. But it had turned into something more complicated and painful than she had ever imagined.

When she had told Shamil that her father was marrying her off to a Saudi man, back when she was seventeen, she wasn't looking for pity or assistance. She was looking for a friend to be there for her. She wanted to say goodbye to Shamil, having accepted her fate as a product her father could sell to whomever he chose. But then Shamil had offered to ask for her hand in marriage, a fake one, and she couldn't say no to his proposal.

They would get engaged and keep delaying the marriage. She could then continue to study and graduate, become independent, make her own money, and choose her own path forward in life once they broke off the engagement.

Shamil had told her plainly—he understood she didn't love him the way he loved her, and he was offering his help as a friend, nothing more. Yet, in a moment of weakness, her emotions tangled with her judgement. A strange connection blossomed within her, unfamiliar and overwhelming, something she had never felt before. Perhaps it was love, she thought, though she wasn't sure. At that moment, she blurted out that she did love him but quickly added she wasn't ready to be anyone's wife.

Shamil's happiness was radiant, almost childlike.

At the time, Laila believed she was doing the right thing, convincing herself that love would come later. She had seen it happen before—Ameena had grown to love Mudhar, Nadia had grown to love Mazen, and countless other women she knew had accepted love as something that arrived after the marriage, not before. Women didn't choose love; they made peace with their circumstances. In a moment of defiance against her father's control over her life, she told Shamil what he wanted to hear: she loved him, and she wanted to marry him—not just to defy her father, but because she believed this was the least painful path. If marriage was her fate, at least she would choose whom to marry.

As time passed, the weight of her deceit began to grow unbearable. Every argument with Shamil felt like proof that their bond wasn't true love. Every kiss reminded her of the lie she had told, guilt gnawing at her until she couldn't contain it any longer. When she finally confessed everything, she braced herself for the worst. But Shamil didn't respond with anger. Instead, he hugged her tightly and promised they would fix things together.

For a while, it seemed like they could. Shamil took her confession in stride, determined to make their marriage work. But slowly, the cracks began to show. Sadness seeped into their lives, first subtly, then all at once. Shamil buried himself in work, retreating into long hours at the office, extended hunting trips, endless conferences, and exhaustive research projects. The man she once thought she could grow to love became a shadow, consumed by his own grief and guilt.

"Divorce me," she had suggested more than once, hoping to free them both. But every time, Shamil refused with an intensity that bordered on desperation. He would remind her of the rules society imposed and the shame a divorced woman would carry. "Divorce dishonours a woman," he would say as if it were a truth she had to live by.

The words suffocated her, each refusal tightening the chains she had hoped to break.

Now, Shamil was back, a changed man in some ways, yet still stubbornly the same. And Laila—she had changed too. Against all odds, she had grown to love him. Perhaps it was inevitable, just as Ameena had learned to love Mudhar and Nadia had learned to love Mazen.

Whether through time, necessity, or shared history, love had found her. But it wasn't the love she had once imagined; it was the love she had come to understand.

Chapter 28: Unplanned Intimacy

Shamil stood in front of his apartment door, the keys warm and damp in his hand. He knew he was late, and Laila must have left already. Still, he wished she hadn't. If only he could open the door and find Zain in his room, fiddling with his laptop and cursing at it, and Laila in the living room watching an Egyptian comedy, painting, or just doing nothing at all—just being there.

The day had been too long, exhausting beyond words, and he needed to rest. Though he had fallen asleep at the hospital, that creaking rust of a bed was hardly restful. He hadn't eaten, and even the best meal would only nauseate him now.

Dragging his feet across the corridor, its carpet conspicuously missing, Shamil noticed flickering reflections on the exposed tiles under Zain's closed door.

"Zain?" he called, pushing the door open to an empty room. A clip showing Zain cradling a blood-covered Amr played in a loop on his laptop monitor. Shamil switched it off and made his way into the living room, where two large travel bags lay by the entrance. Did Laila forget them? Was that smoke he smelled? He checked the bathroom and the kitchen. The closer he got to the cold bedroom, the stronger the smell of smoke became. The bed was as tidy as Laila would normally keep it, and the balcony door was wide open, letting the smoke ride the icy breeze into the house.

"Laila?" Shamil said, stepping onto the balcony. And there she was, sitting on the floor, a cigarette half-burnt in her hand. She had her silver-embroidered abaya on and was still wearing her trainers. "Why are you still here?"

"I'm just getting some fresh air," she sniffled, wiping her face.

"I'm sorry I'm late," Shamil said, crouching in front of her. His voice was low, knowing the night's silence would carry their words into the neighbours' homes. "I thought you'd have called for a taxi by now."

"There weren't any," she said, looking away from him.

"I'll take you now," he extended his hand. "Come on."

"Sit with me," she shuffled a bit, making some space for him.

He nodded, sitting beside her, the corridor's carpet protecting them from the cold floor. "I didn't know you smoked."

"I don't. I just felt like lighting one and… you know," she shrugged.

"Watch it burn?" he said, picking up the cigarette from her hand and taking a pull. It burned his eyes and cut short his breath, forcing him to cough the smoke out. "I still can't do it," he muttered, handing her the cigarette back.

"Neither can I," she said, putting it out.

"You were crying."

"Smoke got into my eyes."

"Laila…"

"I'm fine." She dusted the ash off her lap. "I've just spoken to Nadia; he's been asleep since he arrived."

"Alhamdulillah," Shamil said, haunted by the images of Zain's bloodied hands pressed against Amr's chest.

"I called you, and you didn't answer," Laila looked at him, her voice trailing off. "Sometimes, I expect too much of you."

"I should have been here," Shamil lowered his head in shame, the dirt smudged into his glasses suddenly becoming noticeable. He took his glasses off and wiped them with his shirt before casting them aside. He rubbed his eyes hard, his eyelids heavy and sticky with sweat. "I saw it all happening in my mind. Still, I chose to remain in the hospital."

"You had to help," Laila said, her gaze lingering on his tired eyes before settling on his shoulder, where she rested her head. "He's safe now."

"I'll fix this," Shamil said, Laila's physical closeness warming his heart.

"We'll fix it together this time," she crossed her arms around her chest, moving her body closer to his.

"Let's go inside," Shamil said, feeling her shiver beside him.

"A cuddle would keep me warmer," she said as their eyes met.

A cuddle was exactly what Shamil needed.

If he could read her as well as she could read him, their life together would have been perfect. He had failed the test of Laila so miserably that he had given up trying to take it. She was the one who had coerced him into leaving her and moving to London to start a new life where she could join him later, where they could get divorced and choose their paths in life unswayed by society or family expectations.

She had pushed him out of her life, and he had bitterly complied. And there she was, asking him to cuddle her and keep her warm, and again, he complied.

He pulled his arm around her, and she nestled into his lap, her head now resting on his chest. She glided her hand over his shirt until two stone-cold fingers landed on his bare neck. An accidental touch that sent a tremor of passion jolting through every nerve in his body. She felt it too, he could tell, as she swiftly pulled her hand into a loosely clenched fist that rested on top of his heart.

"Did I hurt your arm?" he asked, remembering how he had pulled her inside the house, gripping her as if she had been a suspect.

"It's okay," she replied, sweeping her soft hair to one side like a silk blanket that enveloped them both. It smelled like jasmine petals, mild and sweet, a scent that banished the smoke that had choked Shamil.

He wished he could stay there forever, her body entwined with his, sharing warmth as they waited for the nightmare to pass. Instead, all he could offer her were a few minutes of unplanned intimacy. Never had he thought about or desired anyone else besides her, even during his loneliest nights in his small room in London. Even though he knew she didn't love him in the same way, the depth of his feelings for her remained unwavering. He had resigned himself to the reality that he would always be in love with her, whether she was by his side or in the arms of another. Her happiness was the only thing that truly mattered to him.

The fences rattled with each distant blast, a now-familiar backdrop that no longer startled Shamil as he held his sweetheart close.

Hours slipped away like seconds, her shallow breaths a soothing rhythm against his chest. With a tender kiss on her head, he woke her, whispering that it was time he took her to Zain, the darkness of night their only cover.

Chapter 29: To The Statue

Shamil woke to Mudhar's voice, urgent and insistent, sneaking through the apartment windows and shattering what little sleep he had managed. He sprang out of bed and dashed to the balcony, his skin prickling from the morning chill.

"Baba, wait!" he shouted, scrambling back inside to grab a wrinkled shirt off the floor before bolting downstairs. He had overheard Mudhar mention attending Amr's funeral—a perilous decision. "You're not going to the funeral," Shamil said, standing in Mudhar's path.

"I'm just joining the prayer, Son," Mudhar replied calmly. He wore his meticulously ironed white gown, reserved only for funerals. "I knew Amr's family well. Besides, Zain has asked me."

"There won't be any police," Shamil warned, hastily buttoning his shirt.

"I don't need protection."

"You're injured. No one will blame you for not going," Shamil pleaded.

"If we don't attend the prayer, people will think we condone Amr's killing, and we don't," Mudhar stated firmly, reaching out to straighten Shamil's shirt. "No one will harm me; I've done this city enough favours."

"I can't let you go alone," Shamil insisted.

"Then come with me."

"I need to stay with Zain."

Mudhar sighed, his calm breaking for just a moment. "He's safe at Nadia's; Laila and Ameena are there now, and I made it very clear this morning that he doesn't step a foot outside the house. Call him if you're worried."

Shamil hesitated, his phone heavy in his hand. He didn't need to call to confirm it; the answer was as clear as the cold morning air: Zain would want him to go to the prayer and honour Amr's memory. It would only take them an hour, two at most, before he left the funeral for Nadia's.

"Just to the prayer, okay?" Shamil said, dusting off his trousers to make them look presentable. They were heading to the mosque, after all, where wearing clean clothes and scented oils was customary.

Pulling a small bottle of scented oil from his pocket, Mudhar poured some into the palm of his healthy hand and smoothed it through his hair until it evaporated. He then poured a few more drops of oil and tried to tame Shamil's ruffled hair. The scent was too strong for Shamil's liking, but the act of his father fixing his hair as if he were still a little boy brought a fleeting sense of comfort. No matter his age, Mudhar's presence always made Shamil feel secure. But now, Shamil felt that his own presence might provide his father with that same sense of security.

"God shall reward every step you take to the mosque with abundance," Mudhar quipped, imitating Ameena's usual reminder to attend Friday prayers. It was Ameena's persistence and preaching that had finally converted Mudhar and got him to pray daily.

He had never set foot inside a mosque before marrying her, and he hadn't stopped visiting mosques since their wedding.

Walking beside his father, Shamil couldn't help but reminisce about the days he and his childhood friend, Alaa, had made the same journey to the mosque. Each step was carefully counted, a game to see how many they could squeeze in between his parents' house and their destination, believing that the more steps taken, the higher the reward. But on the day of Amr's funeral, there was no counting. Mudhar and Shamil moved with purpose, their strides long and hurried, eyes darting around for any sign of the rebels. None were to be seen. Not the rebels, not the police, not even the army. The city seemed to have been handed back to its citizens, allowing them to mourn their loss without interference.

Shamil stayed close to his father, ready to react at any moment. The crowd around them built up slowly, the air thick with grief and anger. Those who recognised Mudhar approached him to offer their salutations and respect. Some questioned his presence, fearing for his safety, but the majority welcomed him as one of their own, united in grief.

In all the years Shamil had attended Friday prayers at Al-Fawwaz Mosque, he had never seen it as packed as it was on the day of Amr's funeral. The streets teemed with people; some hid their faces under masks and balaclavas, but the majority had nothing to hide. Thin, colourful plastic rugs lined the street to accommodate the praying masses, and young men stood guard at all side exits.

The closer Shamil got to the mosque, the more confident he felt about joining the prayers. The crowd's solidarity emboldened him, transforming his apprehension into a quiet but determined defiance; he was going to honour Amr and walk to his funeral.

"Arise to the prayer," declared the imam, prompting the hundreds that had gathered on the street outside the mosque to form prayer lines. Shoulder to shoulder, Shamil stood next to Mudhar, reading Al-Fatiha for Amr's soul as the clouds cleared up the way for their prayers to ascend through the heavens.

"To Jannah, heaven, we march. Martyrs in millions," shouted a masked man standing at the front of the prayer line.

"We answer your call. We answer your call, dear God," shouted another, sparking a tsunami of similar chants from all present. Then, the march began.

Once he finished praying, Mudhar affirmed, "We'll walk with them. Zain would want us to."

Shamil nodded, looking around the clogged street. At least two thousand men, young and old, were walking behind Amr's coffin. Their voices rose to the sky with mournful chants, and their feet shook the ground.

A mile into the march, Mudhar's hips couldn't take it any longer. "I'll head back home," he said, stepping aside to catch his breath.

"Men don't walk half a funeral, Hakim," Amr's uncle said to Mudhar, disappointment evident in his tone. He'd been walking at the front beside Amr's coffin, then trailed off, cheering on the marchers and shaking hands with those he'd recognised.

"I'll walk in my father's place," Shamil interjected, knowing that shame would have easily swayed his father into limping through the entire distance.

"God bless you," Amr's uncle said, clapping Shamil's shoulder. Then, he made his way through the mourners and returned to cheering them on.

"I won't stay beyond the burial," Shamil said to Mudhar before he rejoined the crowd.

The closer they got to the graveyard, the louder the chants grew, and the more vigilant Shamil became. His eyes locked onto a few masked men aggressively shaming passersby into joining them. Initially, he didn't think much of it—he wanted everyone to participate. The higher the number of mourners, the lower the chances of arrests if the procession turned into a protest. But as he looked closer, it became clear: something sinister was brewing.

"No face mask, Doctor?" A familiar voice accompanied a hand landing heavily on Shamil's shoulder.

Shamil pulled away, his fist clenched, ready for any confrontation. "Only criminals hide their faces," he retorted, unable to identify the man, whose face was completely obscured by a keffiyeh and thick sunglasses. A white imprint on his black hat read 'Bless me, Mother'. Was he one of Jassim's men?

"I wonder what pen I should use to write your report," the man taunted. "It must be black, you know, more official that way."

Shamil frowned, fighting the urge to tear the keffiyeh from the man's face. "And I'll use red to write yours since you're as present here as I am."

"Of course," the man scoffed. "You could have at least covered your face." He gestured to his own head as if Shamil should have known that covering up was an obvious precaution. "It's about to get ugly." With that, he melted back into the chanting crowd.

Shamil slowed his pace, the graveyard almost within sight, every instinct screaming at him to turn back. That man had to be one of Jassim's. Why else would he be so cryptic and camouflaged? Should Shamil cover his face now, step aside, and watch how things unfolded? Or should he simply turn around and leave?

There wasn't much time to think. The chanting suddenly ceased, and the marching crowd stood still as a cool, dusty breeze swept through them. Shamil couldn't hear what the imam was saying near the gates— there were at least fifty rows of men between them, their muffled chatter drowning out the prayers.

"I haven't seen any policemen today. Where do you think they are?" a young man in the row ahead of Shamil asked his companion.

"Cowering in their holes like the scared rats they are," another replied.

"The army has been called into the city. They're around the city hall and Al-Assad's statue. Look, my brother took this photo just now from the square. Do you see the soldiers?"

"Nothing can stop us now— we will go and tear that statue down."

"Yes, we'll show others what a free city looks like."

"Let's occupy the city square. It'll become our freedom square."

"To the statue, guys. To the statue."

The phrase spread through the crowd like wildfire.

"The army is there," Shamil shouted, but no one paid attention. "Don't go to the statue!" he tried again, attempting to block their path. But his efforts were futile against the surge of determined men.

Losing his balance, Shamil fell to the ground, marchers nearly trampling him. A few men stepped aside, helping him to the pavement as the throng pressed on, chanting, "The people want to bring down the regime."

Shamil stood up again, shouting louder, but his voice was drowned out by their cries for vengeance. He could have turned back; let it all unfold as it was destined to. He should have. But a massacre was imminent; he could sense it and even smell it in the air. If anything he had seen and researched on the internet had been true, the National Hospital would be overwhelmed, just like in other cities. Following similar events, people died on the floors, their lives hanging by a thread that the mere presence of a doctor could have saved. He had to help, but first, he had to ensure his son was safe.

Slipping into a side alley, away from the commotion, he called Laila.

"Where's Zain?"

"He's right next to me," she answered. "Uncle is here too."

"Give him the phone," Shamil quickly checked the time on his phone—it was twenty past two. "Zain doesn't leave your sight," he said the moment Mudhar's voice filled his ear. "I'm going to the hospital. It's not looking good. Don't go home or anywhere near the centre."

"Son, just come home," Mudhar pleaded, but Shamil's decision was already made.

"I'll be fine," Shamil hung up.

Had he spoken any longer, Mudhar and Laila would have guilt-tripped him into abandoning his duty as a doctor, as a human, and would have had him lock himself up at home with them.

At first, Shamil walked. Then he sped up a little. Then he ran as soon as he heard the first rattling round of gunshots. He prayed for sanity to prevail, for those shots to be warning shots, and for things to calm down and return to normal. But when the shooting continued as he gasped for breath near the hospital's Emergency Department's entrance, hope dwindled.

At the gates, Ayman stood guard; two soldiers alarmed next to him.

"Any injuries yet?" Shamil asked, trying to catch his breath as he scouted the abandoned waiting area.

"Were you there? Did you see what happened?" Ayman asked.

"I was at the funeral, yes. They went to the square, and the army is there now. I think there—" A barrage of thunderous gunfire, unlike anything Shamil had ever heard, silenced him.

It didn't seem real. Not at first.

Ambulance sirens faded into the distance. The thundering clashes died out. The world around Shamil went silent. And for a moment, his heart stood still.

What the hell am I doing here? Why am I still in this horrible place? It hit Shamil hard. He should have been abroad already with his family, but somehow, he ended up here, a nightmare unfolding before him.

Stay focused, he snapped out of it as the chaotic murmurs of the living resumed, and the screams of the bereaved echoed from afar. He knew what was coming; he had seen it happen in other cities, but still, he didn't know what to hope or pray for or whether praying was going to be of any help. His stiffened legs were rooted to the ground beneath him as a wailing ambulance screeched past, almost crash-parking into the gates.

"In the name of the merciful," Shamil muttered to himself, leaning forward to help the paramedic open the backdoors while Ayman held the trolley, waiting to see what was in the back of the ambulance.

It was the river.

The river of raging spirits Shamil had left minutes ago had turned into a stream of silent angels that spilt out the back of the ambulance the moment he opened its doors. He couldn't tell how many there were. One after another, their corpses slid on top of each other and down to his feet, pushing him and Ayman back with their trolley.

Oh, how he wished what he saw wasn't real. That the eyes of these angels could blink. That the light was still in them, and he was just unable to see it.

Chapter 30: The Tough Weakling

Growing up, Shamil was a thin teenager, more reserved than boisterous, preferring the quietude of his thoughts to the chaos of confrontation. His baggy school uniforms hung loose on his slender frame, and his ordinary haircut reflected a preference for simplicity over style. He wasn't exceptionally skilled in sports, a fact that made him an easy target for bullies. This bothered his parents far more than it did him. Shamil believed that true power lay in the strength of one's mind, will, and spirit. And he saw no reason to endure physical pain to prove his masculinity. When faced with threats, he enlisted bigger bullies to defend him, offering high marks on exams as payment. To Shamil, this was the rational approach. But, to his father, Mudhar, it was anything but manly.

"What if you were on your own? What would you do?" Mudhar once asked a teenage Shamil, trying to coax him into taking karate classes.

"Why would I ever be alone?" Shamil shrugged off the question, retreating to his room, feeling the weight of his father's disappointment.

Mudhar didn't see the man he hoped his son would become until a sweltering day in May 1996. He had recently bought a new Jeep and planned a family trip with Nadia and Mazen to the Euphrates. As they neared the roundabout by the new bridge, a gigantic truck appeared out of nowhere, set on a collision course.

The inevitable crash happened at such an angle that the Jeep's sturdy frame bore the brunt of the impact, sparing them from being pulverised.

When the ringing in Shamil's ears subsided and his vision cleared, the first thing he saw was his father's head bleeding against the steering wheel. Mazen was unconscious, while Ameena and Nadia were engulfed in hysterical screams. He must have struck his head; the spider-web crack on the windshield left little for doubt. Still, Shamil had to assess the situation with rapid clarity.

His forehead was wet, but whether it was sweat or blood didn't matter as long as it stayed out of his eyes. He needed to see, to focus. There were no other cars involved. He could smell the diesel leaking, though it hadn't ignited yet. They had to get out. He grabbed Mudhar's arm, dragging him out of the Jeep, knowing he was in the most perilous position if the frame gave way.

"We're fine. Just get out of the car now," Shamil called out, hoping his voice would cut through Ameena's panic. He then helped her and Nadia onto the pavement, waving frantically for taxis to take them to the hospital.

A spirit of calmness had settled over him, driving him to take control when no one else could. In those critical moments, lives hanging in the balance, he acted with a commanding presence that planted a seed of pride in his father's heart. Mudhar never vocalised it, but Shamil knew he had, in that instant, become the man his father had always hoped he would be.

When Shamil opened the back of the ambulance on the day of Amr's funeral, that very same spirit rushed back to aid him. Once again, lives were at stake, and he had to take charge.

He eyed the scene, then quickly crouched in front of a young boy. He couldn't have been older than thirteen; his thin moustache barely had taken shape. Shamil didn't know why he picked him; his injuries were fatal. Listening to his heart wouldn't change a thing, but Shamil did it anyway. Did he hope for a heartbeat? Or was he that incompetent? It didn't matter.

Fidgeting, Ayman stood in front of Shamil, sinking his fingers into a saline infusion bag. He was as pale and clammy as Shamil and perhaps as clueless.

"Ayman, I don't..." Shamil choked.

Ayman looked back at him, walls of tears building up in his eyes. Clutching the saline bag firmly, it became a fidgeting extension of his arm. He did not say a word.

Unlike Ayman's, Shamil's eyes remained dry. Was he dead inside already? Did his instinct take over, signalling it was time for 'fight' and not 'flight'? Or was he still trying to make sense of what he had just witnessed?

It took him a minute before he could navigate through those thoughts building up inside his skull like steam fighting its way out of a pressure cooker. A minute or two that lasted hours in his head. He was aware of every detail. The stink of raw meat was so suffocating he could taste it. The thick, warm blood of the victims that seeped down his thighs and into his trainers.

Their unblinking eyes.

"Get help!" Shamil snapped at Ayman. "Get everyone here, consultants, nurses, everyone!"

Ayman nodded, glancing at him briefly before he dropped the saline bag and bolted through a crowd of spectators that stood behind them, speechless. Joana, the head nurse, was among them. In her thin shadow hid two washed-out student nurses awaiting her wisdom.

"This is what you get when you don't listen. Let them be a lesson to others," she muttered, to Shamil's disbelief.

How dare you? Shamil turned back and glared at her as she stood there, arms crossed, with a sadistic smirk on her face.

"We had everything, and now the country is lost because of their foolishness," she told one of the guards.

What a horrible thing to say it was.

She wasn't a prime example of compassion to start with, but her words still shocked Shamil. Whether she was with the regime or against it, she was a nurse, and he expected some humanity from a nurse. Had it been appropriate, he would have screamed at her to let her know how obnoxious her comment was and asked her to get the hell out of his sight. But he needed every helping hand, even the dirty ones.

"Can you fucking help?" he shouted over his shoulder.

"Go!" Joana instructed her students as if her only job was to stand there and grimace. "I'll go speak to the manager about this," she added, retreating through the emergency department's central corridor and not paying attention to the two men rushing past her.

"Good riddance," Shamil said aloud. Perhaps not loud enough for her to hear, but loud enough to release some of the anger inside him.

We can save them; we still can. Shamil felt reassured as he saw the experts coming.

Mr. Omar, the on-call consultant that day, slowed his pace as he arrived at the scene. He pulled a procedure trolley from the surgical emergencies unit and then parked it behind Shamil.

"He's still warm. Should we continue with chest compressions, or should we move on to the next one?" Shamil asked Mr. Omar, his hands already parked on top of that silent chest.

Mr. Omar said nothing and just looked at Shamil, his eyes wide open.

"Hakim? Start or move on?" Shamil insisted, every second mattered.

"Arrrr…" Mr. Omar looked at Mr. Haji, standing right next to him.

Mr. Haji looked back at Mr. Omar, then at Shamil. He was the head of the surgical department and the most senior surgeon in the governorate. His presence anywhere in the hospital would normally command respect and awe— only this time, it was as if he wasn't there at all. Not as Shamil wanted him to be.

"For God's sake, please, do something!" Shamil shouted at them both as his hands automatically started chest compressions on the teenager's body lying in front of him. They were the most futile chest compressions with no rhythm to them and no real drive.

Tears flooded Mr. Haji's eyes as he put his hands on his head and started weeping; the sight was too much for him to handle.

A few steps back, he shuffled until he crumbled down the wall behind him.

"God almighty have mercy on us. Kind God, be kind to us," said Mr. Omar and Mr. Haji together, overlapping in an unplanned synchrony.

That's all the help Shamil got from them: tears and prayers. Two of the hospital's highly regarded pillars of respect, knowledge, and experience were reduced by the gruesomeness of what was between Shamil's hands to a crying infant and an echoing totem.

Shamil was on his own, after all.

"Let's get them onto the trollies," Shamil said, turning to the student nurses. We'll take them all inside to resuscitate and see what we can do there."

The students were quick to react and help, and then some civilians, Ayman, and the rest of the available staff joined in.

"God, please let one of them survive this," Shamil prayed as he pushed the trolley carrying the last of the injured to the resuscitation room. Another pulseless, warm corpse he was, just like the seven he had seen before him, yet Shamil still hoped for a miracle. God was there; he felt his presence with every atom of his being, but he couldn't understand why God was watching and not intervening - he failed to see his wisdom.

The dead lay still on top of the examination beds and the bloodied floors. How could anyone survive bullets that burrowed through their foreheads and rib cages? Nothing Shamil could do would change that outcome. Not one of them survived.

Whoever pulled the trigger knew precisely where to shoot. They shot to kill, and they killed to teach the civilians a lesson: Whatever life they thought they had wasn't their own. It was the regime's to take whenever they deemed necessary, something Shamil had already known. Their lives were worthless.

How naïve I was, Shamil wept inside, looking at the bodies piling up around him in the resuscitation bay.

He was so stupid, so idealistic, so in denial. What was he thinking, getting his hopes up? He should have just accepted the reality of what he had witnessed and stood back mourning just as Mr. Omar and Mr. Haji did. They knew better.

"We should leave, Hakim; there is nothing for us to do here," Ayman said, clutching Shamil's arm and pulling him away from the resuscitation bay towards the surgical unit.

Glaring at his own feet, Shamil realised his presence had made no difference. His knowledge was useless, his steady hands were useless, and even his prayers were useless. The only difference his presence had made was his footprints crossing others on the blood-stained floors.

He wished he could go home and pretend that day never happened, but he couldn't. Bringing the dead back to life was evidently not within his power, but tending to the sick ones who stood there watching in horror was.

Entering the surgical unit, Shamil turned his attention to a man groaning in agony—a living person.

"Are you injured?" Shamil asked the man who was twisting down on the unit's floor.

"No," the man cried, barely breathing. His knees were bent halfway as he squeezed his stomach with both hands. "My stomach, it's like I am being stabbed."

Shamil sat down by his side and lifted his hands to examine the man's stomach, only to realise he hadn't taken the blood-tainted gloves off yet and that every piece of his clothes was as tainted as those gloves were.

"I'll be right back," Shamil said, heading to the private examination room to get washed and changed. The moment he entered that room, he felt his strength fading away.

Whatever spirit he had in him, guiding his every decision earlier, had abandoned his worn-out body, leaving him to pick up the pieces.

"God, give me a little more strength," Shamil muttered.

His knees bent against his will, bringing him closer to the ground. He sat there, hands in his lap as if he were praying, and befittingly, the only answer to his prayer was the tears that rained on his palms unannounced.

Peeling off the bloodied gloves, he cast them aside, his hands faltering as he scrolled through his phone. His thumb hovered over Laila's name, unwilling to press the call button. He needed to hear her voice, to share the crushing weight of his failure, the raw pain that ravaged him. He needed her presence, yet the thought of dragging her into his turmoil, of making her witness his helplessness, was unbearable. He had already burdened her too much; she shouldn't see him broken and weeping.

Wiping his face, he scrolled up, halting at the first name in his contact list—Alaa.

The heaviness in his chest deepened. He missed his friend, his brother, his steadfast companion. He would have wept in front of Alaa, and Alaa would have punched some sense into him. He had barely spoken to him in five long years, yet if Shamil were to call, Alaa would answer with the same warmth and love as if they had never stopped talking. Still, he couldn't bring himself to do it. What if Alaa didn't answer? What if he was now in a different realm where he could never answer?

Shamil couldn't face it, not now.

Turning off his phone, he mustered his remaining strength and walked over to the nearby sink. He needed a change of gloves, clothes, and even skin, yet all he got was a change of heart.

If he had stopped them from going to the statue, they wouldn't have died. If he had spoken louder, sooner, clearer, some of them might have listened, and with that, they would have been spared. All he wanted when he came back to Syria was to get his family out, but having seen what he had seen, he knew he had to do more.

He just couldn't define "more" yet.

T Hashem

Chapter 31: Solitude

Jassim sat at the head of the mahogany table that centred the dining room in his river villa. His wife, Noura, moved slowly around the table, setting down a steaming pot of lamb stew. He gazed at her with a mixture of affection and sadness— the effects of last year's stroke evident in the slight tremor of her hands. The once sharp-minded Noura was barely recognisable. She had insisted on cooking tonight, and Jassim had allowed it, knowing how much it meant to her.

"Smells wonderful, Noura," he said, forcing warmth into his voice as he spooned a portion of the stew onto his plate. The truth was, Noura's cooking had never been her strong suit, and it had not improved with her declining cognition. Still, he smiled at her as if she had prepared him a feast.

She smiled back, her eyes not quite meeting his. "It does smell wonderful," she said softly, as if she had forgotten she had made it.

He nodded, swallowing a mouthful of the overly salty stew. Perhaps he deserved it salty, considering what had transpired in Ar-Raqqah earlier that day. His calculations had been grossly underestimated. Instead of the anticipated six thousand mourners, over fifty thousand had attended Amr's funeral. More than half had surged towards the statue square, his operatives fanning the fire of their rage, triggering chaos and panic among the soldiers stationed there. The lethal response had led to a massacre, far surpassing the acceptable casualties he had envisioned.

"Oh dear," Noura gasped as distant echoes of sporadic gunshots pierced the silence of the evening.

Her spoon slipped and splashed drops of the red sauce onto Jassim's hands. She reached for a tissue, and Jassim quickly held her hand, squeezing it gently.

"It's fine, sweetheart," he reassured her, wiping her hand and then his.

At least it was only the echoes she heard, not the screaming of those who were shot or their grieving families. That would have deteriorated her mental health even further, a distraction Jassim couldn't afford.

He had warned General Saleem about what would happen, but Saleem had chosen to antagonise him. Their superiors wouldn't blame those deaths on Jassim—he was simply following orders. Saleem would soon have to contend with the fallout, scrambling to contain the situation.

Still, too many had died, Jassim brooded as he finished cleaning his hands. He had hoped the army would retreat and protesters would take over the square, shaming the general in the process. He would have then negotiated a deal with heads of tribes, just like he had done when he was first assigned to SAFI's Al-Jazeera Branch, bolstering his position further within the region. But with so many youngsters dead, he doubted a deal would appease the calls for vengeance without significant concessions on his side. Shamil would undoubtedly take his son abroad, further tarnishing Jassim's reputation. He couldn't compromise— it would only paint him as weak and expendable. Blood had already been spilt, and there was no turning back.

"Why did we leave the guest house?" Noura's voice broke through his thoughts, bringing him back to the present.

"You said you wanted a day by the water, so here we are," he replied, though she hadn't said it.

She nodded, seemingly content with his answer, and returned to her meal. Jassim watched her, his heart heavy. He would have never left her side, but it was apparent now that she wasn't going to be safe in Ar-Raqqah. Even with his operatives securing his villa and the roads leading to it, it wasn't safe enough for Noura. She had to leave.

Jassim pushed back his chair, leaving his half-eaten meal behind, and walked into his office. He lit a cigarette and took a deep pull before he dialled Mudhar's number. "You don't leave Nadia's house no matter what happens in the city the next few days," he instructed Mudhar.

"Are the rebels advancing?" Mudhar asked.

"If they do, I'll send someone to escort you to Deir Ezzor," Jassim said calmly. He stopped short of revealing the full truth.

"Isn't it safer in Jazra town? With Mezar?"

"I don't have enough eyes there," Jassim admitted. He had concentrated all his efforts on Ar-Raqqah events, and should any threat come to Mudhar and his family in Jazra town, Jassim wasn't confident his help would arrive in time.

"What about at your villa?"

"You'll be least safe here." Jassim coughed up thick phlegm tinged with streaks of blood, a now daily sight that no longer bothered him. "Your bunker is bigger than the one we have here anyway," he added jokingly. He had always mocked the bunker Mudhar had insisted on adding to his house plans.

Mudhar had believed that war between Syria and Israel was inevitable, and he didn't want to be caught unprepared. Ironic that that very bunker would serve to protect them against their fellow Syrians instead.

"I pray we never need it," Mudhar said, his voice subdued, and then they both were silent for a few seconds.

"I didn't order the shooting," Jassim said.

"I know, cousin."

"But now my hands are tied," Jassim added, almost whispering, as though confessing to the walls of his office. He needed to say it aloud, even if it changed nothing.

"There's no other choice," Mudhar said, his tone calm and reassuring.

Jassim didn't need Mudhar's approval—at least, that's what he told himself. But the decision to authorise lethal force bore down on him like an iron yoke. Hearing Mudhar's agreement lightened it just enough to breathe. Enough to imagine that when the time came to face the angels guarding the gates of hell, he'd have an answer ready. "It wasn't just me who thought it necessary," he'd say, the words an attempt to justify, to share the burden of his guilt.

If Mudhar—a man who had spent his life saving others, a God doctor whose hands had pulled people back from the brink—had deemed it inevitable, then surely Jassim's own conscience could demand no more. Or so he told himself.

Returning to his dinner table, Noura still there, her plate untouched, Jassim forced down another bite of stew, its saltiness barely noticeable now. His stare locked with determined intensity.

For Adil. For his legacy.

It was time for the rebels to meet their God.

Chapter 32: The Doors Remained Locked

Shamil lay on a floor mattress at Nadia's house, earplugs in place, staring at the wall's peeling paint. He traced the patterns formed by the mould, fighting to keep his eyes open despite his exhaustion. Every time he closed them, haunting images of the massacre's victims filled his mind.

Nadia's house had always been a sanctuary for Shamil and his family, especially during the early years when Mudhar was starting his medical career and money was tight. Holidays were a luxury they couldn't afford, so Nadia's garden became young Shamil's playground. He camped there, built sandcastles, and dug water tunnels, creating memories that now seemed like distant dreams.

In the aftermath of the massacre, Nadia's house became their refuge, safely distant from the violent clashes erupting in the city centre. Mudhar had asked Jassim to host them at his river villa, but Jassim had declined, claiming it wouldn't be ideal. As if hiding from violent uprisings could ever be ideal. Shamil wouldn't have gone to Jassim's place anyway. He refused to give Jassim any more ammunition to use against him; Jassim already had plenty.

Turning to his side, Shamil glanced at Ameena seated on the carpeted floor across from Nadia, a coffee tray neatly placed between them.

Their dresses, one deep blue and the other rich green, looked remarkably alike, distinguished mainly by the amount of gold embellishing each. His gaze then shifted to the diesel heater, where a loaf of bread hung on its side, its edges turning crusty brown, its smell heavenly. Yet, he felt no desire to reach for it and take a piece—chewing on anything after what he had seen the night before felt like sinning.

He sighed and paused the white noise playing on his phone. Despite the noise-cancelling promises of his earplugs, Ameena's and Nadia's muffled voices had broken through, their casual chatter pulling him unwillingly into their conversation.

"Just tell me how, and I'll make it," Ameena said.

"I'll prepare the mix myself, and you can stuff the vegetables," Nadia replied.

Shamil sat up, removing his earplugs.

"Fine," Ameena said, setting her cup down, the weighty bracelets on her arm clinking together loudly. Sham, do you prefer Nadia's stuffing or mine?"

Shamil sighed, fixing his hair. On any other day, he would have complimented both of their cooking, managing to avoid upsetting either of them. Today, it seemed ridiculous that they bickered over spices when dozens of families had lost their sons.

"Ask Laila," he said, leaving them and heading to the kitchen, where Mudhar and Mazen, Nadia's husband, were having tea.

"Excellent timing, Hakim," Mazen cheered, grabbing the teapot. "I added cinnamon to yours."

Shamil took his cup, the cinnamon scent wafting up with the steam, bringing with it memories of a simpler past.

"You're looking well, uncle," Shamil said, recalling the last time he'd spoken to Mazen on a video call. Mazen had had a heart attack and was hospitalised for a few days. Shamil had called him every day, checking up on him and reassuring Nadia.

"Once death knocks on your door, you pray to God it never knocks again," Mazen joked, patting his now shrunken abdomen, clearly proud of how much weight he'd lost.

Shamil forced a smile. He'd seen enough death the day before and couldn't stomach any further mention of it. He put his cup down. "Any news from Jassim?"

"He wants us to remain at Nadia's; the curfew will last for three days," Mudhar answered.

"Can't we head to the village? We can spend a few days there," Shamil asked, hoping that once they were there, their path East would become easier.

"The rebels are about to take it, son," Mudhar said, his face conveying what his lips won't say. It was too late for them to go anywhere.

"They won't enter Ar-Raqqah, though," Mazen interjected. "The army has sealed off the city, and Jassim is ramping up arrests. It'll be over soon; God wills it."

"Baba, come quickly," Zain said from the living room. "It's begun."

Shamil dashed towards the living room, and Mudhar and Mazen were close behind.

The neon light flickered hysterically as they all sat before the ancient TV, its grainy screen broadcasting live images of protesters congregating on Tal-Abyad Street, two blocks from Shamil's apartment.

Lines of protesters slowly advanced towards a group of soldiers who had cordoned off the roundabout leading to the mayor's house.

"Go back! Don't come any closer!" the soldiers shouted, their voices tense, their gestures frantic.

"Go back. Listen to them," Shamil pleaded aloud, knowing his voice couldn't reach beyond the walls of the house.

"We're your brothers," some civilians said to the soldiers.

"We're all on the same side," another added, and for a moment, the soldiers seemed hesitant. Their rifles weren't pointed at the rioters— after all, they were all Syrians.

Shouting didn't help. Gesturing didn't help. The civilians advanced further, and the soldiers, looking confused, began to draw back.

"Look at how courageous they are, standing up to the armed soldiers," Zain said as the civilians appeared to hold their ground.

"What courage?" Shamil shouted, pointing his hand at the TV. "This is stupidity and an unnecessary waste of life should the soldiers shoot."

"The entire world is watching, Baba. The soldiers can't shoot when they're being broadcast live. It will be used as evidence," Zain said softly.

"Evidence?" Shamil was lost for words. The evidence online was overwhelming.

Still, it hadn't stopped the army from committing crimes in other cities, and it sure hadn't stopped them from massacring Ar-Raqqah's youth just one day ago.

"The army, the people, are all one hand," chanted the protesters, closing the distance to the pleading soldiers.

A handshake united two Syrians on opposite sides of the conflict: a soldier following orders and a civilian believer. Then, a kiss on the forehead roused the crowd.

"The army has defected. God is great; they're on our side!" shouted the protesters closest to the soldiers. The chant spread like wildfire.

'The army has defected' was a death sentence, no matter how Shamil looked at it. If the soldiers had indeed defected, their comrades would treat them as traitors and shoot them on the spot. If they hadn't, the mere accusation would force them to prove their loyalty by shooting the rebels and their civilian sympathisers.

The handshake turned into a push, then into an assault stance.

"Get back! Get back, or we will shoot!" shouted the soldiers, raising their rifles at the advancing unarmed civilians.

A visibly distressed soldier fired a shot in the air. The rioters persisted, chanting that they wanted to be martyrs.

"Go back," the soldiers pleaded one last time, then fired a round of bullets into the chanting youth.

Silence followed as bodies fell. The first bullets the soldiers fired at the civilians seemed to be the hardest—the thousands that followed became routine.

Why did the protesters advance? Shamil grabbed his head in shock at what he had seen. Why couldn't they stay where they were and build their numbers slowly? They doomed us, Shamil turned his face away.

"Why are they shooting again?" Zain said, a horrified look on his face.

"Why wouldn't they?" Shamil was now yelling, his heart pounding with every word.

"It's not the time for this," Mudhar said, turning the TV volume down.

"But they're fighting for our freedom," Zain insisted.

"That's not how you get your damn freedom," Shamil said, storming out of the living room and slamming the kitchen door behind him. Rage and fear knotted inside him, and saying anything else would have only made things worse. How could he explain to his son that the soldiers were now murderers? The blood on their hands had stripped away their humanity. And those who observed the killing would start picking up arms to shoot back. How could he show him that life mattered more than any slogan and that now they had moved from demanding freedom to demanding vengeance? A cycle of bloodshed that, if it gained any further momentum, would become eternal.

Death surrounded them; Shamil knew that it was only a matter of time before it paid them a visit. He lowered his head in the kitchen sink, his stomach turning violently. Had there been any trace of food in it, it would have splattered all over the dishes Nadia had left in there.

Was it right for the protesters to advance despite being told otherwise? Was it right for the soldiers to shoot at the protesters? Was it right for the protesters to carry arms and defend themselves in return? Did any of them have a choice in what they did, or were they simply doing what seemed right in the moment? What about all the others who weren't involved in making those decisions yet found themselves caught up in their consequences? What choice did they have?

"Heaven is for those who spend to help when prosperous, those who keep their anger at bay, and those who forgive," Shamil's heart recited to solace his boiling head as he paced the kitchen, trying to think things through. But all he could see was death.

"Where's your faith, Son?" Ameena joined Shamil in the kitchen, closing the door behind her. "You're burning yourself out— you can't keep doing this."

"Mama, any minute now, the rebels could assault the city for vengeance. A stray bullet could hit you in the head. An air raid that follows. I..." Shamil choked. "I can't see any of you getting hurt, I... I won't survive it."

"Habibi," Ameena said softly as she rushed toward Shamil, wrapping him in a warm embrace. One that Shamil desperately needed. "Let me tell you one thing," she said, sitting on a chair in the kitchen, and Shamil followed suit.

"Remember when Nadia was in a car accident, her head split open? Your grandmother was so annoyingly calm, without a single tear in her eye. I looked at her, wondering how she could be that cold when Nadia was gasping for breath.

I heard her say to Nadia, 'Daughter, God gave you to me, and I have been a good mother to you. If He grants you life, then He trusts me with you, and I will spend the rest of my life repaying Him. If He takes you, then I will be happy you're going to His heaven, my sweet angel.' Faith is what kept your grandmother strong, and it is what's keeping us strong. You need to let go, Son; God is our preserver."

Shamil nodded in silence, resting his head on Ameena's shoulder as she gently stroked his back. The scent of cardamom coffee surrounded him, blending with the steady beat of his mother's heart, a fragile comfort amid the turmoil. He wished it were that simple. Yes, he was a believer, but even the prophet said not to put oneself in harm's way and call it fate when harm ran them over. Actions had consequences, and he wasn't going to surrender responsibility just because that was what was written for him.

"We'll all come with you when the time is right. Are you happy now?" Ameena's voice was a balm, lifting some of the weight from Shamil's heart.

He knew she didn't mean it, but he was so tired that he was willing to overlook her lie, to bask in the comfort it momentarily afforded him.

The windows remained shut. The doors remained locked. For three days of relentless fighting, Shamil and his family huddled inside Nadia's tiny house, just as they had during every sandstorm that had swept through their city. And just like all those storms before it, this one, too, was bound to pass.

Chapter 33: The Siege of the Snail

In the days that followed the massacre, Shamil often found himself hiding on Nadia's roof, seeking solace amidst the noise that disrupted his every thought. The city, under curfew, felt like a prison, but he still had to pick himself up every morning to get bread from the nearby bakery during the two hours the army allowed civilians to move about.

It was as if he was the snail from a childhood game his neighbourhood kids used to play. The Siege of the Snail, they called it. One of the boys would draw a circle on the tiled floor using salt and place a snail in the centre. The snail would try to crawl its way out of the circle, but every time its delicate eyes touched the salt, they would shrink in horror back into its shell, leaving a streak of thick tears. Moments later, its curious, slightly damaged eyes would slowly creep out, scouting for a new route. It would try a different direction until it hit the salt again and shrink back into its shell.

Young Shamil used to watch the snail with sympathy, wondering why it ever left its shell. It was safe inside, away from the kids and the world. Every time it ventured out, it got hurt, yet it kept trying.

Fast forward twenty-five years, and Shamil found himself just as terrified of the outside world as he had imagined that snail to be. Yet, he went outside anyway, during the permitted hours, roaming the streets of a city in mourning. Life inside a shell, no matter how safe it felt, wasn't a life at all.

Some nights, he slept on a floor mattress until he couldn't sleep. Then, on the corridor's carpet, until he couldn't. Then, at every corner of Nadia's house, until one night, sleep abandoned him completely. How could his eyelids be so heavy, yet his eyes be so wide open? Climbing onto Nadia's roof, he lay his head down on the cold tiled floor, hoping his brain would freeze and He would pass out. His brain froze, indeed, and a nasty migraine kicked in.

It was three in the morning, and the final generator on the street had sputtered to a stop, plunging the neighbourhood into silence. The streets were deserted, as expected—only the reckless or desperate would dare step outside so late, defying the curfew. And for a December night, the air was unusually mild, carrying with it a strange stillness, as though the city itself was holding its breath.

Shamil turned to lie on his back and stared up at the sky, looking for his lucky star. Instead, his view was blocked by a thick wall of dusky clouds with burnt edges, the acrid scent of fires from sabotaged northern oil pipes tainting the air.

If only things were as they used to be before he left for London. He would have been playing games with Zain, deliberately losing just to hear his laughter once more. He would have slept for hours, even days, with the front door wide open, blissfully untroubled by who might come knocking. And he would have been close to his sweetheart, Laila—the unshakable foundation of his being.

"Are you awake?" Zain's whisper broke the night's silence.

"Yeah," Shamil replied, sitting up as Zain joined him, clutching a pillow.

"I brought the PSPs," Zain said, laying the pillow next to Shamil. "Can we play?"

"I haven't played in years."

"The new Naruto is easy; you'll learn it fast," Zain assured him, quickly setting up the game.

"If you're going to play games, then put your jackets on," Laila whispered, tossing their jackets at them. "And keep it quiet; we're only guests here, remember?" She disappeared downstairs.

Shamil gestured for silence, and Zain showed him he'd muted both devices. They played multiple rounds, Zain winning each one. He didn't laugh as Shamil had hoped, but his wide smile brought much-needed joy to Shamil's heart. As the sky lightened, Shamil's wrist began to ache, and he set the PSP aside, conceding defeat.

"Getting rusty, old man," Zain teased, turning off his device.

"It's a hard game," Shamil said, elbowing him gently.

"I wish we did this more often," Zain said, looking down at his PSP.

Shamil wanted to hug him, but he knew tears would follow, ruining the moment. "Whenever you want to play, I'll never say no."

"Maybe when this is all over?"

"Inshallah, it will all be over soon."

Zain clenched his PSP tightly. "I didn't want this many people to die."

"Sweetie, it's not your fault," Shamil said, pulling him closer. "How could you have known?"

"You knew it, and I didn't listen."

"I still screwed up," Shamil sighed, haunted by the images of the unblinking angels.

"You saved people."

"I saved no one."

"But you tried."

"And I failed."

"You still tried," Zain insisted, his gaze dropping. "When I heard the first shot, I ran away immediately. Amr tripped and fell behind me, and I didn't go back to help him."

"Zain..." Shamil's heart ached with each word.

"They shot him once, and I didn't help him, even though I could have," Zain continued, his voice breaking, tears streaming down his face. "I just watched them shoot him over and over and only moved when others ran to shield him, and the shooting stopped."

Shamil lay his hand on his shoulder, squeezing it gently but purposefully. "I would have done what you did, son. It's only human."

"No, you wouldn't have," Zain sobbed. "You would have jumped in to help him. You always help everyone," he continued, crying harder as Shamil pulled him in and kissed his head. "I thought you were a coward for leaving me and Mum here, but it was me who was the coward."

Pain festered inside Shamil's chest as he held his son tighter, wishing he could take it all away. He could only be there for him, offering what little comfort he could in a world gone mad.

"What happened?" Laila joined them on the roof. "You're going to wake them up!"

"He's ok," Shamil said, kissing Zain's head once more and helping him wipe his tears.

Zain nodded, wiping his face. "I'm fine, mama."

"Did he beat you that badly in the game?" Laila attempted a joke, undoubtedly sensing how hurt Zain was.

"He wishes," Zain chuckled, a hint of maturity twinkling in his congested eyes.

Laila settled beside him, fixing his hair, before she gently teased his thin stubble. "Who once told me that men don't cry?"

"Not me," Zain's smile slowly returned. He grabbed Laila's hand and pecked it gently before cuddling it as he lay on his side, resting his head in her lap.

She caressed his hair as he closed his eyes while Shamil gently patted his back, as if Zain were back in his cradle with two loving parents by his side. It was a reflection of a loving family, always together. It was what Shamil had been holding onto ever since he and Laila decided to separate.

Was he refusing the divorce to protect her and Zain from the stigma associated with it, or was he trying to protect himself from losing them? Was he still afraid of finding out whether she had ever truly loved him? How selfish of him.

He looked at Laila, every heartbeat calling her name. The silence between them was heavy with unspoken words, but in that moment, the silence said enough.

Chapter 34: The Mare

Jassim sat behind General Saleem's desk, his fingers tapping a rhythm to a combat song on the armrest of the leather chair. Framed pictures of Saleem posing with senior members of the Al-Baath party filled the wood-covered walls, soon to be removed in disgrace.

The door swung open with a bang, and Saleem stormed in, his thick face contorting in fury. He stopped dead at the sight of Jassim lounging in his chair, a knowing smirk hovering at the corner of his mouth.

"What the hell were you thinking? Disrespecting me in front of my subordinates?" Saleem barked.

Jassim leaned back further, his smirk widening as he gestured to the chair opposite him. "Sit, General, this will only take two minutes."

Saleem's eyes narrowed to slits, hesitantly stepping forward, then sinking into the chair, his posture cautious and rigid; every muscle seemed tense.

"Good man," Jassim began, his tone deceptively calm. "I'll make this offer once only, and you'll be wise to accept."

"You're a relic, Jassim," Saleem scoffed. "There's nothing you can offer."

Jassim's smirk didn't falter. "We're going to let the rebels take the city."

"I'll burn the city down before I give them an inch," Saleem's face beamed with arrogance.

Jassim leaned forward. "You'll vacate your posts and retreat all units into section seventeen, pending further orders."

Saleem glared at him. "You're going to trap the rebels in the city?"

Jassim tapped a sealed file on Saleem's desk. "More details here; I'd start reading now if I were you."

Saleem scoffed, leaning back in his chair, his arms crossed. "What happened to all your talk about 'no civilians should die'? Or have you finally decided 'collateral damage' doesn't matter?"

"If any civilian were to die, it would be at the hands of the Jihadists," Jassim said, his tone as cold and sharp as a blade. "They wanted an Islamic state, didn't they? Fine. I'm giving them exactly what they want. Let them choke on it. Let's see how long it takes before they're begging us to come back and clean up the mess."

"You've lost your mind, I swear."

"You'll also provide artillery cover for when my men retreat to Deir Ezzor."

"All right, your two minutes are up," Saleem got up and gestured for Jassim to move. "Get out."

"General, I'm not here to argue."

Saleem bleeped through his radio. "Two soldiers to my office, now."

Jassim's eyes gleamed with an unsettling amusement. "I really didn't want to do this," he said, turning the computer monitor to face Saleem and pushing the keyboard towards him.

Saleem reached for the keyboard, his fingers trembling as he clicked on "play." His face blanched, and the screen reflected the horror and rage in his eyes.

"You son of a bitch," Saleem whispered, his voice breaking.

"There's only one bitch here. Unless you're watching a different video than the one I saw."

Saleem sat stunned, ignoring the calls of his soldiers outside his office's closed door. If their roles were reversed and Jassim had been the one exposed in that video, he would have put a bullet through his own skull without hesitation. But then again, Jassim was too clever ever to be caught indulging in such twisted perversions.

He sauntered around the desk to stand over the humiliated general, the video of Nizar pounding Saleem still playing on the monitor. "Now you know your place," Jassim said softly, his hand striking Saleem's cheek in a subtle yet degrading slap. "You'll report to the ministry that this was a mutual decision and that you believe it's imperative we act with haste. I expect the withdrawal to be complete by Friday."

Chapter 35: The Hand Behind the Trigger

In a dream, vivid and disturbingly real, Shamil found himself back in the chaos of an emergency, but this time, he wasn't in Syria. He was in a London hospital, the familiar sterile air filled with the sharp beeping of advanced machines his homeland could only dream of. The boy from the massacre was there, lifeless beneath him, his small chest rising and falling only under the force of Shamil's hands.

But this was different. Here, he wasn't alone. Help was just a call away. Shamil could dial 2222, and within moments, a team would materialise to save the boy. He shouted, "Put out an arrest call!" as his hands pressed down in rhythmic chest compressions. This time, they felt effective and purposeful, as if life itself was within his grasp.

And then, impossibly, his body transformed. A third arm emerged, checking the boy's femoral pulse—it was strong, steady, mirroring the rhythm of the compressions. Then a fourth arm inserted a cannula, adrenaline flowing into collapsed veins. A fifth arm materialised, calmly transcribing every action, recording the miracle as it unfolded.

The miracle came. The boy's pulse returned. His lifeless eyes blinked open, now filled with life. But there was no gratitude in his gaze.

"You could have saved me," the boy said, his voice cold and accusing, his face twisted into a furious glare.

Shamil froze, his hands still pressed against the boy's chest. Then he saw it: the boy's ribs began to tear through his skin, his delicate cage splintering as if shattered by the force of Shamil's compressions.

"No," Shamil shouted, glancing around in desperation. He had called for help. Where were they? Why wasn't anyone coming?

One by one, his miraculous arms disintegrated. The fifth turned to ash, then the fourth, then the third, leaving him with only the two he started with—helpless, tremoring, still locked in the futile act of compressing a chest that could no longer hold life.

"You could have saved me," the boy's voice echoed, relentless, like a broken record stuck on its most damning phrase. The words wrapped around Shamil, tightening like chains, binding him to a guilt that felt heavier with every repetition. His hands moved on their own, pressing down, refusing to stop, refusing to let go.

The room around him began to dissolve, the sharp beeping of the hospital machines distorting, warping, until the sound melted into a thick black tar. It oozed from the walls, slithering across the floor, climbing up his arms. The tar seeped into his skin, cold and suffocating, swallowing him inch by inch as the boy's words echoed louder, each syllable sinking deeper into Shamil's core.

"You could have saved me."

Shamil closed his eyes tightly, holding his breath, forcing himself out of the nightmare that had taken hold of him. He woke with a jolt, his body drenched in sweat, his chest glued to the damp mattress beneath him.

Of all nights, the one night he had decided to sleep at his apartment, the one chance for a rare moment of rest, and the nightmare had stolen it away.

Muttering a verse of the Quran, he blew three times over his left shoulder, then, still trembling, he stepped into the bathroom, turning the shower to its coldest setting. The icy water poured over him, shocking him awake as he tried to scrub away the lingering black tar of the nightmare as if it were something real clinging to his skin.

His thoughts raced, sharper than ever. He knew he had to get his family to safety abroad. But he couldn't just walk away. Not now. Innocent lives were being taken with frightening ease, and Shamil couldn't stay on the sidelines any longer. Mudhar had told him about Jassim's decision to authorise lethal force, and that meant the death toll would only climb higher. The war needed to end—Shamil didn't care who won anymore. Neither the regime nor the rebels seemed willing to stop it, leaving civilians caught in the crossfire, paying the price for both sides' arrogance.

When the numbing cold of the water overtook the pain of his thoughts, Shamil stepped out of the shower. He dried himself quickly, wrapping a towel around his shoulders, and moved to the heater in his living room. The warmth radiated against his skin as he picked up the mobile phone with Zain's accounts on it and then scrolled through the Facebook profile. The Messenger was locked; Zain had refused to accept new messages. The last status update remained the same, untouched for days. But the insights on Zain's posts were staggering—hundreds of thousands of followers, millions of readers.

The reach was unparalleled, a voice that carried farther than Shamil could have ever imagined. At first, the thought of using that account the way Jassim had used it sent a chill through him. It felt dangerous, like holding a loaded gun, his finger hovering over the trigger, unsure of the destruction it might unleash. The words he might post could carry unbearable consequences—a single misdirection could cost a life, a dozen lives, maybe even more.

But those exact words could also save lives. If chosen wisely and if aimed precisely, they could bring about the change Zain and others have been fighting for. Shamil's voice would be heard, unlike on the day of the massacre. The page wasn't different from any weapon. A weapon didn't act on its own; it wasn't the tool that caused harm but the hand that guided it, the mind that set its course. It was the intention behind the act that determined whether it would destroy or protect. And that, Shamil realised, was a choice he had to make.

He stared at the screen, the cursor blinking at the ready. The question lingered: What could he possibly say? What words could cut through the noise, through the grief and the anger and the deafening silence of inaction? He couldn't just beg them to stop. *"Please, end this war,"* had been said too many times, it lost its meaning. His words needed to hit harder, something triggering, something outrageous—something that would make the rebels take their responsibilities seriously and start protecting the civilians who had risked everything to support them.

His fingers hovered over the keyboard, and the words came:

"The Syrian Free Army has left us to die alone. We have been betrayed. And mark my words, soon SAFI will enter every house in Ar-Raqqah. If you were an opposition supporter, it's time you switched sides."

His heart raced as he read them back. He could almost feel the chaos they'd create, the fear they'd spark, the anger they'd channel. For a second, it felt like the right thing to do, the only thing to say.

But then he moved his hand over the backspace key before pressing it. Slowly, the words disappeared, each letter vanishing into the quiet of the room. It wasn't that it was wrong to say—it was that he couldn't betray his son's trust, not now, not when everything else was already falling apart.

Switching off the phone, Shamil slipped it into the back of his closet, burying it under a pile of clothes as if hiding it could keep its power at bay. He hoped he'd never have to turn it on again. Grabbing his thick jacket, he pulled it tightly around himself, bracing against the cold, and headed out the door. A taxi idled at the curb, and hastily, he climbed in, giving the driver directions to Nadia's.

Chapter 36: On Edge

January 2nd, 2013

"It's been lifted?" Shamil asked, checking his phone.

"An hour ago," Zain confirmed, showing Shamil an update on Facebook.

"Could they be lying?" Shamil said, concerned that such a rumour might be a prelude to another riot or, even worse, a rebel attack.

"Baba, look at the video—it's from today," Zain tapped on his phone, showing footage of military vehicles leaving the city centre.

"Have you heard anything from Jassim?" Shamil asked Mudhar.

"Still unreachable," Mudhar replied.

Shamil got up and peeked outside Nadia's front door. The street was slowly filling with neighbours' chatter, and a few civilian cars passed by, their passengers casting wary, confused glances. Something didn't add up. While there had barely been any confrontations between protesters and the army the day before, there was no strategic advantage that he could think of for the military to leave the city centre and head back to their posts, potentially exposing themselves to attacks from both the protesters within the city and the rebels outside.

He rechecked his news feed, confirming that, indeed, some units had begun retreating from the city centre, which pro-regime pages cheered as "mission accomplished."

"It looks legit," Shamil said, still scrolling through his feed.

"Can we go home now, then?" Ameena asked, some joy finally glimmering in her hazel eyes. She had undoubtedly missed her comfortable bed and automatic ovens. Sleeping on a floor mattress for five days must have wrecked her spine, and her temper had been making her discontent clear.

"Let's take a ride around the city first, see what's going on," Mazen suggested.

"You're not going anywhere," Nadia interrupted, firmly clutching Mazen's arm. "We'll wait until we hear from Jassim."

But Shamil couldn't wait. If the army's retreat was indeed a prelude to something more sinister, the sooner he figured it out, the more time he'd have to react. Nadia's house, remote and sufficient to protect them from stray bullets and petrol bombs, wouldn't be safe if rebels invaded the city. In such a case, with subsequent regime air raids, they would all be much safer in Shamil's parents' house, where they had a bunker.

"I won't be long," he said, slipping on his trainers. Grabbing his SAFI lieutenant ID—just in case—he took Mudhar's car and set off for a drive around the city. Nadia's warnings weren't going to stop him, and no matter how much Zain had pleaded, Shamil wasn't going to take him along. This was something he needed to do alone, free from distractions.

Gripping the steering wheel, Shamil scanned the battered streets of Ar-Raqqah, searching for any signs of impending trouble. The rain had stopped, and a faint breakthrough of the afternoon sun cast a grim light on the aftermath of the violent clashes between soldiers and protesters.

Bullet holes peppered the fronts of buildings, soot and oil smeared parts of the city's ancient wall, and smoke still lingered in the air.

He manoeuvred through the debris-strewn streets, his tyres crunching over broken glass, spent bullet casings, and the charred remains of broken branches. The city, wounded as it was, seemed to stir back to life. Driving by Al-Naim Square near his apartment, he watched their beloved pie maker sweeping away the shards of his shattered storefront, his eyes darting nervously at every sound. Across the street, a woman scrubbed soot from her windows, her hands shaking but determined, while a single policeman directed traffic away from Al-Amasy Street, where most of the government buildings were.

Turning a corner, Shamil directed his gaze towards a long queue outside a bakery and an even longer one in front of a pharmacy. Had they run out of bread during the curfew, and now was the time for resupply? Or did they sense that something was coming and wanted to ensure they had enough bread and medicine? Both seemed plausible, and Shamil wished it were the former. Quick, anxious glances were exchanged between strangers, parents gripped their children's hands tighter, and everyone moved with a hurried, purposeful stride as if lingering too long might invite danger—an abnormally normal sight.

The army had left the city, but where were the rest of the police? He'd driven through half of the city's main streets, counting less than a dozen guarding the mayor's palace and official guest houses and three at the gates of the National hospital. It didn't add up.

Ayman? Shamil spotted him dragging his feet toward the national hospital. Slowing down, he honked twice to grab his attention.

"Hakim!" Ayman turned around, clutching a plastic bag with his white coat inside. "God has sent you!"

"Come, I'll give you a ride," Shamil said, opening the door for him.

Ayman jumped in, his hair shaggy and lacking its usual shine. "Hakim, I'm begging you with all that's dear to you," Ayman said, glancing around suspiciously as he settled into his seat. "My brother is at the hospital's detention. The bastards have beaten him, and now they want us to treat him so that he's fit for surgery. You have to help me."

"What surgery?"

"They say it's appendicitis, but they're lying." Ayman pulled an envelope from his pocket. "Wahid had his appendix removed when he was eleven; this is the report."

Why else would they operate on him? Uncertainty troubled Shamil as he glanced at the report. He recalled the late-night card games with Adil and the others from SAFI, the camaraderie laced with dark humour. They would joke about getting new kidneys or livers, should their excessive drinking ruin the ones they had. The way they spoke of it, as though there was an endless supply of organs waiting on shelves, ready to be picked up at a moment's notice, had struck him as absurd.

At the time, Shamil had brushed it off, unwilling to entertain the possibility. It was too outrageous, too cruel. People didn't simply disappear to become spare parts in some sinister economy.

He couldn't believe it, wouldn't believe it. But now, after witnessing the regime's cold efficiency in extinguishing lives without hesitation, the impossible no longer seemed so far-fetched. The idea of organ trading, once dismissed as a cynical jest, now hung before him as a chilling and plausible truth. He felt an urgent need to reassure Ayman, even though he had no idea how to help. " I haven't been able to reach Jassim all day. Only he can help your brother now."

"This can't wait, please, Hakim."

Shamil nodded, his grip tightening on the wheel as he glanced at the streets ahead. After a moment's hesitation, he made a sharp U-turn, heading back toward the hospital. Helping Wahid was urgent, but the thought of gathering information lingered in the back of his mind. The hospital had always been more than a place for healing—it was a crossroads, a hub where SAFI operatives often gathered to trade whispers and intelligence. If there was anything worth knowing, Shamil hoped to find it there.

He parked in the rear garage, closer to the barracks where Ayman believed his brother was being held. Scanning the scene, Shamil noticed a prison van idling opposite the barracks, its engine rumbling. Two guards stood nearby, their eyes flitting between their phones and occasional worried glances. They seemed to sense something was amiss, or perhaps they, too, were kept in the dark by their superiors.

If Ayman's brother was in the barracks, Shamil could get him to the main hospital by having him fake an illness severe enough to convince the guards. But how does he then lose the guards and sneak Ayman's brother into his car?

They would likely stick close, even in the main hospital. And how much time did Shamil have to execute this plan? A sense of foreboding hung in the air, growing heavier with each passing second. The longer he waited, the more it suffocated him.

"Park near X-ray and keep the engine running," Shamil told Ayman, getting out of the car and making himself presentable.

Nodding at the two guards, he entered the barracks, almost choking on the stench of feet, cigarettes, and dampness. It was as if light had never penetrated despite the many windows. The last time Shamil was there to examine a prisoner, the central area was packed with hospital guards and police officers who were drinking tea and playing cards. Now, the double-decker beds were empty, and so were the teacups left on the main desk. To his left, a metallic door was open, revealing a narrow corridor connecting the main area to the holding cells.

"Where are the detainees?" Shamil asked the prison officer who emerged from the corridor.

"And you are?" the guard inquired.

"Lieutenant Shamil, SAFI."

"Salutations," the guard said, seemingly unimpressed. "We're transferring them now."

"Where to?"

"Deir Ezzor."

"I need to speak to one of them."

"Go ahead," the prison guard said, then walked past Shamil. He wasn't even bothered to ask for an ID. "They're all in the room directly in front of you."

Shamil proceeded through the grey-walled narrow corridor. The further he went, the more pungent the stench of rot and sweat became, and the smaller the space felt around him. Entering the last holding cell, he found three prisoners lying on dirty, skin-thin mattresses: no pillows, no sheets, and barely any clothes on them. Bruises of different sizes and ages, some surrounding deep and shallow cigarette burn marks, marred every visible body part. They lay there motionless, indifferent to Shamil's presence.

"Who's Wahid?" Shamil asked, but neither moved. "I'm with your brother Ayman."

"Ayman?" said the man lying opposite, turning to face Shamil. "Where is he?"

Shamil crouched by his side. "He's waiting outside. We need to go now."

Wahid recoiled into the corner as if stung. "Please don't hurt me. I swear I'll never protest again."

"I'm a friend. I won't hurt you, but we have to move quickly." Shamil raised his hand gently, trying to calm him down.

Wahid struggled to open his swollen blue eyelids wider as if needing to confirm Shamil was real. "Just tell him I'm sorry. Tell my mother to forgive me."

Shamil was alarmed — the sounds of the guards grew louder, discussing readying the prisoners. He looked at the other two men, emaciated with little hope left in their eyes, and wished he could take them all. It wasn't possible. He wasn't even sure he could sneak Wahid out alone. Even as a lieutenant, he didn't have the authority to remove prisoners without appropriate clearance. However, as a doctor, he could take Wahid to the hospital's principal building. But only Wahid.

"I need your names." Shamil approached the other two prisoners, hoping to elicit a response. "Your names and phone numbers. I can tell your families that you're being transferred to Deir Ezzor."

One of the prisoners, a gaunt figure with hollow eyes, responded with a hesitant murmur, giving a name and a few phone numbers he still remembered. The other prisoner, however, remained motionless and silent, his gaze fixed on some distant point that seemed to exist beyond the rotten wall of that cell. It was as if the horrors they had witnessed had drained him of any hope or will to communicate.

Shamil couldn't help them all; hard as it was, he had to accept that and focus on what he could do for Wahid.

"Listen carefully," Shamil whispered, the commotion of the guards growing louder. "I need to get you to the hospital, but you need to act like you can't breathe and that your chest is hurting a lot. Okay?"

"Just let me speak to Ayman," Wahid said, tears now streaming from his swollen eyes.

"There's no time," Shamil said, grabbing his hand. "Ayman is waiting outside."

"What if they find out I'm lying?"

"They won't," Shamil said, hoping he would comply.

Wahid stared at the metallic door, wrapping his arms around his shoulders, shaking his head as if the mere thought of freedom disabled him. Still, Shamil wouldn't abandon him, no matter the consequences. Unlike the unblinking angels of the massacre, Wahid's pulse was palpable, and Shamil had to ensure it stayed that way.

"What if I make it impossible for them to find out? Can you handle the pain until we get to the hospital?" Shamil asked, and Wahid nodded. "Here's what we're going to do," Shamil pointed to a particularly bruised spot on his chest. "I'm going to punch you here. It will hurt, but it will make it convincing. Can you trust me?"

Wahid ran his hands across his chest as if already feeling the punch.

"You have to be strong, okay? For Ayman and your parents," Shamil tightened his grip on Wahid's hand.

The plan was insane; Shamil knew that. But it wasn't as inhumane as leaving Wahid to be taken back to the prison, where he would be tortured to death. Shamil had taken an oath to do no harm, yet sometimes, in medicine, a potentially harmful intervention was necessary to save a life. This wasn't any different. He had to cause Wahid pain to save his life; it was the only way.

Palpating Wahid's ribs, Shamil felt some crepitations, a sign of a previous fracture—the ideal site for his hit. It had to be convincing. Gathering his fingers into a flat fist, Shamil delivered a calculated punch, strong enough to cause instant pain but weak enough not to displace Wahid's ribs.

Wahid's scream reverberated off the cell walls, a raw and piercing sound. Shamil gripped Wahid's arm tightly, supporting him as he struggled to stand. The metallic clanging of the gate echoed in the confined space as the guards burst in, slamming it into the wall with a forceful shove.

"Help me get him up," Shamil barked the moment the guards entered the room.

"What's going on?" one guard asked, assisting Shamil in lifting Wahid.

"He coughed and then started shouting," Shamil explained, his eyes on Wahid's face, now turning blue. His punch had been stronger than anticipated. "Breathe. You have to breathe."

"He's faking it," the other guard said dismissively. "They do this to stop us from transferring them. Sneaky bastards."

"He's punctured his lung," Shamil's voice rose with urgency. "He'll die if we don't take him now."

"He'll be fine," the guard insisted, trying to yank Wahid away from Shamil. At that moment, Wahid coughed up blood, splattering the guard's uniform.

"Happy now?" Shamil retorted, panic mounting. Wahid was bleeding internally, and every second was critical. He cursed himself for the punch.

The guards, now alarmed, helped Shamil manoeuvre Wahid toward the hospital's main building. As they passed where Ayman was parked, Shamil made a quick gesture.

Ayman bolted toward them, his face pale with fear. Shamil snapped at him, "Prepare a chest drain kit and wait for me."

"Where?" Ayman asked, his voice shaky.

"You know where," Shamil replied, his tone harsh. He couldn't afford to show any sign of affection towards either of them that might arouse the guards' suspicion. "Move it! NOW!"

Blood rushed back to Ayman's face, and he sprinted ahead.

"He's got a pneumothorax," Shamil announced to the radiologist as they laid Wahid on an empty trolley in the X-ray room. Shamil recognised the radiologist, though he couldn't recall his name. "You'll have to wait outside," he instructed the guards.

"We're not leaving him," the guard declared, suspicion in his eyes.

"The radiation will fry your balls," the radiologist said, pointing to the waist shield he was wearing. The guards exchanged uneasy glances.

"In or out?" Shamil demanded, blocking their path.

"Be quick," the guard closest to Shamil relented, stepping outside with his partner, and Shamil slammed the door shut behind them.

"This is Ayman's brother, right?" the radiologist asked.

"Yes," Shamil confirmed, examining Wahid's chest. He had good air entry on his left side, and his vitals, though shaky, were stable for now. "I need to get him out of here."

"Use the back exit," the radiologist said, helping Shamil push the trolley toward the door.

"What about you? The guards..." Shamil began, but the radiologist cut him off.

"I'll say you hit me," he said, opening the back door.

Shamil nodded gratefully and slipped out, pushing Wahid as fast as he could, only this time he wasn't pushing him to the resuscitation bay like he did with the young men he'd seen the day of the massacre; he was pushing him away from it.

Chapter 37: The Memo

Shamil glared into the sink, the water swirling down the drain like a bottomless pit as he scrubbed Wahid's blood from his hands. The memory of inserting the chest drain lingered in his mind, a damning reminder of how close he had come to losing him. He had managed to save Wahid's life, but the recklessness of his actions haunted him, just as the nightmares of the massacre did. Was there another way to free Wahid from that dungeon without risking his life? Or had Shamil been so consumed by his drive to help that he arrogantly believed his plan was infallible?

A knock on the bathroom door broke his reverie.

"Hakim?" Ayman's voice called softly from behind the closed door.

"I'm coming," Shamil replied, quickly drying his hands and stepping out. "Is he okay?"

"He's sleeping now," Ayman said, offering a glass of rose-flavoured water. "Mother made this for you."

Shamil took the glass, the aroma instantly refreshing him as he took a sip. The cool liquid soothed the acidity that had built up at the back of his throat. He gulped down half of it as if he hadn't tasted anything so delicious in months.

"You're having lunch with us," Ayman said firmly.

"I can't," Shamil protested, glancing at the clock on the wall.

"I'll call your wife. Don't worry."

Shamil finished the rose water and handed the glass back to Ayman. "I really can't stay. Something felt off in the city."

"I spoke to Shareef earlier. He said that he's leaving the city this evening and that we should stay indoors for a few days," Ayman replied.

"Did he say why?"

"He's always a drama queen, probably exaggerating."

"Can you call him for me? I need to ask him something."

Ayman picked up his phone and dialled Shareef, but it went straight to voicemail. He tried the landline with no success. After ten minutes of fruitless attempts, Shamil told him to stop before they both went into the living room where Wahid was lying down, a chest drain helping him breathe.

"I was never that scared in my life," Shamil admitted.

"You saved him," Ayman said.

Shamil took a deep breath, unable to shake the unease. "I almost killed him."

"He was dead without you. At least now he's with us."

Shamil nodded, taking a final glance at Wahid. He was stable. Yes, Ayman was grateful, and Wahid's mother, and perhaps even Wahid himself would be, once the opioids wore off and he woke up. Still, the realisation of how close Shamil had come to ending a life scared him deeply. He had always lived by the principle of doing no harm, yet time and again, he found himself teetering on the edge of causing it.

"Make sure you get him to a hospital," Shamil said, handing Ayman some cash. "Perhaps a private hospital?"

"Hakim," Ayman began before Shamil cut him off.

"Unnegotiable."

Saying goodbye to Ayman, he drove to Shareef's house, Ayman's instructions guiding him. He hoped that he could find some answers. Jassim hadn't admitted it, but Shamil would have bet thousands that Shareef was one of his men, keeping an eye on how things were at the hospital. He would undoubtedly know something, and Shamil had to catch him before he left the city.

Shareef's house was at the eastern edge of the city, where most of the police resided. Their jobs meant they could purchase lands and apartments in that area at a substantial discount subsidised by the Syrian regime—another one of the regime's loyalty schemes.

That day, the police neighbourhood felt like a ghost town. The few cars left were filled beyond capacity with bags and luggage. To Shamil's luck, Shareef was still there, loading the last bag into his pickup truck.

"Shareef, remember me?" Shamil asked, walking to him.

"Hakim, why are you still here?" Shareef said, stepping closer to Shamil. "Didn't you get the memo?"

"Jassim's memo?" Shamil asked. The only 'memo' they received was Jassim asking them to stay put for a few days.

"The army's memo," Shareef said, gripping Shamil's shoulder with a force that conveyed the urgency before he thrust his phone towards Shamil.

Shit.

Chapter 38: Pride is a Dangerous Quality

Laila crouched in Nadia's cramped bathroom, a space barely large enough to turn around in. There was no bathtub to soak her body in, nor a proper shower that she could use standing. She turned the hot water tap off, grateful she hadn't accidentally used the diesel tap this time. She had done that before, twice even, thinking it was the cold-water tap, only to be met with the shocking smell and sticky thickness of diesel.

It was her turn to wash. Nadia's heater could only provide for two people a day, so she filled a bucket with hot water, the steam curling up and fogging the flickering light bulb overhead. She knelt on the rough tiles, pouring the hot water over her head. It cascaded through her hair and down her back, a soothing heat that somehow washed away some of the stress of the cold, hard reality around her.

Should they have left with the smugglers? Would it even have been possible, given that Jassim had known about it all? Laila's mind raced as she poured more hot water on her head. Shamil had been right all along, and she could have been more vocal in supporting him. Instead, she let her doubts win.

Perhaps she was even a little selfish. Somewhere in her heart, she wanted to sabotage their escape, fearing that once they were abroad, Shamil would divorce her - just as she had asked him to. Just as he had promised. The thought of being without him was unbearable. She now loved him more than life itself, and she had to tell him that.

He should have noticed it, anyway. She couldn't have been more obvious about her feelings—painting her face with makeup, asking him to sleep beside her, the lingering touches and gazes. How couldn't he tell she was so madly in love with him now that she would rather stay and die in Syria than face a life without him as her husband abroad?

Laila sighed, gathering her hair into a wrap and squeezing out the water before drying herself with a towel. She checked her reflection in the fading, steam-covered mirror. The dark circles around her eyes looked slightly better now that she had had a proper cleanse.

Entering Nadia's bedroom, she tied her damp hair into a bun, making sure she didn't wet anything in her path, before she settled on Nadia's bed, facing a mould-speckled wall. If only Nadia had accepted Jassim's gifts, her house would have been so much better. Pride was a dangerous quality, one that Laila herself was guilty of. She should tell Shamil how she felt and get it over with. Enough with the amateur gestures and childish games— they were both grown-ups. But how would she phrase it? How would she explain to him that her feelings had changed and that, this time, it was real? What if he rejected her? It would crush her, and then he would pity her. She couldn't accept that. It had to be real for both of them— they had suffered long enough.

Grabbing a pen and paper, Laila wrote, "Dear Shamil," then crossed it off, chuckling at how corny that sounded. "I must tell you this before something happens to us." She paused writing. What if something was to happen to her? To him? To Zain?

She had to finish that letter, no matter what words she used. Shamil had to know.

Folding the paper of her 'initial thoughts', she tucked it safely underneath her mobile's cover and headed to the living room; Nadia had announced that supper was ready. And before Laila could swallow the first bite, the honking of the car as it screeched to a park by the house had Laila's heart sink.

Shamil banged the front door, and Zain opened it hastily. "The rebels are here," he said, barely catching his breath.

Chapter 39: The Startled Prey

Jassim's bodyguards hustled him through a concealed passage beneath his villa, the damp walls closing in around them. Their frantic steps echoed through the tight space, their faces tense and perplexed—they, too, did not see it coming. The stench of cow dung and human waste clung to the air, making it hard for Jassim to breathe. He slipped on a muddy step, his knees hitting the ground with a loud thud. He cursed under his breath as his guards helped him up, only for him to push them away. It wasn't the first time he had to flee from terrorists or escape an assassination attempt; they didn't have to rush him like startled prey.

Emerging from the rancid tunnel, Jassim inhaled the fresher air, grimacing at the sight of the murky banks of the Euphrates River. A small boat awaited him, hidden in a bamboo grove a few dozen metres away.

As they crossed to the south bank, Jassim watched his villa engulfed in flames, his heart pounding with rage. How had his informant missed this until the last minute? Was his network compromised? Did Saleem play a part in this betrayal? It wouldn't be long before he found out, and heads would roll.

Grabbing his satellite phone, he dialled Noura's number. She answered instantly, and relief washed over him—she had made it to Damascus safely.

"How bad is it?" he then asked his driver as he climbed into the jeep.

"It's a disaster, Sir," the driver said grimly. "The Islamists have taken all the outposts around the city."

Jassim's eyes widened in alarm. Although it was his plan all along to have the rebels and their terrorist Jihadist allies gather in Ar-Raqqah city, making it easier to bomb them, he hadn't expected them to move in with such force and speed. He had arranged for Mudhar and his family to be taken to Deir Ezzor while he dealt with the rebels in Ar-Raqqah; only now, he wasn't sure his escorts could deliver them safely, not when the Jihadists moved that fast. He quickly dialled Mudhar's number, but there was no answer. He tried the landline, Shamil's apartment, the clinic—nothing. He wanted to call Nadia's house but hadn't memorised her number; there was never a good reason to do so.

"How many do we have left on the ground?" Jassim asked.

"Just a few," the bodyguard replied.

"Connect me," Jassim ordered, and the bodyguard dialled a number on his phone.

When the other side picked up, Jassim seized the phone from the bodyguard. "This is Colonel Jassim," he barked. "Go to the Waters States, South of the White Garden, Mazen Deratly's house. It's a corner house with a big garden. Once you're there, you call me. Understood?"

He hung up and redialled Mudhar. Still no answer.

Cursing, Jassim repeatedly slammed his fists against the back of the seat in front of him. His escorts stayed silent; their eyes turned away. The flawless plan he had thoroughly devised now teetered on the edge of disaster, and his actions could cost him the few family members he still cared about. The rebels couldn't have moved that fast without inside help.

Did that cursed Saleem really think he could outmanoeuvre Jassim? Take credit for his plans and use the Jihadists to eliminate him? It was a grave miscalculation. Jassim vowed to make an example of Saleem, ensuring that treachery was met with a vengeance unparalleled.

If Jassim were to take the risk, he would drive into the city, pick up Mudhar and his family—Shamil included—and deliver them to safety in Deir Ezzor. But the plan was fraught with danger, a move so predictable that anyone who knew the depth of Jassim's loyalty to Mudhar could anticipate it. Jassim wasn't that naive. Such a choice wouldn't only expose Jassim to near-certain capture but would also place Mudhar and his family directly in harm's way.

Jassim had warned Mudhar to stay put. He had sent his operatives to alert them and help them escape the city. He had ensured the eastern roads to Deir Ezzor were secure. He would wait for them there, but his duty towards Mudhar was fulfilled, and his focus should now be on Noura and Noura alone.

"Damascus or Deir Ezzor, Sir?" the driver asked.

After a long pause, Jassim answered, "Deir Ezzor."

Chapter 40: The Invading Liberators

Shamil hit the gas, speeding East to Deir Ezzor, the only direction the military memo advised the rebels weren't advancing from. In the backseat, Laila clutched Ameena's hand, her eyes darting nervously out the window. Nadia remained silent by their side, holding onto her seatbelt. Zain shared the front seat with Mudhar while Mazen was crammed with the bags into the third row.

"Dear Almighty, safeguard our route," Ameena prayed, and Shamil hoped that God would answer her prayer. He needed all the help he could get.

"We'll be fine; they haven't entered the city yet," Shamil replied, trying to keep his voice steady. "Shareef said the eastern exit is our safest bet."

"We should wait for Jassim's escorts," Mudhar said, failing to reach Jassim on his phone. "Have you seen the rebels yourself?"

"No, but Shareef was sure the rebels have taken all of the outposts around the city, and it's only safe to head east," Shamil slowed down to where a queue of cars had formed near the eastern outskirts.

"Shareef, Shareef, Who the hell is Shareef?" Mudhar snapped. "If anything, we should be home in case we need the bunker until Jassim's escorts arrive."

"Calm down," Ameena said, and Shamil didn't have the patience to respond. He didn't need to see the rebels himself to believe that they were going to take the city any second.

With the army's withdrawal and the vanishing of government officials and the majority of police officers, it was obvious something was brewing in the background. The rebels' taking all of the outposts in less than three hours meant only one thing: the city had been handed over to them. The question that he couldn't find an answer to was why.

"Zain, is there anything online?" Shamil asked, joining the queue of cars. About two hundred metres away, a makeshift roadblock had formed, and armed men in civilian attire were checking the leaving vehicles.

"The opposition is asking people to stay in their houses and close the doors," Zain answered, tapping on his phone's monitor.

Shamil peered out the window, the queue barely moving. "I'll be back," he said, getting out of the car and walking towards the roadblock.

Pacing there with caution, he observed a dozen armed men forcing passengers out. He couldn't make out what they were saying to each other, and it didn't take long before it became clear. They were bandits, taking advantage of the lack of security to extort families for their money and belongings.

He froze in place, thinking about what he could offer them in exchange for a safe passage. He had enough cash on him, and he could offer the bandits a big chunk of it, but what if that wasn't enough? What if they wanted it all? What if they recognised him and his family, took their money, and shot them right there and then? Was it safer to go back to his father's bunker?

He walked closer to the roadblock, straining to hear what the men were demanding.

Suddenly, a few drivers attempted to force their way through, only to be met with rapid gunfire. The bullets shattered the air, sending their cars careening into the valley below.

Panic spread across the remainder of the queue, drifting off the road or backing into each other, and Shamil's legs propelled him back into the car, cursing as he jumped back into the driver's seat.

"They're bandits," Shamil said, reversing the car quickly, barely escaping hitting the one behind him. "We'll try another road," he added, checking the rear mirror to see if any of the armed men were following.

"Take us back," Mudhar insisted.

"Shamil, take us home," Nadia pleaded.

"And then what?" Shamil shouted; the nagging was disrupting his focus. "Wait to be bombed?"

"We'll hide in the bunker," Mudhar shouted back, his voice drowning the gunshots that echoed behind them. "Jassim will get us out."

"Son, just take us home," Ameena pleaded. Shamil's knuckles whitened as he tightened his grip on the steering wheel. He wished he could hit a mute button somewhere for his brain to be able to process everything. He couldn't take them against their will; had anything happened on the road, they would have blamed him forever. Besides, he had no idea where he was taking them. He thought they could stay in the countryside for a day or two and see how things unfolded in the city before they decided their next steps, but seeing how bandits were already rife, staying in the countryside without any weapons to protect themselves would have been as risky as staying in his father's bunker.

What if, by thinking he could take them to safety, he ended up harming them like he did earlier that day with Wahid, Ayman's brother?

Turning the car around, Shamil sped through the streets as the sounds of explosions grew closer. Smoke billowed from burning buildings, and debris littered the roads. Armed men on motorcycles and pickup trucks filled the streets, and it seemed that, suddenly, everyone had a weapon except for Shamil and his family. He really should have taken Jassim's pistol.

As he drove past Al-Naim Square, just a few blocks from his parents' house, an explosion sent a lamp post hurtling towards their car. With lightning-fast reflexes, Shamil swerved onto the pavement, narrowly missing the men standing there. He quickly manoeuvred back onto the road, heart pounding, and sped towards home.

They reached his parents' house in a breathless rush, and it felt like a miracle they made it back in time. As soon as they locked the bunker's heavy metallic door behind them, more explosions rocked the city above, the sound reverberating through the reinforced walls.

He had always hated that damn bunker, but tonight he was thankful for it. He turned on the backup batteries, connected as many lights as there were plugs, and made sure his phone was fully charged. "Any updates?" he asked as Laila and Zain scrolled through their notifications.

"The Free Syrian Army says they've begun their operation to liberate Ar-Raqqah," Laila said, her voice shaking.

"Al Nusra Front, too," Zain added, holding up his phone. "They say half of Ar-Raqqah has now been liberated, and the regime forces are fleeing like rats."

"Any mention of Jassim?" Mudhar asked, grabbing Zain's phone.

"They've surrounded his river villa and are asking him to surrender," Zain pointed at another status update on his phone. "His operatives are still fighting back."

Nadia gasped, nearly fainting before Mazen helped her down.

"They're also marking the houses of anyone affiliated with the regime," Zain continued. "But not us—they didn't add us to the list."

"Not yet," Mudhar interjected grimly.

"They won't," Shamil said, hoping it was true. The only reason he and Zain had managed to escape Amr's wake was because Jassim's men had stirred the crowd to root for them, reminding everyone of Mudhar's good deeds as a doctor and Zain's role as a rebel. But could he count on that now?

He sat beside the metallic door, scrolling through the rapidly increasing online posts and images of the chaos engulfing Ar-Raqqah. The overwhelming theme was the rebels facing minimal resistance, the army barely reacting, and the city's police forces severely overwhelmed. It was as strongly evident as the scent of bleach that filled the bunker—the rebels were mere hours away from completely controlling Ar-Raqqah.

"Zain," Shamil called him to his side. "Are you ok?"

Zain nodded, a familiar determination emanating from his eyes. "We'll win this."

"Have you spoken to any of your rebel friends today?"

"I don't use that Facebook profile anymore, Baba," Zain said, lowering his voice. "It's just that after Amr died, I..." he seemed lost for words.

"I understand," Shamil kissed his head, unable to tell him that they may need his help.

An hour passed, Shamil going through every possible escape scenario before Zain jumped up, his face beaming with joy.

"God is great; they've taken the whole city!" Zain said, playing a video on his phone.

"Seriously?" Mudhar grabbed Zain's phone and turned up the volume. An overjoyed roar of armed men and civilians echoed around the bunker.

Then, other posts followed, as did videos and live feeds from every corner of the city. Shamil played one from the statue square, while Laila played one from Al-Naim square, their audio overlapping with Zain's phone. Soon, echoes of chants from their street pierced through the thick walls of the bunker.

"Should we go outside?" Mudhar said, getting up and grabbing a torch light, only for Ameena to snatch it away from his hand.

"No one goes anywhere," Ameena frowned, pulling him back next to her. "Sit down and let this night pass."

"They're broadcasting from our street now," Shamil said, showing Ameena his phone.

"What if the air raids begin now?" Nadia said. "Can we wait a bit longer?"

Shamil met her gaze in silence. While waiting to see if the regime would retaliate seemed like the logical choice, he couldn't shake the thought that the chaos on the streets might provide just enough cover for them to head north through rebel-controlled territory. If only more people were fleeing the city—yet from everything he'd seen online, it seemed as if no one was leaving. They all remained in their homes, clinging to hope, awaiting liberation.

"We'll wait an hour and see," Shamil concluded, his eyes fixed on the monitor on his phone.

At first, his suggestion seemed to have calmed his family down, but as the chanting around them grew louder and the sounds of bombs and bullets became scarcer, it was hard to justify remaining entrapped in that airless cell.

"I'm going outside," Mudhar said as he rushed to unlock the bunker's gate, Ameena darting at him with her eyes.

Shamil followed Mudhar into their street, cautiously peering through their netted metallic front door before they opened it.

"Congratulations!" their neighbour, Abu Mahmoud, cheered loudly, his little girls holding onto his trousers. "God is great!"

"God is great," Mudhar replied, daring to step further into their street. Dozens of men and children ran past them, cheering as they flew the Syrian opposition flags and banners.

"Father, your car," Shamil said, counting bullet holes that had gone through it. "Good thing it didn't catch fire."

"We're lucky there was barely any fuel in it," Mudhar said, checking the damage. "They hit the engine as well."

"Metal can be fixed," Abu Mahmoud interrupted. "Let's celebrate now!"

Shamil nodded, conflicting emotions churning within him as he watched Mudhar surrender to peer pressure and clap with Abu Mahmoud. Was this really what the people wanted? It sure seemed like it—their laughter and cheers were genuine. But were they aware of the consequences and willing to face them? Had Shamil been so blind to the people's true desires, their yearning for freedom, regardless of the cost?

He glanced at Zain standing beside him, his wide smile bringing an unusual sense of calm to Shamil's heart. Friends and acquaintances high-fived Zain, clapped his shoulder, and hugged him as he cheered them on. He clearly wanted to join the celebration, but his feet remained rooted to Shamil's side.

"Are we really free, Baba?" Zain asked as if he couldn't quite believe it.

"It seems like it," Shamil squeezed his shoulder. "But we still must leave."

Zain looked up at him, joy filling his eyes. "I don't have to hide anymore, do I?"

"One step at a time, son," Shamil replied, cautious about his son's safety. "We don't know how the regime will respond."

Zain nodded, taking small, hesitant steps as his friends cheered him on. Soon, he was off the ground, locking arms with others on the street, forming a circle and jumping up and down in jubilant abandon.

At twenty past midnight, the streets of Ar-Raqqah were as alive and packed as the Eid Market. Crowds spilt into the streets, cheering, shouting, and crying—an eruption of emotions that seemed to have no boundaries. Pickup trucks with mounted guns roared through the streets, their drivers honking incessantly as masked rebels waved flags and fired shots into the air. The city was wide awake.

Shamil stood in his parents' doorway, watching the chaos unfold. He smiled as Zain locked hands with other youngsters as they jumped and cheered for the rebels. Yet, behind the cheers, there was unease. Shamil could feel it—an undercurrent of fear that crept through the alleys and lingered in the eyes of those who weren't shouting.

"You don't cover your face if you have nothing to hide," Nadia muttered behind him, crossing her arms as she glared at a motorcade of rebel pick-up trucks and passing through Shamil family's street, a group of civilian motorcyclists trailing them, and cheering them on. "Only thieves and murderers wouldn't want to be identified," she said.

"They won't have to cover their faces anymore, Grandma," Zain said as he joined them, pointing at some motorcyclists who had begun to take their balaclavas off. "We're all free now."

"We're all doomed," Nadia whispered, her voice breaking as she turned to hug Shamil tightly as if saying goodbye before she left with Mazen.

Shamil nodded to himself, his desire to flee the country untouched by the scenes around him. The rebels had taken the city, and the regime hadn't yet retaliated, but he feared this was no reprieve.

It was only the beginning. The danger hadn't subsided—it had doubled. He would wait for dawn, for the full extent of the rebels' rule to reveal itself, before making his move.

"Baba, they have prisoners at Al-Naim Square," Zain said, holding his phone in front of Shamil.

"They're going to execute them," Abu Mahmoud, their neighbour, said grimly.

"No way," Zain scoffed. "They'll just parade them around."

Shamil took the phone, scrolling through the updates as the chants around them died down. The crowd shifted towards Al-Naim Square like a flock of entranced birds changing direction. A strange, subdued atmosphere settled over the streets, heavy and gripping, as if the city itself were holding its breath. Shamil followed the crowd, his gut twisting with dread. He needed to know if Jassim was among the prisoners.

As he and Zain reached the square, the sight stopped him cold. A group of bearded men stood in a line, their eyes darkened with kohl, their bodies wrapped in traditional Afghani dress. They wore explosive vests strapped to their chests, and each man gripped a large machete that gleamed under the dim streetlights.

In front of them, five kneeling policemen, blindfolded and battered beyond recognition, were bound together. The crowd, thousands strong, surrounded the scene, muted.

"This isn't real," Shamil whispered to himself, but every detail told him otherwise. It was real. Terror had taken form and was standing before him.

"Tonight, we deliver justice," one of the men announced, his voice booming across the square. "This is the Almighty's wrath." He swung his machete.

The blade didn't cut cleanly through the first policeman's neck, but the wound was deep enough to send blood spraying across the square. Gasps rippled through the crowd, and the silence shattered into screams and murmured prayers.

"Why are you doing this?" Zain shouted, his voice breaking. "They were unarmed! Why did you kill them?" He tried to move closer, but Shamil swiftly grabbed him.

"Stop," Shamil hissed, pulling him back.

"They can't do this!" Zain cried, his voice rising. "You can't do this!" His words echoed through the square, drawing nods from a few in the crowd.

"This boy is right," an old man said, stepping forward cautiously. "We need fair trials."

"Why are you defending the murderers?" someone else shouted, and another joined in. "Today's the day for vengeance. Go cry in your mother's lap if you're too weak to see it."

"We are the Almighty's hand!" the bearded man shouted, lifting his bloodied machete toward Zain. "This is His judgement. Takbeer!"

"God is great!" the crowd roared in response. "God is great! God is great!"

Shamil tightened his grip on Zain's arm, feeling his muscles tremor. He yanked him away, retreating into the crowd. Some jeered at them as they passed through them; others turned their backs and left. Maybe, like Zain, they had battled for a dream, only to find themselves trapped in a nightmare.

Chapter 41: Godsent

Al-Naim Square had once been a sanctuary of innocence for Shamil, filled with memories of carefree childhood days. It was where he first learned to do backflips as a teenager and where he had his first ice cream with Laila. Countless nights were spent there, lying on its grass with his best friend Alaa until past midnight when all the shops had closed.

Now, Al-Naim Square was tainted by a single horrific image that haunted Shamil's mind: a policeman being beheaded as Jihadists cheered. That gruesome sight had shattered his perception.

If only he could reach into his brain, dig out that memory with his nails, and toss it into the burning tyre at the corner of his street. Instead, the images seemed to expand, showing him what could be his and his family's future. Perhaps Jassim was right all along, trying to spare the city the wrath of the Jihadists.

It was too late now, the city was gifted to them, and Shamil needed to leave. He quickened his pace, his grip on Zain's arm firm and unyielding; and as they rounded the corner to his street, the glare of a foreign ambulance's lights greeted him. Its sirens were silent, but the bright, almost blinding beams illuminated the road, making it difficult to discern what was unfolding. Behind the vehicle, a shadowy figure loomed, half-hidden in the artificial light.

The closer Shamil got, the clearer the figure became. Behind the ambulance stood Mudhar, his arms wrapped around the paramedic.

But it wasn't just any paramedic. Shamil's steps faltered, his breath catching. That familiar frame, the tall, confident stance, and the unmistakable, infectious laugh—it was a face he hadn't seen in over five years but one he would never forget.

"Alaa?" Shamil said, hardly believing his senses.

Alaa turned around, the smile fading from his dusty, tired face. "There's the exiled," he said, his peaceful green eyes locking onto Shamil.

The weight of the night—the terror, the despair—seemed to lift momentarily. How strange that one night could bring both demons and angels.

"You wish," Alaa replied, hugging him back just as fiercely.

"Are you with the rebels?" Shamil asked, stepping back as Zain jumped between them.

"Uncle Alaa! I knew you'd come!" Zain's excited voice cut through the moment as he pushed between them, throwing his arms around Alaa.

"Our little rebel," Alaa said, ruffling Zain's hair with a fond grin. "See, you got what you wanted," he added, muting the beeping radio on his belt.

Zain's enthusiasm faltered. His eyes, reflecting the horrors he had witnessed at the square, glanced up at Shamil, then back at Alaa. "I didn't fight for terrorists to take over," he said, his voice low but firm.

Alaa's smile dimmed. "None of us did," he said quietly. "But we can't dwell on that now. We need to get going."

"Going where?" Shamil asked.

"Turkey. Where else?"

"Now?"

Alaa shook his head, his grin returning faintly. "Don't be ridiculous. We'll leave in the morning."

"I don't have a passport," Zain said.

"Neither does Laila," Shamil added, unsure if it was possible to enter Turkey without official documents.

"I can get you through with the ambulance. We have a free pass at the border," Alaa said confidently, though his tone betrayed his exhaustion.

"Is it safe?"

"It will be."

Shamil stared at him, his mind puzzled. It couldn't be this simple. Was fate offering him a lifeline, or was Alaa playing some cruel joke? "Don't bullshit me, Alaa."

"I'm not," Alaa said with an exaggerated sigh, muting his pager again as it beeped incessantly. "For fuck's sake, they're relentless. Listen, I need to drop these supplies at the hospital. Come with me," he added, and without waiting for Shamil's response, Alaa was already behind the steering wheel, starting the engine.

Shamil bit his lip as he replayed the gruesome scene at the square in his mind. He would have rather left the city right then and there, but something in Alaa's steady demeanour eased the panic clawing at his chest.

"We'll just deliver the supplies," Alaa reassured him. "If they need a hand with the wounded, I'll help out, and then I'll bring you back home. I promise."

"Go help, son," Mudhar said, giving Shamil a gentle push toward the ambulance.

Shamil's feet moved on their own as if operating on autopilot, carrying him into the ambulance without resistance. The act felt forced, his instinct screaming to say no—to avoid witnessing more horrors like the executions at the square. But the words refused to come. He was a doctor, and that duty, ingrained in his very being, overpowered his fear. His help might be needed at the hospital, and he couldn't turn away.

"I'm coming too," Zain said, jumping in the back of the ambulance, and Shamil didn't object.

"I still can't believe this. God must have sent you," Shamil said, fastening his seatbelt.

"For Zain, not for you," Alaa teased, winking at Zain through the rearview mirror. "God doesn't favour the stone-hearted."

"Indeed, he doesn't," Shamil said, wondering if God was still testing him.

"Five years of silence," Alaa replied, his voice growing sharper. "If I were a dog, you would've checked on me once or twice."

"I have no excuse," Shamil admitted quietly.

"Good. You'd better think of one, though," Alaa said, his tired face hardening into a rare frown. "Once we're out of this mess, you'll have one chance to explain yourself. Then, and only then, I'll decide if you're worth forgiving."

Shamil knew Alaa well enough to recognise the truth behind his words. The anger was real, but Alaa had already forgiven him. That was the kind of friendship they had. When Shamil had left for London, his heart had been too weary to show care for anyone.

But now, battered by the events since his return, he found himself unable to suppress the emotions stirring within him — for Alaa, for Zain, for Laila. Perhaps even for everyone left in this broken city.

Looking ahead, Shamil's gaze followed people driving around, celebrating the liberation and flying the Syrian opposition flags. Some were removing burning tyres to the sides of the roads, while others were clearing out broken glass fragments and bullet shells from their front doors and balconies, and wherever the ambulance passed, people stopped what they were doing and cheered for it. "May God protect you. Live long, our heroes," they chanted.

"Heroes don't behead people," Zain scoffed.

"Heroes save lives, like your father and I do," Alaa punched Shamil's thigh gently.

"I saved no one," Shamil cleared his throat. "I cried at the national hospital more than I'd worked."

"You should have called me."

"I was scared."

"Of?"

"Learning your fate," Shamil answered, almost choking on it.

Alaa nodded, inhaling deeply before he let out a big sigh. "Come, let's see what they need," he said, pulling the brakes.

He picked up a large, sealed box from the back of the ambulance, with Shamil and Zain following him through dozens of civilians that gathered around the emergency department's gates. There were very few casualties; the rest had come to volunteer and assist. It should have felt natural, this rush to aid the injured, an instinct as old as humanity itself.

Yet, in this moment, it felt hauntingly unnatural. Not when the Jihadists were lining the corridors of the hospital like a rosary of black explosive beads. Working near a policeman who had a pistol strapped to his belt wasn't as threatening as working next to a masked man with an explosive belt strapped around his waist. A pistol was threatening only when it was pointed at Shamil, and it was never pointed at him. An explosive belt, however, always pointed at him.

"Brother, why do you shave your beard?" a Jihadist draped in a black Afghan dress stopped Shamil at the gates, glaring at him as if shaving the beard was the biggest of sins.

"I have a skin condition," Shamil lied, knowing that in Islam, rules could be broken when ill.

"The more you suffer, the higher the reward," The Jihadist insisted.

Shamil shook his head, refusing to engage. His stubble, too long for regime officers who demanded a clean shave and too short for Jihadists who insisted on full beards, had somehow become a battleground for their ideologies. It was absurd—fixating on facial hair while the wounded lay bleeding around them, and the echoes of public executions still lingered in the air.

Focus, Shamil told himself, shaking off the distraction. He looked around the chaotic unit before his eyes settled on a man cradling what was left of his hand. Two volunteers worked to stop the bleeding, their efforts frantic and uncoordinated.

"Let me see," Shamil said, stepping in and taking the man's arm. The volunteers held the pressure steady as Shamil carefully peeled back the blood-soaked bandages. "We can handle this here. I just need—"

A firm hand yanked him backwards before he could finish.

"No one treats this bastard," a different Jihadist growled. He grabbed the injured man by the back of the neck and dragged him off the treatment bed like a sack of grain.

Instinct kicked in, and Shamil stepped forward, shoving the Jihadist's arm away. "Hold on, brother. What did he do?"

"He's an informant," the Jihadist snarled.

"I swear I'm not!" the wounded man shouted, his voice trembling. His skin was now ashen, and not just from the blood loss.

"Shut your mouth, you—" The Jihadist's fist flew toward the man's face, but Shamil moved, swiftly blocking the blow before it could land.

"Have patience, brother," Shamil said, his voice steady despite the adrenaline pounding in his veins. "Let me bandage his hand. Then you can arrest him."

The Jihadist glared at Shamil, his rage simmering, but before he could respond, other civilians stepped in, pulling him away.

"You think being a doctor will protect you?" The Jihadist hissed, his fury finding its new target. "Once we're done with the regime scum, we're coming after secular infidels like you."

The words jolted Shamil from the autopilot trance he'd slipped into, his steps faltering as he processed the scolding. Suddenly, the explosive vest strapped to The Jihadist's body felt all too real, and Shamil couldn't stop picturing it detonating. Rule number one in any emergency scenario—the first lesson drilled into him during his training in London—echoed in his mind: Ensure your own safety first before you approach.

Tightening the bandage around the wounded man's hand, Shamil then grabbed Zain's arm and rushed out of the surgical unit.

"I can't do this," Shamil whispered to Alaa, pulling him away from prying ears.

"What happened?" Alaa said, holding two large boxes of latex gloves.

"That lunatic called me an infidel for trimming my beard."

"Yeah, they call everyone who's not like them an infidel. You'll get used to it."

"I don't want ever to get used to it. I am sorry, but I am leaving," Shamil said, pulling his hand in front of Alaa.

"A handshake? Really?" Alaa said, gesturing to one of the Jihadists that he was leaving. He tapped Zain on the shoulder to get moving, and soon, they were all back in the ambulance.

"Are you one of them?" Zain asked, and Shamil dreaded hearing the answer.

Alaa's shaggy beard had planted some doubts in him. Still, Alaa wasn't wearing the same black Afghani dress as the other Jihadists. He wasn't particularly preachy or patronising like them, and Shamil had spent too many drunken nights with him in the past to believe that he was suddenly an Islamist.

"These people are thick as a block of wood," Alaa tapped his skull. Their minds are completely blocked. It's scary, to be honest, but we'll outnumber them."

"You, as in The Free Syrian Army?" Zain asked.

"Exactly. Syria must remain secular."

"Then why are you growing this horrendous beard?" Shamil said, resisting the urge to brush it tidy and shave it even. He didn't want the kind face of Alaa to carry such a mark of terror.

"It has its uses," Alaa patted it. "We have a common enemy now with the Islamists, but we might have to fight them once the regime is out of the picture."

"Another war?" Shamil asked, his stomach turning. It was as if the Syrian dish of misery lacked another bitter ingredient.

What little hope he had of a peaceful future for Syrians was slowly fading. When he left Syria in 2007, he knew that it would always be there for him should he ever decide to return. But after

Alaa and he were back home that night, he feared that once they fled Syria, there wouldn't be anything left to come back to.

"Alaa, my son, you bring light with your presence," Ameena said to Alaa, shaking his hand. If he were any other man, she wouldn't have touched him as per customs—but to her, he was family.

"The light is yours, Auntie," he smiled. "I see the spearmint plants I bought are still alive on the balcony."

"I'll brew you some tea from their leaves," Ameena offered, but Shamil almost interrupted her. It didn't feel like the right time for tea or any other pleasantries.

"Nothing would make me happier," Alaa said, pulling a chair to sit around the grapefruit tree.

"Did they kill Jassim?" Mudhar asked the question Shamil had been waiting to ask, and Ameena lingered to hear the answer.

"We don't know where that monster is," Alaa grimaced. "He'd left young recruits guarding his empty river villa and must have fled it somehow."

"He's still family," Shamil said, worrying Alaa's words would hurt Mudhar.

"He'll get from God what he deserves," Alaa said as silence prevailed for a few seconds. "We all will."

"Enough about Jassim," Shamil said as Mudhar gestured a silent prayer. "We'll take the ambulance in the morning; there's lots of space inside."

Alaa forced a smile on his tired face. "Inshallah."

"Will it be safe?" Mudhar asked.

"I would never put your life at risk, Uncle," Alaa answered, glancing around the courtyard as if looking for something. Zain, grab that big diesel tank. We'll need it for the road tomorrow."

"Let's have some mint tea now and rest. It has been a long night," Ameena rejoined them, Laila trailing her.

Alaa hurriedly rose and approached Ameena. Taking the tray from her, he nodded a silent greeting to Laila before distributing the cups, handing the first one to Mudhar.

"So, now we just wait?" Laila asked.

Shamil offered a brief nod, his reply concise and immediate: "Yes."

Chapter 42: On a Roof, by a Chimney

Shamil sat beneath the grapefruit tree, the cold breeze carrying its sweet fragrance through his parents' courtyard, cleansing the air of diesel and gunpowder. Gunshots reverberated through the roof gap, making it impossible for Shamil to distinguish between celebratory fire and active fighting. He watched Alaa, who laughed and chatted with his family, seamlessly filling a void Shamil hadn't realised was there. He knew he could never be the friend to Alaa that Alaa was to him.

"A good friend is one that transforms you into a better version of yourself," Alaa once recited in an Arabic literature class at school, holding a piece of paper with his sweaty hands and drawing smiles on his classmates' faces. "A version you didn't know existed until you met them. They'd spice you up with sea salt and caramel if you were a plain vanilla ice cream and sweeten you up with honey if you were a boring chilli dip."

Alaa was the spice in Shamil's life, and Laila was his honey. They were inseparable. In the ideal future Shamil had envisioned as a teenager, he saw his children with Laila playing alongside Alaa's kids, all of them enjoying shisha by the Euphrates. That was happiness, he had thought, unaware that real happiness would become fleeting moments he would be too guilt-ridden to notice.

"Rifle or pistol?" Alaa asked, snapping Shamil back to the present.

"What for?" Shamil responded, glancing at his watch. It was almost four in the morning, and Mudhar and Ameena had already fallen asleep.

"Let's go to the roof," Alaa gestured, his expression serious.

"Is everything all right?" Shamil asked as they climbed the narrow staircase.

"Yeah, I just didn't want the others to hear us," Alaa said, glancing over his shoulder. "They'd worry needlessly."

Now Shamil was worrying.

"We can't go tomorrow, can we?" Shamil sighed, his shoulders slumping slightly.

"It's not that simple," Alaa said, lighting a cigarette with a flick of his wrist. He inhaled deeply before continuing, his eyes staring at the horizon. The air on the roof was cooler, and the city stretched out beneath them, a screen of darkness and sporadic flashes of gunfire. "The factions rushed here with no clear strategy. It was an opportunity they couldn't miss."

"The army's retreat?" Shamil asked, his mind racing.

"The Jihadists have been dormant around Ar-Raqqa for over seven months now, not shooting a single bullet. Then all of a sudden, in the last two days, they blew up every single military outpost," Alaa explained, his tone grave. "Other factions felt threatened because if the Jihadists take over Ar-Raqqah, can you imagine the headlines?"

"Terrorists taking over a Syrian city," Shamil said, a cold realisation hitting him like a punch to the gut.

"Exactly," Alaa confirmed. "So, the other factions had to rush here to compete for control of the city with the Islamists, leaving behind bandits on every exit route."

"Allies of convenience?" Shamil questioned.

"More like an inconvenience," Alaa said, blowing out a cloud of smoke. "Tensions are already high, with Islamists wanting Sharia law and seculars wanting a free Syria. They've now been forced to converge in one place; they'll kill each other in no time or divide the city between them."

Converging in one place, Shamil thought, spacing out. It was all starting to make sense now—this was Jassim's plan all along. "You don't chase rats into their holes— you lure them out with the promise of a trophy. The bigger the trophy, the more the rats, the larger the kill," Jassim had said. Only now, the trap Jassim had designed had hundreds of thousands of civilians in it.

"Pistol," Shamil said, wishing he wouldn't have to use it. "I'll take the pistol."

"Good," Alaa patted his shoulder. "My friend Yamin will join us in a few hours. The more guns, the better."

"How long do we have?"

"We'll leave at ten," Alaa answered, pulling a small bottle from his trousers. "For now, we're going to sit here and enjoy this!"

"You're mad!" Shamil glanced over his shoulder, then around at the neighbouring roofs. There was no one nearby, and a few red lights flashed in the distance.

"I promised my mates to drink in their name on the night we took over Ar-Raqqah," Alaa opened the small bottle. "Sharing it with you wasn't something I'd ever imagined possible."

"And you think drinking now is a good idea?" Shamil said, crouching and pulling Alaa down with him. The last thing he needed was someone spotting them on the roof and reporting them to the Islamists.

"We're alive, aren't we?" Alaa smiled, holding the bottle in front of Shamil. "One sip for me?"

Shamil looked at the bottle, the smell of its arak overpowering. He never liked alcohol— it was the adrenaline and rush it brought him, breaking laws and societal norms with Alaa as a teenager, that held its only appeal. "I can't, I'm sorry."

"Ok. Either you're having this drink with me, or I swear on everything I hold dear, I'll drop you off at the border tomorrow, and you'll never see my face again," Alaa said, his eyes defiant.

Reluctantly, Shamil took the bottle and raised it to his lips. The harm from a sip of alcohol paled in comparison to the trauma of witnessing Jihadists behead people.

"To survival," Alaa said, his voice barely above a whisper.

"To survival," Shamil echoed and downed a sip.

Minutes later, more sips followed.

Shamil hadn't realised how much he needed that drink. The tragedies that had plagued his days became distant memories, and all he could feel after the fourth sip was the heavenly warmth of his parents' chimney on one side of his face and the cold breeze on the other. He took his shoes and socks off and caressed the roof tiles with his bare feet.

"I still haven't seen any new Tom Cruise movies. Not without you around to make fun of them," Shamil said, reminiscing about all the nights they'd spent mocking movies together. It was their tradition.

"I stopped watching altogether," Alaa answered, the bottle swinging empty in his hand. "Our whole life is a horror movie right now."

"Mother would say everything happens for a wise reason," Shamil said mockingly.

"Just like the wise reason that had you leave your family," Alaa scoffed, concealing the empty bottle in his vest. "Why did you leave us?" he asked, and Shamil didn't know the answer anymore.

He hadn't left for money—his parents had more than enough, and he stood to inherit it all. It wasn't for better career prospects either—he could have been one of the top surgeons in Ar-Raqqah if he'd stayed, without the exhaustion and underpayment he faced with his work in the UK. For all the hundreds of extra hours he'd worked covering for absent colleagues, they wouldn't even grant him a few extra days of compassionate leave. It was as if none of that dedication mattered. He used to tell himself that it was to atone for his sin of marrying Laila, for falsely assuming that she would love him back when she had become his wife. But if atoning for his sin was why he left, why hadn't he brought Laila to the UK sooner? He had many chances to do it, but instead, he kept making excuses, prolonging the process.

"I had to," Shamil said, the only answer he knew. One he had been telling himself for years.

"I kept on visiting your family to check up on them and to ask about you. You'll never find a brother like me, you idiot," Alaa wiped his eyes, trying to mask his emotion with a laugh.

"I know," Shamil's heart now ached with sorrow. The reason for his departure was becoming painfully clear. It had been easier to maintain the illusion of a distant, functioning family, convincing himself that it was the physical distance that had kept him from fully embracing their love. He had shut himself off from new relationships, clinging to the belief that someday Laila would be his. He had been that selfish. "I hate your disgusting Arak."

"It is disgusting," Alaa chuckled, lying on his side to face Shamil, his hand pressed against the warm chimney pipe.

"Do you think we missed our chance to leave the city?" Shamil asked as the first light of dawn began to break through the night sky.

"My God, Zain's right—you've become so obsessive," Alaa remarked, and Shamil frowned, puzzled. When did Zain have the chance to catch up with Alaa? They had been together the whole time, and Zain hadn't mentioned speaking to Alaa in over a year. Shamil pushed the thought aside, unwilling to linger on it - not when the alcohol had hit him harder than he had anticipated.

"Remember New Year's Eve in tenth grade?" Alaa continued. "We were coming back home really late, and you heard someone calling for help from afar?"

"It was freezing," Shamil said, almost feeling the chill of that night, a question burning at the tip of his tongue.

"I told you we shouldn't go into that dark alley; we could have easily been mobbed or kidnapped, and I begged you not to go," Alaa said. "Remember what you did?"

Shamil smiled, a warm reminiscence touching his heart. "I insisted on going."

"You told me, 'What if someone actually needed help there and we left them?'"

"Yeah, I was really reckless."

"No, you were persistent. You said you could live with being mobbed or stabbed or worse, but you couldn't live knowing that someone needed help, and you just walked away. That old lady we found wouldn't have survived the night if we hadn't found her, picked her up, and helped her back to her house. I mean, who the hell goes out to throw a trash bag past midnight anyway?"

"And she was in a wheelchair."

"In a freaking wheelchair," Alaa squealed, laying his hand on Shamil's knee. "My point is, stop obsessing about what could go wrong and simply enjoy what's already going right."

Shamil nodded, lying down on the roof's tiled floor. The heat of the chimney pipe kept his head warm as Alaa's voice filled his ears.

"I never thought I'd ever leave this land," Alaa began, and Shamil closed his eyes to listen. "When I was in Aleppo, I spent months hiding in the mountains, waiting to return here as a liberator. Next to our camp, there was a large field of dandelions, as beautiful and peaceful as a hundred thousand swaying suns spread across the land.

I was eating zaatar when a bird snatched a piece of bread from my plate and tried to fly away with it. The piece was too large for it, so it dragged it across the dandelion field, stirring up a cloud of seeds. The further it dragged the bread, the more attention it brought to itself, and the more birds flocked around, each snatching a bit, making the seed cloud grow larger. We are those seeds, Sham. One minute, we're sitting home in peace; the next, black crows scatter us around the world for the wind to carry. But, if God wills it, wherever we land, we'll create a home for us. A new dandelion field as vast as the one we left behind."

Alaa's words filled the air, and Shamil lay there, half-listening to the story. He spoke and spoke until Shamil momentarily forgot about the war. The scent of burning tyres faded, replaced by Alaa's cigarette and grapefruit blossoms.

But the war did not forget about him.

A thunderous blast tainted his dreams, and then another one woke him up, gasping for air.

A rocket? A jet? He scanned his surroundings.

"Alaa, look at the sky," Shamil shook him awake. "Get up quickly, we have to go now."

Chapter 43: Breaking the Barrier

The feeble light of dawn seeped through the freezing kitchen window, and Laila stood shuddering, a shattered cup at her feet. It felt like a dire omen, one she struggled to bear amidst the turmoil outside. The sight of those unkempt men turned her stomach. She loathed their shaggy beards and foreign accents, parading triumphantly through the streets, heralding an Islamic Khalifat that would confine her to the shadows, veiled in black.

Her Islam was different to theirs.

She clasped her freezing hands together, fighting to steady her nerves. Every option before her seemed fraught with disaster. Whether they remained trapped or risked the journey north, consequences loomed. Overhearing Alaa's insistence that Shamil carries a pistol for their perilous escape, where bandits roamed unchecked, heightened her anxiety.

She yearned to join them on the roof, to learn more, to find solace, but Ameena wouldn't allow her—it wasn't a place for a woman.

Reaching for the broom, she gingerly stepped around the glass shards with bare feet. Carefully, she swept them up, then mopped the floor clean with water. It felt futile—why bother cleaning when they were about to abandon everything within hours?

Still, she did it anyway; it gave her a purpose.

"You're still awake?" Zain asked, his eyes swollen, not that he had slept at all.

"I'll sleep on the road," Laila said half-heartedly, not believing it would happen.

"Are we having breakfast here?" Zain asked, and it didn't sound like a bad idea.

"If you help me make it, we will," Laila said, putting the broom aside.

Zain got the eggs out, and Laila checked the fridge for cheese. So much food would go to waste, so she had better check with Ameena to see if they could give it all to the neighbours before they left. Abu Mahmoud's little girls would love the rose jam and rice pudding; they would devour them all in one sitting. Oh, how Laila would miss those little girls.

"Zain, stop," Laila said suddenly, the sound of him whisking eggs covering a sinister rumble. "Did you hear that?"

A faint roar, like wind through a crack, grew louder, escalating into a sharp blast before fading.

"An aircraft?" Zain dropped the bowl onto the marble countertop and raced to the roof, Laila close behind.

"Jets are in the air!" Shamil's urgent voice carried from above.

"Get downstairs, NOW!" Zain bolted back down, Shamil and Alaa close on his heels, their faces drained of blood. Laila's instincts urged her towards the bunker entrance, but the thought of confinement stifled her. She couldn't face that suffocating cell again.

"Get the bags in the ambulance!" Shamil said, and Zain followed.

"I'll call Yamen," Alaa headed to where he'd parked the ambulance.

"What do I do?" Laila held Shamil's arm, not wanting to be helpless.

"Help with the bags," Shamil said, banging on the door to where his parents had slept. "Get up, NOW!"

Laila grabbed one of the bags and headed to the ambulance, praying for God's mercy. She'd never seen a warplane flying as close as she did seconds ago; it didn't even seem possible for something that large to move that fast.

"Motherfucking thieves," Alaa cursed, checking his ambulance, its doors wide open, windshield cracked, and back tyres deflated.

"No!" Zain dropped the bags by Laila's side.

"We'll take Yamen's car," Alaa said, swiftly jumping into the back of the ambulance. "The fuckers even took the spares!"

Laila stepped back under the shadow of her in-laws' balcony as another rumble approached. Not that a thin balcony could shield her against a rocket, but she felt safer that way. When the rumble passed, Abu Mahmoud emerged from his house, his daughters crying loudly. Laila rushed to his side and picked one of the girls up, cuddling her closely.

"Why aren't they using anti-air missiles?" Shamil asked, helping Alaa check the ambulance's damage.

"I don't know," Alaa answered, his phone ringing.

Picking the call, he directed Yamin to where he was, and soon, Yamin was parking his jeep in front of the ambulance.

"How many can you fit in your car?" Alaa asked.

"I have space for four more people, five if we push it," Yamin answered, adjusting the Kalashnikov rifle strapped to his shoulder. "We'll have to move now."

"Mum, Dad, get in the car," Shamil directed Ameena and Mudhar to the jeep.

"Son, we," Mudhar began, and Shamil interrupted him.

"Either we're all going, or none of us do," Shamil said firmly. "Your choice; we live or die; it's on you."

Ameena grabbed Mudhar's arm, nodding at him, and he took the hint. They got in the back of Yamin's car, and Zain loaded the rest of their bags onto the ambulance.

"Will it move?" Shamil asked Alaa.

"Not far with these tyres."

"Here, use this," Yamin passed a tyre sealant kit. "It should be enough for two."

Grabbing the sealant can, a thunderous roar had them all ducking for cover. It was the loudest Laila had heard that morning, Shamil's face confirming her worries. Air raids were imminent.

"I have to move, Man," Yamin said as he jumped back into his car. His wife was sitting next to him, cradling their infant. "Just pump the sealant and inflate it."

"You're not coming with us?" Laila asked Shamil, reluctantly handing Abu Mahmoud his crying girl back.

Shamil glanced at Alaa, attaching the sealant can to the tyre, and Laila knew in her heart what Shamil was going to say: "I need to help Alaa; I can't."

"Go with them," Alaa said. "I'll be fine."

"Please take the girls," Abu Mahmoud pleaded, now carrying both of them, their loud cries breaking Laila's heart.

"I can't carry everyone!" Yamin said loudly, visibly frustrated.

"Take the girls with you," Shamil said, taking one of Abu Mahmoud's girls and putting her in Mudhar's lap in the backseat. "We'll be two minutes behind you, Abu Mahmoud with us."

Laila looked at the ambulance, Alaa filling the tyre. The girls could take her place in Yamin's car, and she could stay behind with Shamil. "I'll ride with you in the ambulance."

"You're leaving now," Shamil said, gripping her hand and guiding it towards the jeep. She wouldn't take it anymore. She pulled her hand away, not wanting to be told what to do. She would do what she wanted to do, and right at that moment, she wanted to stay with Shamil.

"Please, Laila, you have to leave now," Alaa pleaded, and now Yamin was cursing.

"Mum?" Zain said, getting out of the jeep.

"Please, for him," Shamil pleaded, and Laila glanced briefly at Zain, then turned back to Shamil. She was willing to risk her life, but to risk her son's as well, that wasn't an option.

Pulling Shamil closer, she handed him her unfinished letter. "Read it," she whispered, kissing his cheek. As their eyes locked, the world outside faded away. There were no prying neighbours, no societal norms to follow, no bombs or fires—just the two of them standing together.

The next kiss came naturally, her lips finding his, soft and warm, conveying everything she had longed to express. "You must read it," she added, her lips parting from his, her grip on his hand loosening but her love lingering in the air between them.

Shamil squeezed her hand firmly, saying, "I will, I promise," before another rumble reminded them they had to get moving.

"Baba, you know I didn't want any of this, right? This isn't why I was protesting," Zain said, pulling his head outside the jeep's window as Yamin started the engine. "I'm so sorry."

"Ten minutes, Habibi. I'll be with you in ten minutes," Shamil said, his eyes visiting Laila's one more time, and Yamin drove away.

Chapter 44: The Rain

"You gonna read that letter," Alaa said, holding the air pump. He had finished sealing the first tyre, using the pump Shamil had picked from the garage, and he was almost done filling the second.

"You heard that?" Shamil said, loading the last bag onto the ambulance. "How can I help?"

"We're almost done here," Alaa said, handing Shamil a pistol. "It's loaded."

"Do you think we'll need it?" Shamil asked, examining the heavy pistol. It had been years since he'd used one, but he wasn't foreign to it.

"Inshallah, we won't," Alaa wiped the sweat off his face, then handed Shamil an empty bottle. "Can you get me water? I'm dying of thirst here."

Shamil nodded, dashing inside his parents' courtyard. In the kitchen, he opened the tap to a weak water pressure, barely dribbling. Checking the fridge, he couldn't find any water left inside it, so he stood by the tap, waiting for the bottle to fill, his patience running thin. It's been about fifteen minutes since his family had left, every second passing an eternity. No more planes were breaking the sound barrier, though, so he took it as a good sign. Perhaps the flights were merely for scouting, not for raiding.

Slipping his hand in his pocket, a burning desire raged inside him to read what Laila had written. What harm could a little peak do while he waited for the water to fill?

"~~Dear Shamil,~~

My love, my companion.

I must tell you this ~~before something happens to us,~~

I love you.

I love you, not as a friend, or a husband, or a father of my child. I love you as my everything.

I can't go on pretending my feelings for you haven't changed; ~~I was just too stubborn to admit it.~~ Our time apart has changed me. I missed your voice, your eyes, and your hands caressing my body. And I wanted you to kiss me again. I want to, and I will always want to, but I am afraid that you have moved on.

I wanted you to come back, not just for Zain, but for me too. You didn't say it, but I feel it, the guilt that has been consuming you. You offered me marriage as an escape, and I said yes to it; you didn't force me. If our marriage was wrong, then tell me, how can a bad thing create the most beautiful, honest, and righteous young man on this planet? A mistake didn't bring about Zain, our best creation; our love for each other did.

If you have moved on, then I will have to live with it. If you haven't, and you still love me, then I am yours.

Sham, you win the race."

The water bottle overflowed, and the ground shook underneath Shamil as a loud blast echoed through the courtyard.

"It hit the Al-Firdous area. We need to leave NOW!" shouted Alaa loudly through the main door. Then, a blinding light and a deafening blast threw Shamil to the ground, shattering the glass around him.

Opening his eyes, the ringing in his ears piercing, Shamil couldn't tell how long he'd been on the ground. He checked his face; pieces of his glasses were embedded in his temple, and his entire body was covered in dust and debris. There were a few specs of blood on him; somehow, his body had missed being hit by the thousands of shards that scattered around him. The ceiling was still there. The grapefruit tree wasn't on fire. So, where was all that smoke coming from?

Alaa? Shamil finally came to his senses. "Alaa," he shouted, choking through the smoke that filled the street.

Stepping outside, he couldn't see Alaa, nor could he see Abu Mahmoud. The ambulance was on fire, and half of it was buried under his parents' balcony. He dashed towards the burning ambulance, only to be repelled with a flash of fire that sucked whatever air was left in his lungs. Then Shamil saw it, and he instantly turned his eyes away. He didn't want that image to stick— Alaa was a beautiful man, and he would only remember him as such.

He cried as he walked away to a safe distance, hoping for a miracle. He wanted to go back near, but he couldn't. The ambulance could explode. The other cars on the street could explode. Another aeroplane could hit them.

"Stay away," Shamil shouted as people from other neighbourhoods started running towards the ambulance. "It's not safe; stay away," he yelled louder, but no one listened.

Why weren't they listening to him? Why hadn't anyone listened?

They gathered around the ambulance, throwing buckets of water on the fire, only for another rocket to hit where the people were gathering.

Shamil was far enough for his body to survive the heat yet close enough for his soul to burn with it.

Why? he cried, curled up on the asphalt. He pressed his hands against his ears, and ash and dust rained on the flesh scattered around him.

"Say nothing shall afflict us, but what God has ordained for us," he recited Ameena's words over and over again until he gathered enough strength to stand up and walk away.

He didn't look back, not once. He couldn't look back. All he saw in front of him was his family waiting for him at Tal-Abyad. Laila was there. Zain, Ameena, Mudhar, and even Alaa were there.

He limped down the city streets to where he thought Tal-Abyad would be. His mind had flushed out all thoughts and left one hanging like a flashing banner in front of him. Get them to safety, it said.

"Kind God, get me back to my family," Shamil prayed yet again, looking around for an escape.

Cars sped past him, packed with desperate families and rebel fighters, their faces pale with fear. Shamil waved frantically at each one, shouting until his voice cracked.

None stopped, and he couldn't blame them. If it were him driving his family to safety, he wouldn't have stopped either. Still, he waved again, his gestures growing more erratic with desperation. Then, a motorcade of rebels roared down the road; some carried the wounded, and others were empty - unlike the night before. One truck screeched to a halt next to his side.

"Jump in; we're heading to the hospital," one of the rebels barked, leaning out of the truck's bed.

Shamil lunged forward, his hands gripping the truck's edge. "Tal Abyad," he gasped. "I need a ride to Tal Abyad. Please."

The driver slammed his hand against the wheel in frustration. "What fucking Tal Abyad? Don't you see the jets?" he said in frustration. "We'll take you to the hospital."

"My family!" Shamil rambled on in desperation. "Please, I need to get to them. Just drop me outside the city; I'll walk," he pleaded as his eyes darted toward a silent figure on a motorcycle parked beside the truck. The man sat still, a Kalashnikov slung over his shoulder, his face hidden behind a thick balaclava.

"I swear you hit your head," the rebel muttered from the truck's bed, shaking his head.

Shamil fumbled in his pocket, his trembling fingers pulling out a crumpled wad of cash. "One thousand dollars," he said, holding it out. "Please. Just help me."

The rebel in the truck looked down the road, his gaze shifting to the sky where the rumble of a chopper drew closer, low and menacing. He banged his fist against the truck's side. "Let's go!" he shouted, and the truck lurched forward, leaving Shamil standing in a cloud of dust.

The motorcyclist hesitated, his engine humming softly as he glanced back at Shamil. Their eyes locked—or so it seemed—and Shamil could have sworn this was the same man who had shadowed him a few nights ago. Then, with a sharp twist of the throttle, the man sped off after the truck. Shamil stood frozen, his legs weighed down by exhaustion and defeat. Just as he began to turn away, the motorcyclist braked abruptly, spinning back toward him.

"You'll pay me in cash, yeah?" the man asked, his voice muffled.

"Yes, yes, and more when you get me to Tal Abyad," Shamil said, clutching the man's arm.

"Hop on, be quick," the man said, gesturing impatiently, then drove off in the opposite direction to where the chopper was coming from. "I'll take you north, but if they stop us at any checkpoint, you're on your own."

"Yes, thank you. Yes," Shamil said, embracing him with both arms, the man's rifle sitting between them.

Fear gripped Shamil the moment he climbed onto the motorcycle. He wanted to close his eyes, to shut out the possibility of an incoming rocket, but he couldn't. His eyes remained wide open, absorbing the chaos surrounding him.

The city was an inferno of devastation. Flames climbed the charred walls of buildings, their roofs crumbling under the relentless assault. Smoke billowed into the sky, a suffocating black veil that turned day into night—those agonising screams of grey-faced civilians holding pieces of their loved ones in their hands.

Thirty minutes. That was all it took to transport Shamil from the heart of the burning city to its quiet outskirts. The further they drove, the slower his heart became. And the lower it became, the heavier it felt. If only he had pulled Alaa from beneath the burning ambulance. If only he had kissed his forehead goodbye. If only he had perished alongside the other innocents— wouldn't that be just?

Weeping, Shamil held onto the man, driving him to safety. The motorcycle bounced in between roads and rough, pockmarked terrain, its tyres kicking up clouds of dust that mixed with the smell of burning rubber and flesh. The landscape stretched out in a dismal panorama; the vast fields were plagued with patches of burnt grass that lay like festering wounds on the surface of the earth. Tall eucalyptus trees standing as skeletal sentinels, their branches twisted and charred. Through his broken glasses, Shamil watched cattle meandering across the land, oblivious to the bloodshed that had soaked into the soil beneath their hooves. Their uncomprehending eyes were blind to what had transpired, and Shamil wished he was as mindless as they were.

"Your phone is ringing," the man said, and Shamil reached for his phone in an instant. How had he missed it?

"Sham, where are you?" Laila said at the other end.

"I'm.." Shamil's voice trailed off, and he held his breath. Any whisper of air would have brought about a flood of tears.

"We're at the border gate. Are you on your way?" Laila's voice started to cut.

Thank God, Shamil prayed, trying to calm himself down. He didn't want to alarm her.

"Sham?" the mobile died, and Shamil was now awake. They had made it to the border, and he was on his way to them. It would all soon be over.

"We're almost there," the man said. "You said your family is ok, right?"

"They are," Shamil said, wiping his eyes. "They're at the gate now."

"I saw you with your father at the funeral," the man said, and Shamil withdrew his hands from around him, looking at the man's reflection in the mirror. Those eyes, he was the man he had spared after he had tried killing Mudhar. "Sometimes I lose myself to demons and do stupid things. Then I hesitate and regret them later."

Shamil didn't respond and looked at the road ahead.

"I'm glad he survived," the man continued. "My aim is normally better."

Was he joking? Shamil couldn't tell. The man's tone was light, yet his words carried a harsh weight, as if shooting someone was a casual pastime. It didn't matter. Shamil was willing to overlook everything, every unsettling nuance, as long as this man would get him to his family.

"Fuck me," the man said, slowing down as a black-flagged pickup truck approached them. He looked around for an alternative route. There was none, and the car ahead flashed its light, signalling him to stop.

"What do they want?" Shamil asked.

"Hide your passport; they mustn't see that you've been abroad."

"We haven't done anything against them," Shamil said, tucking his passport in his underpants.

"You're not one of them; that's enough," the man said, then pulled over as the Jihadist's car stopped in front of them.

Two men emerged from the car, both bearded, both heavily armed. Their faded black Afghan tunics hung loosely over their frames, and what appeared to be explosive belts circled their waists with an unsettling casualness. They moved with a grim purpose, their boots crunching on the gravel as they approached Shamil, conversing in a dialect he couldn't place.

The men's voices were low, their words clipped and urgent. Shamil strained to catch fragments of their conversation, but the foreign cadence eluded him. The colour of their beards was the only distinguishing feature—one deep, coal black, the other shot through with streaks of Auburn. From a distance, they were almost indistinguishable, shadows painted by the same grim brush.

"Assalamu Alaikum, brothers," the young man said, withdrawing his balaclava and forcing a wide smile on his face.

"Wa Alaikum Assalam," answered both beards. "Are you Free Army?" said the one with the auburn beard in a broken Syrian accent.

"We're civilians. We're going to Tal-Abyad," the young man said as Shamil stood there in silence, wishing he was invisible. His head was starting to hurt, and so was his chest. "We barely escaped the air raids on the city; I am sure you know what's happening there right now," the young man added.

"All shall be martyrs, inshallah," Auburn Beard said.

"Including you, too," the young man said.

"God is generous," Black Beard said, pulling his hand forward. Only Tal-Abyad people can go there. I must see your IDs."

"We're from Ar-Raqqah," Shamil said. "My family is in Tal-Abyad."

"ID, now," Black Beard said, grabbing his rifle.

The young man looked at Shamil, silent, then handed over his ID to Black Beard, and so did Shamil.

"Aziz?" Black Beard said, examining the young man's ID. "That's like my uncle's name."

Aziz's fake smile grew tired. "It's a common name."

"Kurdish?" Auburn Beard said, looking at Shamil.

"Arab," Shamil said, pointing at his name. "It's an Arabic name."

"It says here, 'born Kurdish'," Auburn Beard pointed at the registration office's address on Shamil's ID.

"That's my registration address," Shamil argued to deaf ears. "I'm an Arab."

"You're coming to spy on us, eh? Kurdish man," Auburn Beard jeered as if he had stumbled upon a treasure by falsely decoding Shamil's ID.

"Brother, just look at him," Aziz said. "He's bleeding from everywhere; he's a civilian."

"We have no problem with you; you can go," Black Beard said to Aziz, tossing him back his ID. "This Kurd is coming with us."

Aziz clutched his rifle, his eyes locked onto Shamil with a defiant intensity, ready to confront the Jihadists. All Shamil had to do was nod, say the word, or pull the pistol Alaa had given him and start shooting. But he couldn't. How could he ever be ready to shoot another human being?

"Hakim?" Aziz said as Shamil stood there, arms hanging limply at his sides, eyes drifting away and fixating on Tal-Abyad, so close yet impossibly far. "What a shame," he added, and soon, he was back onto his motorcycle, driving away.

Chapter 45: The Will to Kill

Shamil glared at the Jihadists, his concussed mind a storm of conflicting thoughts. Why did he let Aziz go? Why didn't he pull the pistol and end it all?

Killing them would have been so easy— he didn't need to be an expert to deliver a fatal shot. They stood so close that missing was impossible. It was the simplest of tasks, the most obvious choice.

It was the right thing to do.

Yet, each time Shamil acted on what he believed to be right, it backfired—returning when John had warned him not to, engaging the smugglers when Laila had warned him not to, refusing to aid Jassim in halting the rebels, reluctance to join the protesters, Aziz's mother, the village—all these choices had led to outcomes he had neither anticipated nor desired.

He always had a plan and then another to back it up should the first one fail. Yet, time and again, life had demonstrated to him that, indeed, there was a plan—just not his own. It was as if an unseen hand, influenced by his choices but guided by a higher design, was at work. This was God's plan.

"Forgive me, God," Shamil whispered to himself, tightening his grip on the frigid handle. Each heartbeat sent a searing pain up his neck as the time had come for a swift action—kill or be killed.

Auburn Beard must die first; Black Beard must then swiftly follow.

That was the right thing to do.

But what if it wasn't?

What if these two men had misunderstood his ID's details, and once their Emir cleared things up, he would be set free? These men were merely following orders. If he killed them, how different would he be from the soldiers who shot civilians at Amr's funeral? How different from the Jihadists who beheaded the police officers? How different from Jassim? How could he live with himself knowing he had killed two people who might have been innocent? Hadn't he already suffered enough from guilt? Was he willing to trade one sin for an even greater one?

No. He had had enough. His family was safe; his mission was complete. They would survive without him, just as they did before— they had each other, and it was time for him to rest.

"Thus was written that he who takes one life, for no righteous reason, is as if he killed all mankind. And he who saves a life is as if he saved all mankind."

Letting go of the pistol's handle, Shamil climbed into the back of the Jihadists' car. They were taking him to their Emir, and whether he survived that meeting or not, he left to luck, to probability, to chance, and to a higher power.

It didn't take long for him to find out. As the Jihadists drove east towards the town of Suluk, Aziz's loud beeping chased them, his headlights flashing insistently. He gestured for the men to pull over, but they ignored him.

"Brothers, he left his passport with me. He's British. Pullover!" Aziz shouted, pulling alongside the car and gesturing urgently.

Shamil's hand moved swiftly to where he had hidden his passport. It was still there, and it most certainly wasn't British. What was Aziz plotting? Why would he expose Shamil like that?

The Jihadists finally pulled over, and Aziz parked beside them, knocking on Black Beard's window to lower it.

"Tell them who you are," Aziz demanded, glaring at Shamil.

"What?" Shamil was lost for words, not quite catching Aziz's drift. What happened next was too swift for Shamil to comprehend. As soon as the Jihadists turned their heads to look back, Aziz's bullets burrowed through their skulls.

All it took was seconds. Killing was a natural thing to Aziz. He did it so swiftly, emptying the entire magazine, that he left no chance for the two men to react.

"Get out. What are you waiting for?" Aziz yanked the jeep's back door open. "Fucking animals, they couldn't just let us go."

Shamil's eyes fixated on the hollowed faces in front of him as he reluctantly got out of the jeep. Even when he believed he had spared a life, it had been snatched away in an instant, right before his eyes. Riding on Aziz's motorcycle, he clung to his waist, numb to everything around him. He should have felt relief or perhaps even sadness, but he felt nothing at all. Nothing made sense anymore, and he was so exhausted, so desperate that all he wanted was for someone to wake him up and tell him that day hadn't happened. Suddenly, he broke into laughter, which turned into crying, then laughter again.

He embraced his saviour, a cold-blooded murderer, for whom he was inexplicably grateful.

"I can't take you any closer to the gate, but it's just a fifteen-minute walk up this field," Aziz said, stopping at the south end of the border gate road. "Can I have my money?" He extended his hand.

Reaching into his socks, Shamil retrieved whatever money was in them and gave it to Aziz.

"I didn't do it just for the money," Aziz said, pulling him in for a brief hug, seemingly unable to believe how much money Shamil had given him.

Shamil didn't linger by the road. At any moment, another Jihadist could drive by, or a bandit could finish what the air raids had started. He descended into the field, his legs barely carrying him. Every muscle in his body ached, and every bone creaked. He could see the border guard towers, the Turkish flags flying atop them, and he limped faster until his legs gave out and he collapsed. His face caressed the cold dirt as he commanded his legs to move, but they wouldn't. He willed his hands to push him up, but they, too, refused. Every part of him protested its exhaustion, and he closed his eyes, feeling the warmth of red flood his face and drown his vision.

Time stood still, and Shamil found himself back on his parents' balcony, with Ameena sitting across from him, reading his fortune. Her lips moved, but he couldn't hear her. "What did you see?" he asked, reaching for the cup, yet it eluded his grasp. It wasn't there, and neither was Ameena. He looked up at the sky, a blur of cotton white, heavy and close to his skin. He inhaled the cold air, fresh and sterile, burning the back of his throat.

Then, Laila's voice rippled through the white sky as warmth climbed up his hands.

"Sham." Her voice pierced the haze, the steady beeping in the background growing louder.

Was everything a dream? Shamil thrust himself up, a sharp stabbing pain spread through his spine, and Laila' embrace helped him lie back down. "You're ok. You're ok," she sat by his side, her grip on his hand strong. "You've just had surgery."

He looked around the white-walled room, reading signs in a foreign language he didn't understand and checking the beeping machines he knew all too well. His vitals were stable.

"Where's Zain?" he asked, his hoarse voice barely audible.

"He's here," Laila reached for the buzzer. "We're all here, in Turkey."

Shamil stopped Laila from buzzing the nurse, swallowing a painful lump that had formed in his throat. Perhaps some of the things he was beginning to remember weren't real, and he didn't want others to be there when he asked it.

"Alaa.." he choked, and Laila's brown eyes glimmered.

"I know," she said, tears flowing down her face. "Uncle asked them to bury him by the grapefruit tree."

"He wanted water," Shamil said, his words catching in his throat. "He only wanted water," he broke down, unable to say anything else.

Laila drew him into her arms, hugged him as close as Alaa used to do, and he sobbed on her shoulder, the pain of shrapnel piercing through his body paled in comparison to the pain that filled his heart.

Chapter 46: A White Veil

January 5th, 2013

Laila sat by Shamil's side, her heart aching as she wrapped her arms around him. She had never seen him cry like this, not with such unrestrained emotion as if he had been holding it in for years and was finally letting go. He had endured so much, and seeing him now—cuts and bruises marring his body, his face pale and gaunt—was almost too much to bear. Had it not been for the Turkish guards spotting him from their towers as he collapsed in the field, he would never have made it.

When they rushed him to the hospital, the doctors told her he was seconds from death. She had refused to believe them. God wouldn't have done that to him. To her.

Now, safe in her arms, she vowed never to leave his side again. Not ever.

"It's okay. I'm here. We're all here," she whispered, pressing her cheek against his.

He clung to her as if she were the last solid thing in his world. His tears soaked her shoulder, but she held him tighter, just like he'd held her many times before.

The door creaked open, interrupting them, and Zain rushed to Shamil's side, hugging him with an intensity Laila had never seen before.

"I knew you'd make it," Zain said with a tearful chuckle. "How did you get to Tal Abyad?"

Shamil's eyes flickered, looking away, unable to meet Zain's gaze—and Laila felt it in her heart, the weight of memories too painful to share.

"The important thing is that he's here," she said softly, placing her hand on Zain's shoulder.

Zain nodded, kissing Shamil's head. He reached into his pocket and pulled out a phone. "This was Uncle Alaa's."

Shamil took the phone, his fingers trembling as he held it. He looked at it for a long moment before setting it aside, his eyes filled with sorrow.

"Tell him about the border guards," Laila suggested to Zain, an attempt at distraction.

Zain's face lit up a little as he began to recount their journey, his voice growing more animated with each word. Laila watched Shamil's face as their son spoke, seeing the faintest flicker of a smile.

Then, in her purse, her phone rang. She hastily walked into the corridor to answer it, not wanting to alarm Shamil any further; it was an unknown number.

"Hello?" she said, her voice barely above a whisper.

"How is he?" The distinct timbre of Jassim's voice was unmistakable. If she didn't know better, she might have mistaken his tone for genuine concern.

"He's... he's alive," she replied, glancing back at the room where Shamil and Zain were. "Barely."

"And the others?"

"All here."

"Give him the phone," Jassim said, but Laila wouldn't do it. He deserved no gratitude and most certainly didn't deserve any words with Shamil. It had all been said, and it was time they banished him from their lives.

"When he's ready, he'll call you," she said, switching off the phone, her heart racing.

It felt satisfying, even exhilarating, and for a moment, Laila experienced what she had always imagined being Nadia would be like: putting Jassim in his place.

Taking a deep breath by the door, she steadied herself before she went to look for her in-laws. Twenty minutes passed, and she still couldn't find them despite looking at every corner of the hospital. She really should have called them before she switched off her phone.

"Who was it?" Shamil asked the moment she returned to Shamil's room.

"Jassim," she said, and Shamil's face turned serious after he had just been laughing with Zain. "I hung up on him," she added proudly.

"You did what?" Zain squeaked.

"The right thing," Shamil said, reaching for her hand, a smile returning to his face. She met his grasp, and he pulled her to his side. "Zain, can I talk to your mum in private?"

Zain nodded, making way for Laila.

"Call your grandfather, see where they are, okay?" Laila said, loosening her hijab. Shamil's room was a bit too hot for comfort.

"How are they?" Shamil asked as Laila sat on the bed beside him.

"Strong," she replied, still amused by Mudhar asking the nurses where he could find the best kebab shop in town while Shamil was in surgery. Mudhar had insisted he wanted Shamil to have the best meal when he woke up to make up for all the blood he had lost, and Ameena had agreed with him. Laila hadn't understood it at first—how could they be so careless? Then she realised Mudhar simply couldn't stand by idly.

He needed to keep himself occupied, to do something—anything—while his son lay at the mercy of the surgeon's knife.

Shamil grunted in pain as he tried to adjust his position. Laila was quick to help, grabbing the bed controller. "I'm fine," he said, inspecting the bandages over his stomach and the tubes protruding from it. "How long was I in surgery?"

"Six hours."

"I must have lost a lot of blood."

"And a kidney and some liver," Laila said, still struggling to comprehend how one could lose part of their liver, intestine, and kidney and still survive. It must have been a miracle.

"Enough to make a barbeque wrap?" He attempted a joke.

"Not funny!" Laila snapped. "It was serious. They kept saying that you…" her voice trailed off, and she turned her gaze away.

"I'm here now," he said, gripping her hand tightly. "Not in mint condition, but since I won the race, you're stuck with me."

Laila felt heat rush to her cheeks, a flood of conflicting emotions overwhelming her senses. He had read the letter, but was he mocking it or accepting it? She couldn't tell.

"Shut up," she muttered, trying to withdraw her hand, her hijab sliding down her shoulders. Instead, he drew her nearer for a kiss, and she yielded to his embrace. Their lips met in a passionate union, each touch making her want more. Feeling the cracks on his tender lips, she slowed down, worried that kissing him too intensely might make them bleed.

She bit her own lips instead, her forehead now resting against his, their breaths synchronised.

"I love you. I've always loved you," he said, holding her close, just as she'd always wanted.

"I didn't know how to tell you."

"You did, and I was blind," he replied, gently sweeping her hair aside and laying a brief kiss on her lips. "You don't have to wear it anymore."

Laila picked up her white silk hijab, now almost falling off her shoulders. "I know," she said, catching her reflection in the window. Draping half of her head with the hijab like a bridal veil, she then tied it back, just as she always had. Only this time, she liked it.

Chapter 47: The Syrian Dandelion

January 24th, 2013

In a secluded chamber, tucked away from the frantic corridors of the Emergency Department, Shamil raised the back of his bed, his rested gaze fixed upon the glowing laptop screen. The words he typed came naturally as if he'd always known them. As if all the words posted since this account's creation belonged to him, not Alaa.

The Syrian Dandelion Status Update:

"Freedom is a sun that must shine in every soul."

Closing the laptop, he grabbed a cup of spearmint tea Laila had made him, a bitter smile visiting his lips the moment the spearmint's scent filled his head. The first sip was sharp and soothing, much like Alaa's presence had been. And though the pain of his loss was still raw, the memory brought a strange comfort. He sipped the tea again, its warmth spreading through him like a bone-mending potion, and suddenly, it all came rushing back.

"This war will break you unless you're one of the lucky ones," Alaa had said that night on the roof as Shamil fell asleep. "And you're lucky if you've ever had someone you love so much that you hide your sadness and pain from them; the thought of them hurting over you breaks your heart. But you're even luckier if you have someone you love so much that you can't imagine hiding anything from them. They're the rock that anchors you when you're spiralling out of control, and you're their rock when life's wheel turns."

To Shamil, Alaa had been both a source of strength and a reason for vulnerability. He had said that they were all dandelions floating around the world, looking for a new place to call home. Alaa found his underneath a grapefruit tree—a piece of heaven, and Shamil was now at the mercy of the turbulent wind, his family at last by his side, forever hoping.

B"H

The End.

The Syrian Dandelion

In loving memory of A. M. & Husam.

.

ABOUT THE AUTHOR

Dr Thaier Alhusain, AKA Tha'er Hashem, is a Syrian medical doctor known for his contributions both during and after the Syrian conflict. During the early years of the war, he worked in Syria and joined Médecins Sans Frontières (MSF) in April 2013, continuing until August 2014. Following his tenure with MSF, Tha'er relocated to London to pursue a Master's degree in International Health at University College London (UCL).

In addition to his medical practice, Tha'er is the founder of "6abibak," an online Arabic medical journal that has become one of the most widely followed health platforms in the Arab world, boasting over 13 million followers.

Beyond his medical and educational endeavours, Dr Alhusain co-authored a poetry collection titled "Diaspora Hallucinations" with his father, Hashem Alhussein. The collection reflects on themes of survival, love, and acceptance, with profits aimed at assisting families affected by the Syrian Civil War.

Author's Note: While true events inspire this book, it is a work of fiction. All characters, events, and places are products of the author's imagination. Any resemblance to real people is purely coincidental.

Printed in Great Britain
by Amazon